THE DEVIL'S CUP

THE DEVIL'S CUP

A Hawkenlye Mystery

Alys Clare

Severn House Large Print
London & New York

This first large print edition published 2018
in Great Britain and the USA by
SEVERN HOUSE PUBLISHERS LTD of
Eardley House, 4 Uxbridge Street, London W8 7SY.
First world regular print edition published 2017 by
Severn House Publishers Ltd.

British Library Cataloguing in Publication Data
A CIP catalogue record for this title is available from the British Library.

ISBN-13: 9780727893468

Severn House Publishers support the Forest Stewardship Council™
[FSC™], the leading international forest certification organisation. All
our titles that are printed on FSC certified paper carry the FSC logo.

```
 ®
     MIX
    Paper from
FSC  responsible sources
www.fsc.org  FSC® C013056
```

Typeset by Palimpsest Book Production Ltd.,
Falkirk, Stirlingshire, Scotland.
Printed and bound in Great Britain by
T J International, Padstow, Cornwall.

Dedicated to everyone who has come along for all or part of Josse and Helewise's seventeen-book journey; I hope you've enjzoyed it as much as I have.

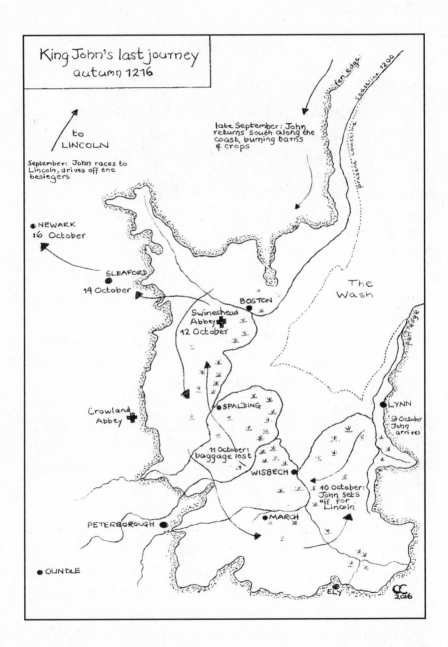

Prologue

Summer 1130

They had punished him.

Some bastard fellow brother must have found out he'd gone absent without leave, and retribution had fallen on him with a heavy hand. Literally, for the first part of the punishment had been a beating. Even as that bloody sadist of a monk was laying on the lash, though, he'd consoled himself with the thought that they'd have beaten him twice as hard and for twice as long if they had known what else he'd done.

It would have been worth it, though. Almost.

But the beating hadn't been the end of it. Now here he was out in the blazing heat, cursing, soaked in sweat, exhausted, dehydrated, mouth so dry he couldn't have swallowed even had he had anything *to* swallow, and he was digging holes. Every time he swung the pick to break up the bone-dry, rock-hard ground, it felt as if his lashed back was on fire.

This was the second part of his punishment, and he had been sent out to dig burial pits. Under the stern and ever-vigilant eye of one of the toughest sergeants he'd ever met – and *that* was saying something – he was working alongside other miscreants, swinging the pick, digging, shovelling, sunrise to sunset, to extend the charnel house

1

where they put the dead. Fifty or more corpses, every bloody day, so that sometimes he wondered how they'd manage to keep ahead of demand.

His years with the Hospitallers were a long tale of disobedience and retribution, for he was not good at taking orders. He'd had far worse punishments than this; once he'd been shut up in the terrible punishment cell for over a week, unable to lie down, unable even to stretch out legs and arms simultaneously. He'd never confessed it to those who stood in authority over him, but that one had almost driven him to the ultimate sin. Only, clever monks that they were, there was nothing in the minuscule, airless, lightless cell, stinking and haunted by other men's agony and despair, with which he could have finished himself off.

They had never found out what he was really like. He had joined the Order in a great hurry and as a last resort, paying his way in with a chest of stolen money, on the run from men who desperately sought his blood. With some justification, since he had just committed brutal murder.

Today, though, he was feeling happy again. Or he would, once the work was over, for it was the last day of his punishment.

The tormenting, terrible hours went on. Around noon, when the tiny, white-hot disc of the sun was at its height, the sergeants brought out water – not enough, never enough – and permitted the punishment detail a short break in the shade. Then it was back to work, and the labour seemed even worse than before by contrast.

As the weary day at last approached its end, his pick struck something hard. With a sigh, he laid down his tool and, leaning right into the deep trench, began to poke around with his fingers. The soil here was clay, and prone to breaking up into huge, cracked lumps, heavy and unwieldy; quite often large pieces of rock were deeply embedded in it. When the edge of the pick or spade caught against one of these rocks, the painful jarring shock ran right up the arms and into the shoulders and back. The rocks were usually stuck fast, and the only way to get them out was to work them free with painful, blistered, raw fingers.

Quite soon he realized that what his spade had struck was no rock. Intrigued, he hastened to get it out of the imprisoning clay. It was filthy, naturally, and at first he didn't understand what it was that lay so heavy in his hands. He gave it a shake. He looked more closely. Then a smile spread across his lean face. Maybe this punishment hadn't been such a misfortune after all.

He straightened up, a hand to his back as if easing aching muscles. His eyes roamed swiftly around the whole area, but nobody was looking his way. Diving back into the trench, he re-buried his find. When, a short time later, the signal came for the end of work, he made sure to leave a small mark beside the trench, just in case he didn't manage to memorize its location.

Not that there was much fear of that.

That evening, he was officially released from his punishment – not without a lengthy lecture on the evils of going absent without leave and a

3

brief homily on how great and generous was the Lord God, who forgave his sinful children again and again – and sent back to his unit. He ate his supper, refusing to allow himself to fall upon the food as he so badly wanted to. It didn't do to reveal weakness, even to his fellow soldiers, and he always played down how deeply he was affected by the punishments. Then, when they had settled down in the long dormitory and the cacophony of snoring told him the others were all asleep, he crept out.

The burial field looked different by night. To his surprise, he felt a shiver of fear. He crushed it with ruthless determination. Keeping to the shadows, he made his soft-footed way to the trench where he had been working earlier. Just as he had anticipated, he found it readily; it was as if its location had been graven on his mind. It was a matter of moments to dig down in the broken-up clay and release his treasure. And then he was out of the trench, off and away, silently crowing at how easy it had been, wanting to shout his contempt for the world to the lonely night.

But he was not alone.

Others had been watching his movements, patiently waiting for their opportunity. He had committed an outrage and, although they had witnessed every day of his punishment, they understood that it must surely be the retribution for a lesser crime. The Knights Hospitallers were disciplinarians and their rule was strict; surely a beating and a few days of digging pits was not sufficient penalty for what this man had done?

It didn't really matter, for they planned their own revenge.

As the Hospitaller hurried away from the burial field, swiftly getting into the concealing shelter of a dark, sunken little alley stinking of sewage, they quietly set off after him. Just as he was about to re-enter the city and return to the safety of the patrolled areas within its walls, they jumped him.

There were three of them: a middle-aged man, his son and his nephew. All three were heavily built and strong; all three were fired with the hot blood of righteous anger. The nephew held the Hospitaller's arms behind him while the father – most affected of all – punched him repeatedly, breaking his nose, splitting his lips and cracking a rib. But the Hospitaller was a fit man, and a soldier; he fought back, managing to free himself from the nephew's grip and landing some telling blows of his own.

All four men were shouting, panting, gasping and, quite soon, howling in pain. Although they were some distance from the city walls, a guard heard them and came hurrying out to investigate.

The violence intensified. It was as if some external force was egging them on; as if an intelligence full of malice was watching with savage glee and hissing *Go on! Go on!* Damaging blows turned to killing blows, and soon the nephew, the guard and the Hospitaller lay dead and bleeding on the still-warm earth.

The older man bent briefly over his nephew, muttering a prayer and touching the bloody, pulped face with a tender hand. Then he stood up and glanced at his son, eyebrows raised in silent

5

query. The son shrugged. 'I'm all right,' he hissed through mashed lips, spitting out a broken tooth. He glanced at his dead cousin, and a spasm of pain crossed his bloody face.

The father knelt down by the dead knight. 'May as well see if he has anything worth taking,' he said. He patted down the body, quickly coming across the treasure. He extracted it from inside the dead man's tunic, looked at it briefly, smiled grimly and hid it inside his robe. Then, an arm round his son to help him along, they slipped quietly away.

The treasure had been above ground for under an hour and already it had claimed three lives.

This was how it began.

The later history of the treasure was a long tale of betrayal and death. A part of it came into the possession of a prince who, wanting to win the heart of the beautiful woman he adored, had it melted down and incorporated into a rich and heavy ring of stranded silver and gold. She agreed to marry him and for a time they were happy. But on her finger the bright, white metal of the ring silently and constantly worked its malice, and she betrayed her devoted husband with his charming and handsome best friend. The husband found out, slaughtered his wife and his best friend in a torment of sexual jealousy, and then took his own life.

Some of the treasure came into the possession of a rich merchant. He used it to oust a bunch of desperate, homeless beggars from the ruins of an old building, for he had purchased the land with the intention of constructing for himself a grand and opulent mansion. But not long after he took up residence, the earth shook in a violent quake, bringing down the glorious new house on top of the merchant, his wife, his daughter and his newborn grandchild.

Other men acquired elements of the treasure, by fair means or foul. But the method of acquisition made no difference, for the treasure itself carried a taint. Always it was the same story: initial delight at taking possession of something valuable at a bargain price, the employment of the new-found wealth for something close to the owner's heart, followed sooner or later by violent and frequently painful death.

That is the way with tainted objects.

One

Autumn 1216

A foreign army had invaded England.

It wasn't exactly an invasion, for Prince Louis the Lion of France was in the country by invitation. A fair proportion of England's subjects wanted him there and, heartily sick of King John, the rebel barons had offered his crown to Philip of France's son.

On 22 May 1216, Prince Louis landed at Sandwich. John had prepared his defences and believed himself ready to throw off the threat, but a storm blew up and scattered his ships. The barons who were still loyal to him, unhappy about trusting the mercenary forces, which were pretty much all John had left, advised retreat, and John agreed. Unchallenged, Louis blasted his way through Kent, to be greeted in London on the second of June by a huge, cheering crowd.

Other lords and leaders whose realms were closer to home had also finally had enough of King John and were preparing to act. The barons in the north had invited the King of the Scots, Alexander II, to take control of Northumberland, Cumberland and Westmorland and, in Wales, Llywelyn ap Iorwerth – already referring to himself as prince – had embarked upon a series of raids whose main purpose was the taking of

English-held castles. John faced enemies on three fronts and, as if that was not enough, many of his people – and not only the barons – were in favour of a change of monarch.

But not all of them: there was a forceful, vocal and well-organized element who remained loyal to John and were hugely opposed to replacing him.

Especially with a prince of France.

The south and the south-east were bearing the brunt of the conflict against Louis and his army. Already one particular place was becoming renowned for its fierce and effective resistance, and this was the Great Wealden Forest. A large part of Louis's force was besieging Dover Castle; fairly pointlessly, since the utter impregnability of the great fortress was making the siege much more demoralizing for the invaders than the inhabitants. The remainder of his army in the south faced a band of rebels whose leader was reputed to be William of Kensham, a former bailiff who was resolutely loyal to the monarch. Willikin of the Weald, as he was commonly known, had gathered together a group of like-minded bowmen. So effective were they at getting under the invaders' skin and generally upsetting the smooth running of Louis's campaign that John himself was moved to send his thanks.

There were other loyal supporters of the beleaguered King within the wide, untamed area of the forest. Tucked away in the House in the Woods, Josse d'Acquin had long ago announced to his large family and his modest household that he would remain the King's man unto death. He had felt, in this time of deep division between the people of England, that it was only fair to state his position unequivocally.

'Prince Louis is very close,' he had said to the kin and the household he had summoned to his hall soon after the French prince had landed. 'Every man and woman here has the right to decide for him or herself who to support, and, the dear Lord knows, King John has done little in the course of his turbulent reign to win his subjects' loyalty. For myself—' he had paused, staring round at the familiar faces of his wife, his adopted son, his own son and daughter, Helewise's sons and their families and the very welcome recent addition – 'for myself, I have known the King since he was a lad. I can't say I have always approved of what he's done, but nevertheless I find that I retain a deep affection for my wayward monarch and I will not act against him.' He heard one or two murmurs. He saw Leofgar's wife Rohaise give her husband a swift look, narrow eyebrows drawn down in a frown. *Ah*, he thought. 'While I will think none the less of anyone who does not feel the same, I must tell you now that I cannot condone any action taken against the King.' He paused again, for this was proving very painful. 'If any of you are compelled by your conscience to undertake such action, then I ask you not to do so under this roof.' He glanced up at the strong old beams supporting his beloved home. Then, once again letting his eyes roam across his audience, he said quietly, 'I will not allow this strife within my

11

country to penetrate and threaten the security and the peace of my own hearth.'

It was rare for Josse to lay down the law to his family and his household. As he walked swiftly out of the hall, he had left behind him a stunned silence.

That had been three months ago. Now, as the autumn drew on, the lines of division had become very clear.

There had been little doubt that Ninian, Josse's adopted son and the child of his lost love Joanna, would support the King. It was a secret known to very few people, but Ninian was John's half-brother. Their paths had crossed once, and the events of that day had, for a time, meant that the King had put a price on Ninian's head.[1] That had not been enough, however, to turn Ninian into a rebel; on the contrary, it seemed to Josse that, despite everything, the encounter had left the young man with a strange respect for John. Perhaps, Josse thought, it was true what the old wives said and blood really was thicker than water.

Now, Ninian headed a band of fighters as ruthlessly efficient as Willikin's bowmen; possibly more efficient, since, knowing the forest and its ways so very well, Ninian had been able to instruct his group in how to move around unobserved and undetected. It was as if, Josse had once reflected with an untypical fancifulness, the forest recognized one of its own and gave Ninian a helping hand.

[1] See *The Rose of the World.*

12

Ninian's mother had been one of the Forest People, one of their Great Ones. The forest, it seemed, didn't forget.

Fighting alongside Ninian were Helewise's elder son Dominic and his boy, Hugo; the elder son, Ralf, was fully involved in a fight of his own, being part of the garrison at Dover. Geoffroi, Josse's son by Joanna, was with Ninian. Sturdy and well muscled at seventeen years old, Geoffroi strongly resembled his father and fought as bravely, and Ninian was glad to have him.

Helewise's younger son Leofgar, however, had taken the side of the rebel barons. It was a cause of distress to his mother; not, Josse thought, because she disapproved of his having taken the barons' side – she was a woman who believed fiercely in encouraging her children to work matters out for themselves – but because Leofgar being with the rebels divided the family.

In addition, Josse strongly suspected Helewise attributed Leofgar's choice of sides to his wife's influence. Rohaise was ambitious. Not content with the comfortable life of a rural lady that Leofgar had provided for her, she wanted to advance him – and herself – to a position of far greater influence. She wanted, Josse believed, to infiltrate the outer circles of court; even, perhaps, the inner ones. She appeared to think that hitching her star to King John's glittering but exhausted train was no use, and therefore had pinned her hopes on the new regime.

Sometimes Josse wondered how she could be so utterly certain there would *be* a new regime.

Josse's other abiding concern was his daughter,

Meggie; more precisely, Meggie's lover, Jehan Leferronier. The two of them had been intermittently together for five years now, and, with Meggie's help, Jehan had rebuilt the ruined and long-deserted forge in the old charcoal burners' camp on the outer fringe of the forest. The business had thrived, for, as Jehan pointed out to Abbess Caliste of Hawkenlye Abbey when he sought her permission for the forge, the Hawkenlye area had been in dire need of a blacksmith nearer than Tonbridge, to save everyone the trudge down the hill to the town and back again whenever a horse needed shoeing, a door needed new hinges or a plough coulter bent by a stone required straightening. The day's work, indeed, was often too much for one pair of expert hands, and Jehan was instructing both Meggie and Geoffroi, when he could spare the time, in the mystical art of smithing. Geoffroi, with his great love of and sympathy with animals, was particularly useful with nervous horses. The constant, hard physicality of the work had completed Geoffroi's transformation from boy to man; now he was taller than Josse, and his upper body was enormously strong.

Meggie and Jehan had also constructed a modest dwelling within the clearing. It was small, consisting of little more than a main room with a central hearth and, through an arched opening in the rear wall, a second, smaller room where they slept, but Jehan had made it solid and sound, and Meggie had made it comfortable and homely.

For all that, it seemed to Josse – who would

never dream of being so intrusive as to enquire – that Meggie and Jehan didn't spend all that much time there together. Jehan was a very hard worker and he was usually to be found just where he should be: in his forge, busy on some task, and often with a small queue of people waiting for him to finish so that he could get on with whatever job they had for him. It was true that he absented himself from time to time – that was something else Josse didn't ask about – but each time he made sure to put the word about that he wouldn't be available for the next week, or fortnight – once it was a month – to save people the time and effort of coming out to the forge only to discover he wasn't there.

And when Jehan was at home, very often Meggie wasn't.

Josse didn't even need to ask where she went, for he knew. She would be at the hut deep in the forest; the precious little dwelling where she had been born, where her mother Joanna had lived and, Josse now understood, had left quite a lot of her essence. With Joanna herself long gone from the world, this was a comfort to those who had loved her. Very few people knew about the hut, and even fewer could locate it. Even Josse, who had been there on countless occasions, sometimes couldn't find it. He told himself it was mere fanciful whimsy to think that the little hut had the ability to hide itself when it – or its occupant – didn't want to be found, but, in truth, that was how it felt.

All things considered, Josse found that he was taking even more pleasure than he had anticipated

15

in the presence of the latest addition to his household: his brother Yves. He had arrived unexpectedly some six months ago and had said straight away, and with typical frankness, that he would like to stay. His wife was dead and he missed her; the wide hall and walled courtyard of Acquin weren't the same without her, and he didn't want to remain there. His son Luke was now master of the family estates, and, as Yves ruefully observed, would do a much better job without his father watching and criticizing.

'I'll wager you didn't do much of that,' Josse had remarked.

Yves had shot him a slightly guilty look. 'I did enough,' he'd replied shortly.

Sometimes, as he and his brother rode out together or sat in companionable silence beside the fire at the end of the day, Josse thought back over their long lives. Yves was the second eldest after Josse and only a year and a half separated them, so they had been each other's natural allies as, one by one, three more little brothers arrived. They had always got on well, and Josse often reflected that they'd have sought each other out as friends even if they hadn't already been linked by blood. Like all young men of their station in life, they'd been separated as they grew older, and their paths had taken divergent courses. Yet always, sooner or later, one would arrive at the other's home, and the easy affection that masked a true and deep love would be re-established.

The prospect of sharing his home with his favourite brother for the foreseeable future – well, until one or other of them died, probably – filled Josse with quiet joy.

On a bright morning around the time of the autumn equinox, Josse sat in his comfortable old chair before the hearth, slowly turning over in his mind the many matters that were of current concern. Sometimes he thought to himself that going through the long list of all the people who were precious to him, pausing for a moment to bring each one to mind, reflect on what they were doing, think about what was happening in their lives and wish them well in their endeavours and, finally, where appropriate – and it almost always was – to send them his love, was a little like telling the beads on his rosary. He hoped this concept wasn't blasphemous – he must remember to ask his priest – but he didn't see how it could be. He was substituting loving thoughts for prayers, of course, but, in his own view, surely loving thoughts were what God would wish?

The House in the Woods was quiet. It was an hour before noon, and the household were all about their duties. Josse was listening out for voices, for Yves and Geoffroi would be back soon, having set out some time ago with another couple of baskets of provisions for Helewise in the Sanctuary. Placed as it was close to the road that circled the Great Forest, it had gained a reputation as somewhere that the desperate would always find help. Helewise and her team of helpers offered simple but nourishing food, medical advice, a shoulder to cry on and, in Helewise's case, someone to pray with. In these hard and dangerous times, the demand never seemed to grow less.

Josse closed his eyes and slipped into a brief doze.

The somnolent peace was broken by the sound of tentative footsteps on the flagstones. Jerked into wakefulness, Josse sat up straight, opened his eyes widely and took on the appearance of a man who hadn't really been asleep but merely closing his eyes in thought.

He focused on the face peering round the half-open door. 'Come in, come in!' he cried. 'It's Brother Watt, isn't it?'

A sturdy young lay brother edged his way into the hall. 'I went round the back,' he said apologetically, bending double in a deep bow, 'but it seems nobody's there, or else they're all so busy that they didn't hear me knock and call out.'

Josse waved a hand. 'Don't worry, you're as welcome as anyone to come in by the main door!' he exclaimed. 'What can I do for you?' Struck by a sudden alarming thought, he added swiftly, 'Is all well at Hawkenlye Abbey?'

Straightening up, Brother Watt made a face. 'Aye, it is. At least, well as it can be, sir, in these times of peril and uncertainty, and the nuns and the brothers are working themselves as hard as ever. But it's not why I've called,' he said sternly, straightening his shoulders as if abruptly reminding himself that he was here on an important mission.

Suppressing a smile, Josse said, 'You'd better tell me why you have done, then.'

Brother Watt reached inside his black robe and drew out an object, partly concealed by his large

18

hand. 'I was to give you this, Sir Josse,' he said, holding it up. 'It was brought to the abbey, with instructions to make absolutely sure it reached you as soon as possible.' He grinned. 'Seems the person who sent it has forgotten where you live!'

And that's the way I like it, and, indeed, have striven to bring about, Josse thought. The House in the Woods was secluded, in its secretive setting deep within the Great Wealden Forest, and few who did not live there knew its location. Sometimes, when he thought about it, Josse remembered Joanna's hut, and how she had seemed to be able to conceal it even from his eyes if she'd wanted to; the thought still had the power to wound, even all these years later. He did wonder, though, if somehow Joanna was exerting her power and similarly keeping the House in the Woods hidden from unfriendly eyes.

But he told himself he was being fanciful.

'Let me see, then,' he said, smiling at Brother Watt. Encouraged, Watt came across the wide flagged floor of the hall in a respectful semi-crouch, and now Josse saw that what he bore in his hand – with the sort of care that suggested it was both very fragile and highly valuable – was a rolled document of vellum. 'Sir, this was delivered to the abbey and taken straight to Abbess Caliste, and she sent for me immediately and told me to bring it with all speed to you.' He bowed so deeply that his forehead all but touched his knees, at the same time holding the rolled parchment up aloft. It was an awkward pose, and Josse instantly took pity on him.

'Stand up, Brother Watt, for heaven's sake,'

19

he said cheerfully, 'you'll put your back out crouching like that! And there's no need for such servitude – it's me, Josse, and you know perfectly well I don't stand on ceremony and I certainly don't bite!'

Slowly and reluctantly, Watt straightened up.

Josse waited, but nothing happened. 'Hadn't you better give me whatever it is you've brought?' he prompted gently.

Watt gave a great start, blushed, and the hand holding the document shot out. Josse held out his own hand to receive it, and Watt thrust it into his open palm and instantly stepped back, as if the document had burned him and he couldn't wait to get away from it.

His curiosity thoroughly aroused, Josse looked at what lay in his hands. It was a large piece of very heavy, expensive vellum, of the finest quality and with a soft sheen. It was pale creamy-yellow in colour, and Josse's name and the destination – Hawkenlye Abbey – had been inscribed in rich, dark ink in a beautiful hand, flowing and even.

Josse turned it over to inspect the seal. This was in vivid scarlet wax, very large and impressive, and it was a seal that Josse instantly recognized. It depicted a crowned man sitting on a throne, sword in his right hand, orb and sceptre in his left.

Then he understood Brother Watt's strange behaviour, particularly the sudden onset of obsequious bowing and the very obvious fear; and it had had little, if anything, to do with Josse.

The document bore the royal seal.

It had been sent by King John.

* * *

Sensing that this was something he ought to read alone, without any witness, Josse sent Brother Watt off to the kitchen in the hope that Tilly had returned and would find him something to eat and drink before he rode back to the abbey. Then, turning his chair so that nobody would be able to stand behind him and read over his shoulder, he broke the seal and unrolled the parchment.

The bulk of the contents was in the same hand as that which had written Josse's name on the outside. It was a typical cleric's hand, and Josse imagined it had been written at the dictation of one of the King's senior advisors. It was phrased in the careful, complicated language of officialdom, and consequently it took Josse a while to extract the meaning.

The missive began with a journey into the past.

In a lengthy paragraph, it set out Josse's life from early boyhood. It reminded him that he had been a page and then a squire in the court of Henry II; that once he had fought alongside the King's sons, Henry the Young King and Richard. *It was just a skirmish*, Josse thought, momentarily putting down the document and smiling happily into the distance as the memory came galloping back. He and some of the other squires had been out with the two princes when they'd encountered a scouting party of King Henry's. Since the princes were at the time furiously angry with their father (*when were they not?* Josse reflected with a smile), they'd attacked the scouts, disarmed and unhorsed several of them, and then invited the youngsters to celebrate with far too much wine. The result had been Josse's

21

introduction to what happened on the rueful, nauseous, shaking, shivering, painful day after a heavy drinking bout . . .

He made himself leave the past and return to the parchment.

The narrative went on to remind Josse of his service to three kings: Henry, Richard and John. In flowery prose that Josse knew was designed to flatter, it set out what an invaluable aid he had always been; how the monarchs, each in their turn, had been pleased and reassured whenever they thought, as they so regularly and frequently did, of the undoubted and eternal loyalty of *Our faithful King's Man down in the South-West*.

South-East, Josse corrected silently. He grinned. *So much for thinking so regularly and frequently of me; they can't even remember where I live.*

He skipped a few lines and went on to the final paragraph. Now the flattery and the roundabout, courtly, wordy tone had gone, for the narrative had turned to matters of immediate importance and not inconsiderable peril. Josse was all but certain he heard his monarch's own voice – impatient, boastful, bombastic and proud – behind the words. The message was quite clear: Prince Louis's advance had been stopped, and he was slowly but steadily being beaten back by the stalwart English loyal to the Crown. The siege of Dover had proved a total failure, Louis's troops were disheartened and deserting him in droves, barons who had previously supported the French prince had seen the error of their ways and were flocking back to fight shoulder

22

to shoulder with their rightful King. Now was the time, the missive concluded, for loyal men to stand up and be counted; now was the time for every true knight to remember his vow of fealty and show his love, his loyalty and his courage. There followed a brief word on the King's present whereabouts and his intentions for the immediate future.

It was a summons.

Slowly Josse lowered the parchment to his lap. Only then, as one end curled up into its roll, did he notice that there was another paragraph. This one was brief, written with the sort of untidiness that suggested the writer had been in a hurry. The monks who taught him in his youth, Josse reflected with a smile, would have been horrified at the scrawl, which in addition was decorated with several blots, as if the writer had impatiently shaken the quill to make the ink flow.

I am surrounded by indecisive men and turncoats, it said. *It is a time for old friends to come to my aid. I want you beside me, Josse d'Acquin. For the sake of the love you bore my father, my brother and, I may hope to say, me, come to me.*

The signature, large and bold, sprawled right across the corner of the document. And there was something else: beneath the black letters something else had been written, but then, apparently changing his mind, the writer had impatiently and violently crossed it out, the ink so thick and the lines inscribed so forcefully that the vellum had been scarred. But, holding

23

the document up to the light, Josse thought he could make out the words: *I am so tired*.

Time passed: Josse could not have said how long. He was musing on the power of words; awed at how just four of them could force their way deep inside him, straight to his heart. His mind was overflowing with vivid, alarming, colourful, sometimes very funny memories, for he had known John in boyhood and the lad had never been one to sit quietly in a corner . . .

He heard the sound of a soft cough, the sort designed not to clear the throat but to alert attention. Looking up, he saw Brother Watt in the doorway.

'Did you wish to speak to me again?' he asked. 'Come closer, Watt, I have finished reading the document you brought.'

Brother Watt came to stand before him. 'Well, yes, sir,' he said. 'Fact is, I've been ordered to speak to your daughter. I mentioned it to Tilly and Gus out in the kitchen – she's a fine cook, isn't she, Tilly? – and they said they didn't know where she was and I'd better ask you.' He looked hopefully at Josse.

'You could, Brother Watt, only she isn't here at the moment,' Josse replied. 'Would you like me to pass on a message when she returns?'

Brother Watt's pleasant and friendly face had gone through several expressions as Josse spoke, and now he simply looked relieved, as if glad that the burden of the messenger's responsibility had been passed on. 'Aye, that I would, sir, and thank you. Abbess Caliste asks if she will come to the abbey as soon as she can,' he said, closing

24

his eyes as he concentrated on repeating the message verbatim, 'because Sister Liese has a patient in the infirmary she's very worried about. It's a woman and she's delirious, ranting about something very evil that's a danger to someone.' He opened his eyes, frowning. 'Or some*thing* – oh, which was it?' He looked aghast. 'I can't remember!'

'Don't worry, Brother Watt,' Josse said reassuringly. 'If this poor woman is raving in fever, then in all probability her words don't mean much anyway, so I'm sure it's not important.'

'Thank you, sir,' Watt muttered. Then: 'You'll ask her?'

'As soon as I see her,' Josse said.

Meggie was on her way back to the House in the Woods. She had been deep in the forest, thinking, communing. She had gone first to the tiny dwelling beside the new forge that she was trying to think of as home, but, once she had done a few desultory chores and swept out the forge, she found she couldn't settle. There was no sign of Jehan – the forge furnace was cold – and she discovered that, unusually for her, she badly needed company. Her father's house called her, and she saw no reason not to answer.

She was very worried about Jehan. She suspected – no, more than that, she was all but certain – that he had joined up with the band of Bretons with whom he originally came to England five years ago.[2] Jehan and his companions had

[2] See *The Song of the Nightingale*.

25

been driven by one single, simple purpose: to a man, they hated King John, because they held him responsible for the murder of their beloved Arthur, the son of Constance of Brittany and her husband Geoffrey, who had been John's brother. Their intention then had been to seek out John and kill him. There was no reason at all, Meggie reflected anxiously, to think any of them had changed their minds since: they wanted to see the King dead. And, apart from the fact that all of them would suffer appallingly when they were caught (Meggie was quite sure it was *when* and not *if*), there was something else.

She knew what the King had done. She knew all his faults, as did most of his subjects after seventeen years of his rule, and she didn't doubt that, even if he hadn't actually murdered his own nephew, he was more than capable of it. When you tallied up all the evil things he had done in his lifetime, she mused, there was no doubt that he probably deserved death.

But she had met him. More than once. And, despite her common sense, the wiser part of her mind and her full awareness that you should never trust a man of power and particularly not a king, something in her responded to something in him. She had fought it, tried to banish whatever it was from her mind and her heart, told herself she was a fool and ought to know better.

But she had never quite succeeded.

I do not want Jehan and his hot-headed Bretons to kill him, she thought as she trudged along. Then – and she had no idea where the thought came

26

from – *He is sick, perhaps already dying, and the thought pains me so much.*

She stopped dead, shaken by the sudden certainty.

How did that happen? she asked herself wildly. Then – and it calmed her a little – she realized where she was. She was deep in the most secret depths of the Great Forest, in the area that had once been the dwelling of the Forest People, her own maternal ancestors among them. If there was ever a spot where messages from another world were likely to reach her – accurate messages, at that – then surely it was here.

She walked on, still a little shaken. To distract her mind, she allowed her thoughts to return to Jehan. She had to admit to herself that life together hadn't been so good recently. She loved him – at least, she amended, she was fairly sure she did – and physically he still had a strong power over her. His dark aspect had always been such an attraction: black hair, long and glossy, eyes that sometimes were as dark and shiny as jet, and the brown skin he had inherited, along with his overall air of *foreignness*, from his grandmother, a woman of Ethiopia. He was beautiful, and she never tired of looking at him.

But, she reflected honestly, you couldn't go on spending all day in bed making love with someone; not, anyway, after you'd worked the initial hot-blooded passion out of your system, and after the novelty of living together had faded a little. Sooner or later, you had to settle down to real life. To work; to cooking, cleaning, washing; to the constant presence of another person; to the expectations and demands of someone else when

27

you were used to coming and going much as you pleased. She had tried very hard, but she hadn't been able to settle to the domestic life that Jehan seemed to be asking of her.

To begin with, as besotted with her as she was with him, he hadn't objected when she took time away from him to be alone in the hut in the forest. Recently, though, he had begun to frown when she announced she was going there for a day or two, as if the prospect of her absence was unwelcome. And, rather more worryingly, he had been saying that the time had come for them to make a deeper commitment to each other, and she knew without him specifying that he was thinking of a child. Forced to look deep inside herself, she had come to the sad realization that this wasn't what she wanted. She knew, as had her mother and no doubt her grandmother before her and all the other herbalists of the forest, how to prevent conception and, although she had never told Jehan, she had discreetly taken the necessary steps. If he wondered why, after five years together, she had not become pregnant, he didn't ask.

She was close to the House in the Forest now. She increased her pace, for she had had enough of her troubling thoughts. *I am too like my mother*, she said to herself ruefully. She knew in her very bones that it would be a terrible mistake to go against her very nature only on the grounds that she loved Jehan and wanted to make him happy. *I would be doing what he wants, yes*, she thought sadly, *but it's not what*

I want. And surely the huge, life-changing deci-sion to bring a child into this hard world should only be made if you are utterly sure that it is the right thing to do and know you would give all you have to make that child secure and happy.

Most women, she realized, didn't have the choice. Thanks to her mother's teaching, Meggie did.

And she wasn't sure at all.

And there was something else: something that had nothing to do with her and everything to do with Jehan. In recent months, he had been different. She had tried many times to work out *how* he was different, and the best she had come up with was that he was often preoccupied, tended to be short with her when she interrupted his brooding – although he always apologized afterwards – and that, most concerning of all, he had taken to being absent, often for several days at a time, with very little reason other than a vague, 'I've been looking further afield for work.' Since they were often so busy at the forge that both Meggie and her brother Geoffroi were called upon to help, this didn't really make sense.

There was something on Jehan's mind and – coming back to her starting point – she believed she knew exactly what it was.

Although she did her utmost to put the dangerous memories out of her mind, sometimes – far too often – she still dreamed of the stocky man with the bright blue eyes who had once offered to teach her how to wield a sword.

Two

King John of England was travelling north.

Since the beginning of September, he had been engaged on the planning and execution of an all-out attack on Prince Louis and the rebel barons. After the success of the feigned advance designed to relieve the siege of Windsor Castle, he had swept in a wide semicircle to the north and west of London, heading towards Cambridge with the aim of cutting off the rebel-held lands of East Anglia and Lincolnshire. The plan was to establish a stronghold at Lincoln, from which his forces would be able to keep the rebels under control.

As if Louis's invasion and the threat of the growing army of barons were not enough, there was also Llywelyn ap Iorwerth in the west, advancing out of Wales, capturing English-held castles and impudently styling himself 'prince'. Also, there was Alexander II of Scotland and the invitation by the barons of northern England for him to take control of Cumberland, Westmorland and Northumberland; how unlikely had it been, John thought angrily, that his response would be to say, *Oh, no, I don't think so, thanks*. To increase the pique of that particular wound, Alexander had recently marched south to do homage to Prince Louis for his new English lands and John, racing to try and intercept him as he hurried north again, had only just missed him. His fury over Alexander's escape was burning up inside him and at times he could barely contain it.

As he rode towards Lincoln on that warm late September morning, the King's depression grew. Reflecting morosely that, since there appeared little in his life to be cheerful about, he might as well run through every last thing that was concerning him, his thoughts turned inevitably to his wife.

It had been sixteen years since he had abducted her from her betrothed, Hugh IX of Lusignan, and, before there had been time for anything but a lot of righteous anger, disapproval and a general wringing of hands, married her. The gossips and the prudish old monks who wrote the accounts of his doings all said it was nothing more or less than strong sexual attraction. They were wrong. That had come into it, naturally – although Isabella had been a child in years, she'd had a woman's body and a woman's subtle mind – but the grand gesture had not been as impetuous as it had appeared, and had mainly been to curb Hugh of Lusignan's alarmingly growing power. Marriage to the daughter of the count of Angoulême would have given Hugh another great tract of land to add to what he already had and, in John's eyes, that hadn't been a good idea at all; if anybody was going to gain Angoulême via marriage to Isabella, much better for it to be him.

With hindsight, however, he wasn't so sure. For one thing, he had made bitter enemies of the entire Lusignan clan, and they hadn't waited long before demonstrating their furious disapproval in the form of rebellion against John's rule in his French territories and an ultimately futile alliance with Arthur of Brittany. Although it was true that, in recent years, Hugh and the rest of the Lusignans appeared to have lost some of the hot heat of their righteous indignation, John did not entirely trust them.

And, over and above all that, there was Isabella herself.

For a time, she had been exactly what he'd needed. She certainly hadn't failed in the prime duty of a queen, having given him five children in eight years, the first two the longed-for boys. The trouble was, John reflected, that he'd treated her like a child – a knowing, subtle, scheming and exotic child – early in their marriage, and it seemed to have become a habit. Whether it persisted at her instigation or his, he never quite made up his mind. It suited him to know she was securely guarded in these dangerous times, and he persuaded himself it was for her protection. She went along with it willingly enough, but his knowledge of her was sufficient to understand that she would not have done so unless there had been some benefit to herself. What that might be, he had not yet fathomed.

She is tired of me, he admitted to himself. She was compliant enough when he bedded her, but he'd had enough women in his lifetime to know when a woman's passion was genuine. Isabella's was not. Despite himself – despite the fact that he knew full well there were few, if any, moments when his queen was left alone – John suspected that she had her eye on someone else.

He was haunted by a conversation he'd once had with her. He'd remarked somewhat bitterly that his marriage to her had cost him dear in terms of what he had lost, and, quick as a flash, she had shot back that she'd lost the best man in the world for him.

Those thoughts were too depressing. With an effort, the King turned his mind back to the present crisis.

He wished he had some means of acquiring an accurate tally of who was with him and who wasn't. The trouble was, to have any value, such a count would have to be taken practically every day, with all the barons of England being asked where they planned to stand for the next twenty-four hours. Sometimes the King despaired of the whole damned lot of them. What sort of a man changed sides depending on which leader was in the ascendant? Even when the vacillating barons were with him, their support was of questionable value if they couldn't be relied upon to *stay* with him.

He longed for the comfort of solid, well-tried friendships; for loyal men whose support he could rely on, and who wouldn't change their minds and dash off to join Louis the instant he managed to advance half a mile or take a couple of puny and strategically unimportant castles.

Which was why, in camp a week or so back, he had yelled for his scribe and had those letters written.

One of which he'd sent to his brother's man, Josse d'Acquin.

From up ahead there was a flurry of activity,

and a small band of men came cantering towards him, their horses sweaty and frothing, the men themselves splattered with mud, one of them with a black eye and another bleeding from a cut on his cheek. The leader pulled up his horse and, not pausing to dismount but attempting to bow from the waist as he sat in the saddle, panted, 'My lord King, good news!' He paused to gasp in another breath. 'Your advance force has driven off the rebels besieging Lincoln and already our troops are entering the town!' The dried mud on his cheek cracked as he beamed his delight. 'Furthermore, I am instructed to tell you that your orders concerning the religious houses and the tithe barns in the vicinity have been thoroughly carried out. The buildings are in ruins, the barns are all burning and the crops are destroyed.'

John nodded. 'The rebels are fleeing?'

'Aye, my lord, in the direction of the Isle of Axholme.' The man risked another smile. 'I wish them joy of it,' he added, 'we've been there already, and we took what we could carry away and burned the rest. Those blasted rebels will find no help or sustenance out there.'

At last, the King permitted himself a small smile. 'Good,' he said softly. Then, turning in the saddle to address his personal bodyguard, riding as always just behind him, he called out, 'Go on into the city and find me somewhere suitable to lodge. With a bath!' he shouted as they hastened away.

This night I shall sleep under a proper roof, he thought, *and, with any luck, lie in hot water and wash the filth of too many days on the road and too many nights in a tent from my aching body.*

He sighed.

Then he put heels to his horse and rode on towards Lincoln.

Josse had not expected his household to greet his announcement with cheers of delight. He had not, however, anticipated quite so much resistance, and expressed so swiftly: the letter from the King had only arrived that morning, and already everyone, from his beloved Helewise to the youngest child of his household servants Tilly and Gus, had managed to find a quiet moment to say, with varying degrees of politeness, consideration and diffidence, that they thought he was making a big mistake.

They all believe I'm too old! Josse thought furiously, pausing in the seemingly endless task of preparing his kit. *They have become accustomed to seeing me pottering about the house and the immediate vicinity, rarely venturing further than the abbey or, occasionally, down into Tonbridge, and they think I am capable of no more!*

It stung to realize that those he loved and respected saw him no longer as the brave, adventurous knight he had once been. But in his heart he still was that man: it might well be that this venture to join his imperilled King would be his last – in fact, in his more honest moments, Josse accepted that it probably would – but that was no reason not to answer the summons! Wasn't it something very special, to have a personal request from King John? One, moreover, on which the King had actually written a few words with his own hand?

Josse still saw those poignant, scratched-out words. And he knew he wasn't capable of ignoring the appeal. No matter how much his family and his servants disapproved, he was going.

He had finished with his gear. His sword shone bright, its edge as keen as he could make it. His knife and dagger were in their sheaths, similarly sharpened, the leather of the scabbards soft and glistening. His mail coat was free of rust, he had shaken the dust and the creases out of his surcoat, and he had packed a leather bag of clean personal linen and a washcloth. His horse, the big, golden-coated Alfred, well fed, gleaming from a thorough grooming, stood swishing his long, dark tail. Josse had managed to convince himself that Alfred, at least, was as eager as his master to be on the road.

When he could think of nothing else to keep him out in the stables, Josse straightened his shoulders, drew a deep breath and went back into the house. He went first to seek out Helewise: of all his loved ones, it was she he must convince. No, he amended, not convince; he didn't think he'd ever manage that. But what he hoped he might do was explain to her that he had no choice, he *had* to go, and he'd much rather do so with her blessing.

He found her sitting on a bench beside the house, catching the morning sun. He sat down beside her and took her hand. 'I—' he began.

But, turning to him with a smile, she interrupted him. 'Don't, my love,' she said quietly. 'I know what you would say and there is no need.' She paused, and he thought he saw the glint of tears in her grey eyes. 'I do not want you to go to the King, but it is not because I believe you incapable of helping him, for he would not have summoned you if he thought you'd be no more than a hindrance.'

A *hindrance!* Josse opened his mouth to protest, but again she stopped him.

'I don't want you to go because I love you,' she said simply. 'You and I are getting old, dear Josse, and we will not have many more years together. I am selfish, perhaps, but I begrudge every day – every hour – that I do not spend with you.'

He tried to answer – to say something jolly about being back safely before she even knew he'd gone – but found he couldn't speak. So he just held her hand a bit more tightly.

'Go with my blessing,' Helewise continued. 'I shall pray for you as often as I can, and keep you always in my thoughts and in my heart.'

He managed to mutter, 'Thank you.'

He thought she'd finished. But, after a while, she said, 'There is, though, one condition.'

His heart sank. 'Oh?'

He saw her smile, briefly. Then she said, 'Take Yves with you for good company and take Geoffroi for his strong arms.'

'But I don't want them to accompany me!' he protested. 'They mean far too much to me, both of them, and I won't have them going into danger . . . Oh.'

Too late, he realized what she'd done; how neatly she had wrought from him that admission. With a very sweet smile, she said, 'Now you know how we all feel about *you*.'

Meggie, too, was preparing to leave. She had arrived back at the House in the Woods to be greeted by her father, bustling about in the stables and the outhouses and apparently assembling, overhauling and cleaning his fighting gear. Even as she was wondering why nobody seemed to be helping him, he explained where he was going and she understood. Belatedly he had remembered to give her the message from Abbess Caliste, and now she was answering it and on the point of setting out for Hawkenlye Abbey.

Now, all appeared to be ready. Josse stood at Alfred's head, stroking the big horse's nose, calming him. Yves was stuffing a warm cloak into one of his bulging saddle bags, muttering under his breath as he went through everything he had packed. Geoffroi was already mounted on his dark brown mare; despite the sense of hectic excitement in the yard, both Geoffroi and his horse exuded an air of calm. Meggie looked up at her brother, and, sensing her eyes on him, he turned and gave her a sweet smile.

I am forgiven, then, she thought, very relieved.

There had been a nasty little scene when Josse had said to Geoffroi that he was to accompany his father and his Uncle Yves on their mission to join the King. Geoffroi had at first looked nothing but delighted but then, very swiftly, the expression of joy had been replaced by one of regret.

38

'I can't come with you, Father,' Geoffroi said. 'I'm needed here, particularly at the forge, where Jehan has far more work than he can manage alone, even with Meggie's help. Much as I'd wish to go, I must remain, and—'

'You can't be of any help whatsoever to Jehan because he's not at the forge,' Meggie interrupted, her anxiety, pain and sheer anger at Jehan's continued and unexplained absence boiling over and homing in on quite the wrong target. 'So you may as well go somewhere where you *can* be useful.'

There had been a stunned, shocked silence. Even as Josse opened his mouth to administer the well-deserved reprimand, Meggie, hearing the echo of her furious words, ran across to her brother, took his big, muscular body in her arms and whispered, 'I'm sorry, Geoffroi, I'm *so* sorry. You didn't deserve that, and I spoke without thinking.'

He had gently disengaged himself and walked away.

Now, his smile had been doubly welcome: it didn't do for loving siblings to say farewell before a potentially risky journey with unresolved distress between them.

The whole household had come out to bid the master farewell, God's speed and safe return; moved, Meggie had to look away.

Like everyone else, Meggie was uneasy about Josse setting out to join the King. She didn't know quite why; it wasn't exactly that she felt he was past his prime, and no longer up to the rigours of the road and, in all probability, some fighting along the way. Her father had been a

39

fighter for most of his life, and she well knew that he could look after himself. No: what concerned her was something else; something to do with deep sorrow . . . Although she tried to banish the images, she kept seeing Josse bent in grief, tears on his face.

Stop it, she commanded herself.

It would be a relief to get to the abbey, where it sounded as if the abbess and Sister Liese had a challenging and absorbing task for her. She tried to turn her thoughts ahead to her patient; a delirious woman, raving about something very dangerous. It was intriguing, to say the least.

But still she found her attention returning to her father and his quest. A sudden thought struck her. Was there time? She glanced around. Tilly had just raced back inside the house, apparently having forgotten to give Josse and his companions the package of food and drink she'd spent the morning preparing. Good: they wouldn't be leaving just yet.

Meggie slipped away from the press of people and ran inside. She hurried along the passage to the place she'd made her own within her father's household, reaching behind the rolled-up mattress for the pack she kept hidden there. Unfastening the drawstrings, she reached inside. The object – so familiar in her hand – was small, but quite heavy. For a moment she held it to her heart. It was her heirloom from her father, and doubly precious because of that. Then she tucked it away inside her gown and went back outside.

Very shortly afterwards, they set out. Josse

and Yves rode ahead, Geoffroi followed, with Meggie walking beside him.

Their route took them initially through the forest, so nobody would ride very fast; Meggie, on foot, could easily keep up. They would continue together until the narrow path through the trees emerged on to the main track that circled the forest. Shortly after that, they would come to the place where the roads parted: one to go on to Hawkenlye Abbey, one to curve northwards and descend to Tonbridge, down in the river valley, and then on, over the North Downs and to London and beyond.

On, in fact, to where the King was.

They went in silence for the main part, each deep in their own thoughts. Once or twice Meggie heard Josse exchange some remark with Yves, and a couple of times both brothers laughed.

Soon – too soon – they came to the parting of the ways. Looking up at her brother, Meggie thought, *I'm so glad he's going. He's like a young Josse, but he has the full strength and vigour of his youth.* She blinked away tears. *He'll look after Father. No need to worry.*

Josse, Yves and Geoffroi dismounted, and each in turn took Meggie in their arms to kiss her. Josse was the last. He didn't speak, simply stared into her eyes. He hugged her very tightly for a moment, then let her go.

She watched as the three of them rode off down the hill. When they were almost out of sight, she gave a last wave – which she doubted they'd have seen – and strode on towards the abbey.

She had the strongest sense that – quite soon – she would be going after them. She didn't know how, or why, but that didn't seem to matter. The foreknowledge was just *there*, firm in her mind, and she knew there was no point in trying to pretend otherwise.

There were rational, sensible reasons why she might feel compelled to go after them. She feared for Jehan, and perhaps her presence in the King's vicinity might somehow prevent him from the consequences of some hot-headed and foolhardy attempt on John's life. Also, if she were nearby, she would be able to help Josse – and, indeed, Yves and Geoffroi too, if they needed it.

Yes. Those were the reasons Meggie would have given had anybody asked her.

But neither was really why she knew she'd soon be heading north. Whatever was behind that strange compulsion, there was danger involved; she was quite certain of that.

Why else would she have been so irresistibly prompted to hurry back inside the House in the Woods to fetch the Eye of Jerusalem?

Three

Jehan Leferronier, mounted on a fine, borrowed bay gelding which was a lot harder to handle than his sturdy ginger horse, Auban, concentrated on remembering all that he'd been told about riding such an independent-minded and spirited animal, hoping fervently that it might take his mind off his worries.

So far, the ruse wasn't proving to be very successful.

In the company of a band of eight including himself, he was riding north. In total, their number was a great deal more than eight, but they had been divided up into small groups in the hope of thus attracting less attention. The measure had been crucial up to now, when they'd been riding through quiet, little-used lanes and tracks in the vicinity of, first, the Great Forest and then the Medway Valley. Although these places were lightly populated, there were always one or two people to watch and take note, and the sheer rarity of strangers passing through some of the most remote areas meant that it was important not to raise too much curiosity. Soon, however, the group would emerge from cover and set off up the main road to London and the Thames crossing, where, with any luck, they would merge with all the other traffic – which would no doubt increase as they neared the capital – and go unnoticed in the crowd.

The morning was fine and sunny, the company was good. Jehan had met up with one old friend, Joséph, and another man he'd known slightly, and the others seemed fine companions, as dedicated to the mission as he was himself. As far as he could tell, anyway, for the band were not encouraged to talk. They had plenty of food and drink, and the supplies would easily last until they could be replenished. His sprightly horse, although very challenging, was definitely exciting to ride, and already he was appreciating the bay gelding's finer points. Jehan was well armed – he was a blacksmith, after all, and probably knew more about preparing a fine blade than the rest of the group put together – and his kit was in good order. And the mission – this long-postponed but vital mission – was as close to his heart as it had ever been.

Nevertheless, he just couldn't stop thinking about Meggie.

He had tried so hard to persuade her to marry him and have his children. It was what he wanted; what he'd wanted almost since he'd met her, and it was why he'd worked so hard to make a living by which to support her, and cobble together a house – it was tiny, but how comfortable and cosy she had made it – in which they could live. But always, *always*, she held back. Once again – for what seemed like the hundredth time – he felt the anger course through him. *Why* did she have to keep going off by herself? What was it about that little hut deep in the forest that called to her so insistently? She'd explained, but it hadn't been much of an explanation. 'It belonged to my mother, and to my grandmother before her,' she had said, that vague, unfocused look in her eyes that came over her every time she spoke of the hut, or her mother, or her early years out in the forest. 'I have to go there from time to time for their sake.'

He was sure there was more to it than that. He suspected that the reason she was so often absent had less to do with needing to look after the little hut – which seemed sturdy enough to manage without any attention from Meggie, or indeed anyone – and more to do with her need for solitude; for time spent alone; for time away from him.

It hurt. What hurt even more was that she seemed somehow to contrive to hide the hut from him if she didn't want to be found.

It made no sense; it was totally illogical; it smacked of magic (and he told himself there was no such thing as magic). But the fact remained, and he couldn't ignore it: twice now, he had gone to seek her out in the little hut and tell her it was time to come home; he knew the hut's location perfectly well, or he had thought he did, and he'd managed to find his way there unaided several times. On those two other occasions, however, it had been different. Once it had been early in February – the first or the second; he wasn't sure – and snow had fallen heavily. Very anxious, believing she might be in trouble, he had gone to help her home. The little hut seemed to have vanished.

He told himself he must have been confused by the thick blanket of snow. When Meggie had returned a day later, rosy-cheeked and serene and clearly quite unharmed, he had said nothing.

The second time, though, had been in fine, sunny weather; in midsummer, as he recalled. On that occasion he had sought her out because he needed her assistance in the forge. As before, try as he might, he couldn't find the hut.

Since then, he had stopped going to look for her.

He didn't like it. He felt that it was wrong for her to absent herself, especially so thoroughly that he was given no chance to go and haul her home if he felt he had reason to, but he realized that she was giving him no alternative.

No. He didn't like it at all.

Too often he found himself alone at the forge and within the four walls of the little cottage. He'd had too much time to brood. And how he had brooded, both on his dissatisfaction with his life with Meggie and also, with a thrill of excitement that had all the appeal of the dangerous and the forbidden, on the current situation in England.

Thinking of this, and in particular the proximity of Prince Louis and his invading force, had brought back all of Jehan's enmity towards King John. *It was not dead but sleeping*, he had said to himself when first it had begun to keep him awake at night. *And now it is time to act.*

He had lost touch long ago with the other Bretons with whom he had crossed to England five years ago. The plan then had been to attack the King through the method of joining forces with his enemy: one of his many enemies. The Breton force had been heading for Wales, to offer their swords to the Welshman Llywelyn and fight with him to bring down the English King. But Jehan had parted company from his countrymen, and because of various events – in no small part because he met Meggie – there had been other preoccupations; he had made no attempt to rejoin his group.

Until now.

He had re-established contact with his Bretons around the time that Prince Louis had landed in Kent. It had involved a trip to the coast, an anxious, desperate time while he tried to locate the place where they'd made landfall five years ago, followed by a very tough interrogation by one of the Breton leaders who suspected he was a spy – he'd eventually managed to convince the man only through the sheer good luck of another member of the group recognizing him – and the telling of quite a lot of lies to Meggie. It had irked him that, although she seemed to expect him not to mind her absences from home for a day, two days, sometimes three or four days at a time, he was required to explain where he'd been and why he hadn't told her he was going away.

He'd made up some story about travelling further afield to look for work; a story he'd used several times since. Business at the forge had, luckily for him, picked up considerably, so perhaps she didn't find it hard to believe him.

He wasn't sure why he had lied. He'd only known he had to; he was utterly convinced he couldn't tell her the real reason for his absences. Nevertheless, sometimes he asked himself *why* he was so convinced. She'd known his purpose when they first met, for he had made quite sure to explain himself. She'd understood, and there was no reason why she wouldn't still understand now. But he'd noticed something a little strange about her: whenever the King's name was mentioned – to be more exact, whenever he muttered darkly about King John not being fit to live, let alone rule – a part of her seemed to withdraw, and her gaze went distant, as if she was looking at things he couldn't see.

It was as if she cherished some sort of feeling for the King, amounting – although it seemed absurd – almost to affection, which was surely unlikely since she'd never met him.

Or had she?

Jehan had lied to Meggie. Wasn't it entirely possible, a nasty little voice said inside his head, that she had lied to him too?

Stop, he told himself firmly. He knew he must not go on worrying over these unanswerable questions, must not continue to torture himself with his anxieties and his suspicions. Apart from the harm he was doing to himself – he had a headache that refused to abate, and wished he had thought to bring one or two of Meggie's remedies – he was not riding out for his own amusement: there was a task ahead, and a very important one, and he owed it to the cause and to his companions to give of his very best.

With a huge effort, he put Meggie out of his mind. She, and the forge on the edge of the forest, and the life they shared together there, were behind him now, and he must learn to make them as distant from his thoughts as they were physically. He had fallen a little behind his comrades, so he put his heels to the gelding's sides, aiming to catch up.

But the gelding was not the calm, patient Auban; he was a horse trained for fighting, and Jehan had been given no choice but to accept the loan. Auban, the leader of his group had told him dismissively, was no mount for a soldier. Now, the sudden stab of Jehan's heels in the bay gelding's sides had caused him to protest, and it was some moments before Jehan had him under control again.

Jehan endured the ribald teasing of his companions stoically. When they'd had enough, for now, of the endlessly repeated jokes about blacksmiths being terrible horsemen, he turned his thoughts to what lay ahead.

The Bretons had a new leader. His name was Yann Duguesclin, and he came from a small market town a little inland from the old port of Dinan, on the river Rance. He was utterly devoted to the cause, yet lacked the hot-headed impulsiveness that all too often had characterized the Bretons' attempts to achieve their purpose. Yann Duguesclin thought like a true leader: he understood combat; he understood troop movement; he understood, in short, everything to do with achieving military success. It was said he had been a mercenary soldier for much of his adult life, although nobody ventured to suggest in whose pay he had fought. Given Yann Duguesclin's views on discipline and his ruthless control of his rebel army, it was wiser not to gossip.

Yann told his troops firmly that there had been enough of throwing in their lot with Welsh princes who might at any time change sides and decide to support the King; enough of meekly following where other men led. Now, he had harangued them, it was time for the Breton band to act alone, and that action was going to be direct: the most direct possible. The group of well-armed, well-mounted Breton fighters heading north towards

East Anglia all knew their destiny: they were going to seek out John of England and, before Prince Louis or the rebel barons or anyone else had the chance to get in first, they were going to kill him.

In the infirmary at Hawkenlye Abbey, Sister Liese watched as a nursing nun tried to administer yet another nostrum to their wild-eyed patient. Sister Audrey, the ageing and rather unadventurous nun who made the herbal preparations, had run through the standard remedies two days ago and was now resorting to vaguely beneficial substances that surely stood very little chance of helping the poor woman. But how they all wanted to help her! Far from showing any small sign of improvement, however, her symptoms seemed to be getting worse. She cried and raved, beating away those who tried to soothe her and repeatedly trying to get out of bed. 'Go! Must *go!*' she kept sobbing. 'Danger! *Must stop!*' You would have thought, Sister Liese reflected, that the poor soul was in the punishing grip of a high fever, yet, other than sweating from her violent struggles, the woman was relatively cool. It didn't appear that delirium was responsible for her acute distress.

The latest remedy appeared to be affording no more relief than all its predecessors. Sister Liese gave a quiet sigh. She wondered what the strange old nun who had been the abbey's herbalist in the past would have suggested. Sister Tiphaine, they said, had an almost magical touch with all growing things and was rumoured to have

50

conversed with the spirits of the forest. 'Super-stitious nonsense,' Sister Liese muttered to herself. Nevertheless, she knew full well that she was fast approaching the state of mind where she'd have authorized any treatment at all if it had promised to work.

Once again, Sister Liese turned to peer down the long infirmary ward to the entrance. Early that morning, at her wits' end, she had asked Abbess Caliste's permission to send for Meggie, and the abbess, bless her compassionate heart, had instantly done so. Now, as Sister Liese waited with growing impatience (she was, she realized, pinning quite a lot of hope on Meggie), she tried to piece together all she knew about the young woman.

They had met, of course, many times over the years, although Sister Liese admitted to herself that this didn't mean she *knew* Meggie; she didn't, not in any meaningful way. *More to do with me than with her*, she thought honestly. Meggie, it was true, had a reserve about her, but the infirmarer knew full well that she had held off from making any approach towards closer friendship with Meggie.

Like old Sister Tiphaine, Meggie too had a connection with the forest. Hers was even stronger, for she was the daughter of one of the strange, powerful Forest People. She had apparently been trained in their ways, even to the extent – or so the rumours said – of visiting the place somewhere in Brittany where the elders of the people were skilled in the treatment of those who were sick in their minds.

51

Sister Liese knew that she must overcome her deep-rooted prejudice about the Forest People and their strange ways. Abbess Caliste had told her so, gently but firmly: 'Whilst it is true that they perceive God in a way that is not the same as ours,' she had once said, 'that is no reason to be suspicious of their methods and dismiss them as ignorant. One has only to look at their skills as healers – again, different from ours but no less effective – to realize that God works through their hands just as he does through yours and those of your nursing nuns.'

The infirmarer had been striving to obey. She felt sure she had made progress. Now, in this current emergency, if help could be found for her patient she didn't really care *where* it came from. She was fervently praying and hoping that the deeply disturbed woman in the infirmary would respond to whatever Meggie came up with, and whole-heartedly grateful that Meggie was on her way.

The distraught woman wasn't Sister Liese's only patient, after all, and people suffering from the pain of injuries, and the distress and anxiety of sickness, needed peace and quiet, and they certainly weren't getting any at the moment. Patients and nuns alike reflected in their tense faces the stress of living with the constant, distressing shouts and screams, and only the deaf and the insensate were spared.

Once again, Sister Liese glanced towards the door. Still no sign of Meggie. *Watching the door isn't going to make her arrive any sooner*, the infirmarer told herself firmly. She turned back to the woman in the bed.

52

It was hard to guess her age. Her skin was heavily lined, giving an impression of advanced years that might be inaccurate. She was small, dark-complexioned and fiery, with black eyes shaped like almonds and set at a slight tilt in her face. She was modest in the extreme: even the Hawkenlye nuns, long accustomed to a life in which nobody displayed an inch of bodily flesh if they could help it, had been taken aback at the lengths to which the raving woman went to keep her garments wrapped tightly around her. It had taken the combined persuasive efforts of the abbess and the infirmarer to encourage the woman to remove the long white scarf wound around her head, tightly fastened beneath the carefully arranged veil and covering both her face, down to the eyebrows, and all of her chin and throat. Her hair, revealed, was black and streaked with grey at the temples and, as soon as Sister Liese had finished inspecting the skull for wounds (she had wondered if the woman's deep distress had been caused by a blow to the head), the patient had rapidly and deftly covered herself up once more.

The infirmarer still hadn't managed to examine her patient below the throat. *It is just as well*, she thought ruefully, *that I don't suspect broken ribs or a cracked pelvis.*

The dark woman had been travelling from the coast towards London, accompanied by her son, when she had taken ill. The son, worried about her mounting distress, had brought her to Hawkenlye Abbey. Now, having handed her over to the nuns' care, he spent most of his time outside in the sunshine. Sister Liese didn't blame him, for his mother was absolutely furious with him. When he ventured inside to see how she was, she instantly began shouting at him in their own language, waving her arms, little hands screwed up into fists as if she longed to punch him, face distorted in fury and spittle spraying from her mouth. Sister Liese surmised, from the woman's repeated shouts of '*Go! Must go!*' that the anger was because the son had interrupted the journey to wherever they were bound and brought his sick mother to the nuns' care.

At times, the haunted, driven look in those slanting dark eyes was quite terrifying.

At the abbey gates, Meggie exchanged a greeting with Sister Teresa, on watch in her little shelter. 'I know why you're here,' the nun whispered, 'and the infirmarer isn't the only one who'll say a prayer of thanks that you answered our call.'

'I was . . .' Meggie began. Then from the infirmary a loud cry rang out, harsh and distressing. 'Oh. I see what you mean.'

'Go on in,' Sister Teresa urged, giving Meggie a little push. Meggie clutched her satchel and hurried off.

The infirmarer strode down the long ward to greet her, one of the nursing nuns hastening to join her, almost as if Meggie's arrival deserved an official welcome. Meggie recognized the younger nun as Sister Maria, and noticed with dismay that the long, plain face – usually the girl resembled an amiable horse – was haggard with anxiety.

'Thank you for coming,' Sister Liese said, giving Meggie a little bow. 'Please, come with me.' Spinning round, she strode back up the infirmary to the recess at the far end. Pulling aside the curtain, she said quietly, 'Here is our patient.'

Meggie tried to take in the whole scene with one quick glance: the patient, emitting harsh little cries, twisting violently in the narrow bed, hands busy pulling, pleating and folding the linen sheet; Sister Audrey, some potion in a little cup that she had presumably been trying to administer, but most of which had been spilled down her habit; another nun, even younger than Sister Maria, whose big brown eyes were full of unshed tears. And, even now hurrying down the ward and almost upon them, a man of about twenty, black hair worn long, tall and broad in the chest, his handsome face creased into a frown. Before the woman in the bed could catch sight of him, Meggie took a deep breath and said, with quiet control, 'I should like a few moments alone with her, please.'

Such was the authority in her soft voice that the cubicle emptied instantly. On departing, Sister Liese – the last to leave – firmly drew the curtains into place.

When the sound of receding footsteps had faded, along with the hissed and angry conversation between the tall young man and the infirmarer, Meggie sat down on the edge of the woman's bed and, for a while, simply smiled at her. The woman's cries slowed and then stopped, and gradually her rapid, gasping breaths calmed. Her hands relaxed, one of them trying to smooth out the bunched, creased sheet. After a while, Meggie covered it with her own. Meeting the woman's wide-eyed stare, she said softy, 'It doesn't matter. There's no harm done.'

She thought the woman had understood. Under her touch, the restless hand trembled and then lay still.

Meggie said, keeping her tone calm, as if this were an everyday conversation, 'There were a lot of people, weren't there?' Slowly the woman nodded. 'Too many, perhaps,' Meggie added.

The woman nodded again, more vigorously.

'They were trying to help you,' Meggie said quietly. 'They were worried about you.'

The woman gave a deep sigh, closing her eyes briefly as if she wished to shut out the world and all its troubles. Meggie was about to speak again – were her tentative words being understood? – when the woman said, 'Yes. I know. They are good but they do *not* help.' A flash of anger crossed the lean face.

Meggie made herself wait until it had passed. Then she said, 'How, then, can we help?'

'*I must go!*' the woman said in a harsh voice. 'I – we – have an urgent mission. There is danger, bad, evil danger, and nobody understands the peril but us; nobody can stop the evil but us!' She paused, then – as if it was a secret and should not be spoken of aloud – hissed, 'Through their greed and their folly my kinsmen began it, although they cannot have known what they were unleashing on the world, and now it is for us to finish it.' The dark eyes flashed with rage and frustration. 'It is our responsibility!'

Meggie studied her patient. Was this the ranting of someone whose mind was unhinged? It seemed wise to explore a little further before deciding.

'*We?*' she said. '*Us?*' The woman frowned. 'You said *we* and *us*,' Meggie elaborated. 'You were not travelling alone?'

The woman shook her head. 'No. I am with my son.' She jerked her head in the direction of the door, at the far end of the infirmary. 'Faruq.' She all but spat out the name.

'He is very concerned about you,' Meggie said.

'He made me come here!' the woman cried. 'But I cannot stay! I will recover, I tell him, I will be better as soon as we travel again, and how *dare* Faruq override my wishes? Must *go!*' she repeated urgently. She threw off Meggie's hand and tried to get out of bed.

'Won't you wait a little, regain your strength?' Meggie suggested mildly, not doing anything to restrain her. 'There is nourishing food here, and a warm bed. Will your journey not be accomplished all the more swiftly if you permit yourself a short delay while you rest awhile?'

The woman paused. She fixed Meggie with an alarming glare, and then very slowly sank back on her pillows. 'Perhaps,' she admitted.

There was silence in the little recess. For a while, all was still; the woman closed her eyes, and Meggie wondered if she had gone to sleep.

Then she sensed a small movement behind her. Turning, she saw the curtains part just enough to admit the tall young man. Catching his eye, Meggie put her finger to her lips and he nodded his understanding. He came to stand right beside

57

her. 'She sleeps?' he asked, his words barely more than a breath in her ear.

'Yes,' she whispered back.

Together they studied the woman. She seemed to have fallen into the deep sleep of total exhaustion. Her body was relaxed, her mouth had fallen open and she was snoring gently, her breathing slow, deep and regular.

The young man's face broke into a relieved smile. 'You have worked a small miracle,' he observed. 'You have done in a few moments what nobody else managed in as many hours.'

'I think she had worn herself out,' Meggie replied.

'Perhaps, but you had the sense to send everyone away,' he said. Meggie thought that it was a little ungrateful to speak of sending away the kindly, concerned nuns who had been trying so hard to help, and it seemed the young man agreed, for swiftly he added, 'They have done all they could, I know.'

Silence fell once more. Then Meggie said, 'What is your mother's name?'

'Hadil,' he said. He grinned suddenly. 'In our language it means the cooing of doves.'

Meggie smothered a laugh. 'Well, I'm sure she lives up to her lovely name under normal circumstances,' she said kindly.

The young man – Faruq – gave her a sidelong glance. He didn't reply.

He moved away a little and stood staring down at his mother, his face unreadable. Meggie took the chance to study him. She saw now that he was a little older than she'd initially thought, for, up close to him, she could make out fine lines around his eyes. Where his mother was small and intense, he shared barely a feature with her, except for his intensely black hair and the tough wiriness of his body. He was tall, well muscled, long-legged and elegant; his skin was pale where his mother's was dark, and his eyes were a mix of blue and green. He was dressed in a shin-length tunic of fine wool, padded hose and good boots, on top of which he wore a good-quality cloak. Like his mother, he was kitted out for riding; Meggie had noticed her cloak, draped across the end of her bed, and the costly boots on the floor beneath it. Underneath the tunic the young man wore a chemise in a fabric that Meggie didn't recognize. It was fine, with a slight gloss, and brightly white.

After a pause, Meggie asked, 'Where are you bound?'

Faruq spun round to look at her. His dark face showed a torment of frustration, and she suspected anger was boiling up, as yet under control. 'It is not important,' he said with cold, firm finality, 'since it appears we shall be progressing no further.'

Four

Helewise shifted the heavy bundle to the other shoulder and trudged on along the narrow, winding track through the forest. It was very early in the morning on the day after Josse's departure, and almost all of her thoughts rode with him.

Although she had kept a smile of encouragement on her face as he, Geoffroi and Yves rode away, with Meggie walking behind, the effort had drained her. Considering that only four members of the large household had left, the House in the Woods had felt alarmingly empty once they'd gone.

She had wandered listlessly from small task to small task for the remainder of the day, finding nothing to take her mind off her anxiety. Tilly, Gus and their children managed the domestic life of the house, just as they always did, and food appeared on the table that evening; a good, solid meal, as if Tilly were exhorting the depleted family to keep up its strength. Ninian and Eloise, too, had their children to care for and, with Josse's absence, Ninian was now nominally the head of the household, which brought its own responsibilities.

One of which, it became apparent straight away, was the provision of food and shelter for what seemed a large band of the bowmen busy harrying the French invader in and around the Great Forest. It wasn't as if they'd taken advantage of Josse being away to start using his house as a place of succour, for Helewise recognized many of the faces from previous visits; that evening, however, was the first time so many had turned up all at once.

The House in the Woods was largely self-sufficient. Out beyond the forest fringes there was a handful of small, inconspicuous fields under cultivation for wheat and barley. In an acre of cleared land close to the house, there was an expertly tended and very productive vegetable garden. For meat, there was lamb in season and mutton for the rest of the year; Josse's sheep shared pasture lands with Dominic's, and the flock was steadily growing. Both men were making good money from the wool, and, in those times of such hardship, having a regular supply of meat was even more valuable than money.

So, feeding the bowmen had not presented much of a problem, although the fare, produced at short notice by Tilly, was simple. They had all then set out bedrolls and settled down for the night in the hall. As one of them remarked, it made a nice change to sleep beside the embers of a good, big fire.

The presence of the bowmen hadn't disturbed her; indeed, it had been quite diverting, for the men had been rough but amusing company. But their visit had served to harden a tentative idea that had been forming in her mind: she did not want to stay at the House in the Woods without Josse. There was no point, she had discovered, in trying to analyse why she felt this way. For one thing, it was such a powerful feeling that she knew it would not respond to logic, and for another, she suspected it had to do with what the House in the Woods would be like if Josse didn't come back, and she couldn't bear even to begin to think about that.

Having made her decision, the next question had been: where should she go? She was welcome

61

at Hawkenlye Abbey – Abbess Caliste had made that perfectly clear – and there was always work there for another pair of hands. *But I left the abbey,* she thought. *I cannot go back.*

Besides, there was another place that was possibly even more suitable . . .

And now, with the sun just appearing above the eastern horizon and colouring the soft clouds pale yellow, she was on her way. She had kept the farewells brief, merely mentioning to Ninian before they all retired the previous evening where she was going, and saying that she would be away for several days.

At the place she was heading for, she would find the constant work that she so badly needed; it was, moreover, a place that was her own, that she had brought into existence and where she was in overall charge. She didn't like to admit that this was a factor in her decision, but she knew that it was. *Pride,* she castigated herself as she shifted the bundle yet again to the less painful shoulder. *Always my pride, that I must ever see myself as the calm, dependable person in authority, whom others leap to obey and who knows what to do in even the most trying of circumstances.*

It was a matter she must take up yet again with her priest. How many times, she mused, had he heard her speak the same words? How many times had she performed the penance, always determined that she would force herself to do better? Well, he – and she – would just have to endure it again.

She was on the final half-mile. As if imposing

a preliminary penance, she made herself walk faster. Thin strands of bramble scratched at her face, she turned her foot on a half-buried root, the bundle felt as if it had doubled in weight and size, so much did the muscles of her shoulders, arms and back burn, and still she forced her pace. At last, aching all over, sobbing for breath and gasping with thirst – for the morning was already warm – she burst into the little clearing before the Sanctuary and, with vast relief, dropped the bundle on to the soft, mossy grass.

It did not take her long to recover for, despite her years, she was strong and fit. She stood up, brushed the leaves and twigs from her dark gown, straightened her headdress and veil, then rolled up her sleeves and opened up the Sanctuary. For now, she had it to herself, for it was still too early for the day's supplicants and nobody had stayed overnight. *Good*, she thought. She lit a fire in the circle of hearth stones in the middle of the room, then, as it took hold, collected a couple of buckets and went to fetch water from the little stream that ran nearby. She put some on to heat, for there was laundry to do and it promised to be a good drying day. Then she tipped a large quantity of stream water over the flagged stone floor and gave it the sort of scrubbing it hadn't received in months.

By mid-morning, when the first of the day's visitors came by, she had finished. The interior of the Sanctuary sparkled with cleanliness, with every pot and knife washed and dried, the simple wooden shelves emptied, dusted and re-stocked, the bedding laundered and now spread out on the bramble and hazel bushes to bleach and dry in the bright sunshine. Helewise had had time to unpack her large bundle – it contained her bedroll, a couple of soft blankets and a change of personal linen – and to tidy herself, too, and now she greeted the arrivals with a serene smile.

Thus the first day of Josse's absence began.

Early that same morning, Meggie, waking to profound darkness and a different smell, wondered at first where she was. Then, stretching, she remembered.

Hawkenlye Abbey was overflowing. The sick, the hungry, the wounded and the plain desperate had always found their way to its gates, and now, when the usual and just about bearable hardships had been augmented by a new sense of uncertainty, the daily, steady trickle had turned into a spring tide. Every bed and makeshift cot in the infirmary was occupied. Every day the monks down in the vale were stuffing sacks with straw to make more mattresses, and they were now erecting awnings to form shelter from the rain, if nothing else, since their guest accommodation had long been filled. Even the beds in the nuns' refuge for penitent whores and unwed mothers were all in use; not exclusively with whores and unwed mothers, for those who were at the end of their strength and their endurance were far too exhausted to be fussy.

Abbess Caliste had offered Meggie the little room where she sat and worked each day, and had herself fetched a palliasse, a pillow and a blanket. Meggie had settled down for the night with her head under the abbess's large, oak table. The room had one small window, set high up beside the door, and its size, together with the room's location in a shadowy corner at the end of the cloister, accounted for the darkness. That, and the fact that it was still so early: now, lying still and listening, Meggie couldn't hear a sound.

She knew she wouldn't sleep again. Propping herself up, arms behind her head, she thought about her father. How far would he have got? They would travel swiftly, for Josse and Geoffroi both knew the terrain very well, at least for the first twenty or thirty miles. With any luck, some time today they'd cross the wide Thames estuary and land safely on the northern side. Their plan had been to keep off the bigger roads and the main thoroughfares, keeping to the lanes, tracks and byways. Josse had told her he intended to avoid London. 'Too full of Prince Louis's supporters,' he'd added.

Prince Louis. Meggie's musings moved to the invader. It was odd, she reflected, that, despite Hawkenlye Abbey being so full, and despite the fact that many had come because they knew a foreign army was somewhere in the land, nobody seemed very worried about it. *It's not their war*, she thought. *It's a power struggle between two men who both wish to rule the land, and whichever one wins, it won't make much difference; not, at any rate, to the vast mass of ordinary people.*

'Kings and princes fight for who owns the land,' Josse had once said in one of his more philosophical moods. 'Everyone else fights for existence.'

Meggie smiled. She suspected he was quite right.

Her mind roved on and an image of Jehan appeared. Where was he? Was he, too, heading north-east? Oh, but he . . .

Deliberately she stopped the thought. It hurt in so many ways to think about Jehan that it really was better not to.

She got up and, with swift, economical movements, shook out her blanket and the thin straw mattress, rolling them tidily around the pillow, fastening the binding and stowing the bundle behind the door. Then she went outside to the washroom. Back in the abbess's room, brushing and re-plaiting her hair, she heard running footsteps outside. There was a peremptory tap on the door, and it opened to reveal Luke, one of the lay brothers, a pitchfork in his hand and a strong smell of horse manure clinging to him.

'You're to come, quickly,' he panted. 'Please,' he added with belated politeness.

'Of course.' Meggie was already stooping to pick up her satchel. 'What's happened?'

Brother Luke was already hurrying back along the cloister, turning back from time to time to make sure she was following. 'It's her in the infirmary,' he said. 'The noisy one.'

Hadil! Meggie quickened her pace to a run and, overtaking Brother Luke, raced to the infirmary.

She forced herself to slow to a dignified walk on entering. The infirmarer was very strict with all her nurses, insisting that at no time did anyone display a sense of panic or undue hurry, lest a nervous, anxious patient be further troubled. As Meggie made her way majestically up the ward, she thought impatiently that it had never seemed so long.

The curtain was drawn across the recess. There was no raucous, angry shouting; no wailing or sobbing. Nothing, in fact, except the mutter of worried voices.

She slipped in between the curtain and the wall and went in. Sister Liese and Abbess Caliste stood, heads close together. '. . . kept a watch, but we've been so busy and I didn't think there was any need,' the infirmarer was saying in an anguished voice.

Abbess Caliste looked up and caught Meggie's eye, then, turning back to Sister Liese, said calmly, 'Nobody did, Sister. Besides, your nurses have all been working so hard and so ceaselessly that sleep was imperative, and it was quite right to send them to their beds and leave just the one nun on duty.'

'She should have . . .' the infirmarer began. But a swift look from her superior silenced her.

The bed was empty: Hadil had gone.

'She's not – I suppose she hasn't merely gone outside for some fresh air, or to speak to her son?' Meggie ventured.

The two nuns shook their heads. 'We have searched, and there is no sign of her,' the abbess said.

'What does Faruq think?' The nuns exchanged a glance. 'He doesn't know, does he?'

'No,' Abbess Caliste said.

Then Meggie understood the urgent summons. 'You want me to tell him.'

'Yes,' the abbess replied serenely. 'You spoke

to him yesterday, Meggie. You have, perhaps, reached the beginning of friendship. It would, I believe, be best that he hear this news from you.'

'Of course,' Meggie murmured. It was hard, as she and virtually everyone else had discovered, to refuse the abbess. 'He's down with the monks in the vale, I imagine?'

'He is,' said the abbess.

Both nuns were looking at her expectantly. There was no alternative but to do as she was asked.

Faruq was standing outside the guest accommodation in the vale, vigorously rubbing his face and head with a length of linen. He was dressed as immaculately as on the previous day, and looked clean and refreshed. Putting down the cloth and noticing Meggie, his expression clouded; she realized that surprising him in his ablutions had embarrassed him.

She stepped back a pace or two, lowering her head.

In a few moments he was standing beside her.

'I'm sorry to disturb you so early,' she said.

He shook his head impatiently. 'It is no matter. What has happened?' She paused, and he said with urgent, anxious irritation, 'Tell me! My mother, is she worse?'

Meggie met his light eyes. 'No. She's gone.'

For a moment he didn't answer. Then, slowly, a wry half-smile spread over his face. 'Gone,' he repeated softly. 'Oh, I should have foreseen this!' His eyes narrowed in anger, but Meggie didn't think it was with her; already she had

68

formed the opinion that Faruq wasn't a man who would punish the messenger who brought bad news.

However, he might well wish to punish those he imagined had been neglectful of their duty. 'There was an infirmary nun on duty overnight,' she said, 'but only one, for all of them are worn out with the long hours of work and it was judged best if—'

He held up a hand, stopping her. 'Please, there is no need to defend them,' he said. 'I have seen with my own eyes how they wear themselves out in their care for their patients.' He hesitated. 'I am angry with myself, for not having the sense to realize what would happen and issue a warning. Even more, however, I am furious with my mother, for she is stubborn, headstrong, and now has put herself in danger, for she is not equipped to travel through an unknown land and, even now, already, she will be at grave risk.'

There was a silence; a heavy sort of silence, Meggie thought. Her mind was working busily, throwing up suggestions, ideas, solutions. She said, 'Yesterday you said there wasn't any point in telling me where you were bound, you and your mother, because it seemed you wouldn't be going any further. I think, don't you, that you should tell me now.'

He stared at her. 'Why?

She sighed. 'Because you and I are going to go after her.'

Faruq and Hadil had arrived at the abbey on horse-back, and their mounts had been tended in the

Hawkenlye stables. Now, only Faruq's graceful arch-necked black gelding remained: Hadil's horse – a grey mare, according to her son – had gone.

Meggie and Faruq stood side by side in the stables, and she sensed his intense frustration. 'Only one horse!' he moaned. 'I will have to go alone, although—'

'You won't,' she interrupted. 'You don't know the countryside round here, and wouldn't know where to begin. I have a horse, and he is nearby. Pack up what you need, tell the kitchen nuns we need food and water, and by the time you've done that and tacked up, I'll be back.'

He began to say something, but she didn't wait to hear what it was. She gathered up her skirts in one hand, ran out of the stable and raced for the abbey gates.

Auban raised his head from his grazing and regarded her with friendly interest. Sweating and puffing, for she had run all the way, Meggie put her arms round his neck and briefly leaned against him. 'We're going on an excursion, Auban,' she told him. He flicked an ear. 'I have to borrow you without your master's permission, but then he's not here to ask, so I have no choice.' She swallowed the emotions that flared up at the thought of Jehan's absence and what it probably meant. 'Come over to the hut' – she took hold of a lock of Auban's long, luxuriant cream mane – 'and I'll fetch your tack.'

She worked swiftly, and soon the stocky horse stood ready. She wondered briefly whether to

70

pack a bag for herself, but time was precious and she begrudged even the few minutes it would take her. She secured the little dwelling, then set off again. She led the horse for the first half-mile, for the track made riding difficult, then mounted up and kicked him into a trot, then a canter.

'Well, then?' she asked.

She and Faruq had left the abbey and drawn rein a few yards from the gates.

Faruq turned to look at her. His eyes didn't quite meet hers.

She said, exasperated, 'Look, Faruq, we need to find your mother because she's in danger, and you said as much yourself. She's also sick. We need to find her *quickly*. I appreciate that whatever you're doing here is your own business, and probably a deadly secret, but if you don't tell me where you were bound, I'll have no idea where your mother might have gone and we'll probably set off in quite the wrong direction and waste an awful lot of time.' She ran out of breath. 'So?'

He was smiling at her. 'I did not hesitate because I was reluctant to share the deadly secret with you. I hesitated because I don't actually know where we were heading.'

'You – *what?*'

He looked abashed. 'We have – had – a destination, a purpose,' he said, 'but I do not know where we must go.'

She shook her head, not understanding.

He watched her. The tension seemed to increase as, slowly, he made up his mind to trust her.

'We came to England because we must seek out the Queen,' he said eventually.

Whatever Meggie had expected him to say, it certainly wasn't that. 'I suppose,' she said with heavy irony, 'there's no point in asking why?'

He shook his head. Then, quickly, he said, 'Please, it is not with the intention of hurting or harming her, or of in any way distressing her – this you *must* believe.'

Strangely, for she barely knew him, she did. 'And you think your mother may know where to find her, and has set off to do so?'

He shrugged: a very foreign gesture, she thought. 'I do not know. Before she told me about the . . .' He stopped. 'Before we embarked on our long journey, I would have said she had no idea about such worldly matters as how to discover the whereabouts of the queen of an alien land, for she – my mother – has always been a woman whose very existence was focused on home, hearth and kin; who rarely, if ever, raised her eyes above her own, near horizon. Now, I have come to see her in another light altogether.'

Meggie suppressed her irritation. *All very poetic and moving*, she thought, *but it's not helping us find Hadil*. 'I know, or can guess, where the Queen is,' she said with some asperity.

'You can?' Faruq stared at her in amazement.

Meggie grinned. 'Don't look so impressed,' she said, 'it's common knowledge.' That was probably an exaggeration, but Meggie had the advantage of frequent contact with Josse, who knew the ways of kings and queens better than most and who, where necessary, could make a very good guess.

Faruq was slowly shaking his head, still, clearly, deeply impressed. 'So, which road will my mother have taken? Which way should we go?'

'We go that way,' Meggie said without hesitation. Pointing almost due west, along the road that wound off around the bulge of the forest, she added, 'If your mother has discovered where the Queen is, that's where we'll find her.'

Five

A mile or so down the road, breaking a silence that had lasted for some time, Faruq said, 'She wasn't really sick.'

Meggie smiled. 'Ah. I see.'

'But she was totally exhausted!' Faruq cried, as if she had demanded an explanation. 'We've been travelling for so long and come so far, and then the sea was very rough when we undertook the crossing – she was so frightened, and it was not easy to calm her – and then she began vomiting, and didn't want me to watch, so it was impossible to help her, you see, and then she insisted we set out straight away, although she was still so very weak, and I . . . well, I said she *had* to have a rest and I made her go to that abbey.' He paused, his expression anguished. 'I just thought she'd get a proper bed for the night, and perhaps a hot

73

meal. I didn't expect those nuns to be so diligent.' He glanced at Meggie, eyes wide in wonder. 'They really cared about her!'

'They did,' she agreed.

He went on looking at her. Then he said, 'You knew she wasn't ill, didn't you?'

'I didn't think the raving was because she'd lost her wits, no,' she replied. He raised a dark eyebrow. 'I've had a little instruction in caring for those who wander in their minds,' she said briefly. Before he could ask, she went on, 'Enough to suspect that your mother was angry rather than mad. I imagine she wasn't at all pleased when Sister Liese insisted on putting her to bed and looking after her?'

Faruq tried to suppress a smile and failed. 'She was livid.'

'And so, cleverly, she fooled us all into thinking she had fallen into a deep, restorative sleep,' Meggie said softly, 'then, once everyone had settled down for the night and there was just one worn-out nun left on duty, she slipped out, saddled her horse and set out to continue on this vitally important journey of yours.'

Faruq said, 'I hope that nun won't get into trouble. It wasn't her fault, I'm sure of that. My mother can be very crafty.'

Meggie nodded. 'I'm sure. No, I don't believe she will.' They had come to a stretch where branches bordering the track swept down low, so that for a while they had to ride single file. When there was room to ride abreast again, she said, 'Will you not tell me about it? This journey, or quest, or whatever it is?'

'No.' He frowned, shaking his head. 'I have told you already more than I ought to.'

'You had to, or else I'd have had no idea how to set about following your mother!' she said crossly.

He inclined his head in acknowledgement. 'True. But, you see, in truth I don't know the whole story, not from the beginning. My mother refuses to . . . She and her . . .' He stopped, and she had the impression he'd just forced himself to bite back whatever he'd been about to say. 'As to what I do know, she made me swear, on everything that is most dear and precious to me, that which I hold deepest in my heart, not to reveal our purpose.' His light eyes were fixed on hers. 'It is dangerous. Believe me, there is such grave danger, and we . . .' Once again, very firmly he shut his mouth.

'If you've taken such a solemn oath,' Meggie said after a while, 'then it wouldn't be right for me to try to persuade you to break it.' He gave her a look of such gratitude that she was deeply moved. 'But if circumstances change and you discover you need someone on your side, and perhaps that entails a little explanation, then I'll respect the need for secrecy. And I'll do my best to help you,' she added.

He smiled. 'Already you are helping me.'

'Yes, so I am.' She smiled back.

It was around noon, to judge by the sun's position, that they found Hadil.

They came across the grey mare grazing beside the road. She was still saddled, and a large, soft leather bag was secured behind the saddle. She had a broken rein and there were grass stains on her right shoulder.

Meggie and Faruq hurriedly dismounted, and Faruq quickly secured the horses, looping their reins around the branch of a beech tree. The mare, whickering a greeting to her stable mate, moved over to the tethered horses. She was lame, favouring her right foreleg.

Faruq muttered something; words of fear and anxiety, from his tone, in a language Meggie didn't understand. The meaning of the lame mare, her stained shoulder and the broken rein was only too clear. Together they began searching.

It was Meggie who found Hadil. She lay half asleep, or perhaps half conscious, in soft grass a few paces back from the road. Her face was shaded by a mass of ferns, which concealed much of her body. It was only the scarlet fringe of the shawl she had wrapped around her that had caught Meggie's eye.

She called out to Faruq. Even as he came pounding over to her, she was already crouching at Hadil's side. She took one of the woman's hands in both of hers. The flesh was cool, but not cold. Hastily Meggie's fingers went to the upper side of the wrist, searching for the pulse of life that beat there. At first she couldn't detect it. Then she moved her fingers slightly and there it was. Slow, but quite steady. She said calmly, 'She's alive.'

Faruq gave a sort of sob, and began a long, soft, monotone muttering that Meggie guessed was a prayer. With quick hands she began feeling for injuries. There was a large bump on the right side of Hadil's forehead. Her right arm was very swollen; it was either broken or badly sprained. There was a cuff at the end of the sleeve of her soft white undergarment and already this tight band had made the hand puff up alarmingly. Unable to fathom how the cuff fastened, Meggie drew out her little knife and cut it. It seemed to her – although she knew she was probably being over-optimistic – that straight away the hand began to subside. She ran her fingers up and down Hadil's forearm again, then, gently laying it across the woman's breast, resumed her examination.

She was very aware of Faruq standing over her. He had finished his prayers and she could hear his rapid breathing. He had the good sense to keep quiet and let her get on with her task.

After a while, she sat back on her heels and said, 'She has probably broken her arm; one or both of the bones below the elbow. I can treat it, but not here, although I can make her a little more comfortable so that riding won't be too painful.'

He nodded. 'What else?'

Meggie looked down at Hadil. 'She banged her head, probably when her horse fell, as both her injuries and the horse's are on the same side.' She bent down close to Hadil, and said gently, 'Hadil? Hadil? Can you hear me? It's Meggie, from the abbey, and Faruq is here with me.'

Hadil's eyes fluttered open. She looked at Meggie, and at Faruq behind her, and gave a groan. She said one word, very sharply – Faruq gave a gasp – then closed her eyes again.

'What did she say?' Meggie asked him in a whisper.

Faruq was shaking his head. 'I will not tell you.' His face wore a strange expression: half disapproving, half awestruck. 'I had no idea she *knew* such words,' he muttered.

Meggie chuckled. 'It appears she's not very pleased that we've caught her up.'

He, too, laughed briefly. 'I believe you are right.'

'I don't think she knocked herself out,' Meggie said, 'because it looks as if she was able to crawl from wherever she fell – which must have been on or close to the track – to this well-shaded spot. But she's had a blow to the head, and she's hurt her arm quite badly, so what we must do is take her somewhere so that she can rest and be well looked after. We'll—'

'I'm not going back to that abbey.' Hadil's eyes were still closed but she spoke with total authority.

'Mother, you *must*,' Faruq said. 'You need rest and care, and we—'

'I will not go to the abbey,' Hadil repeated, quite a lot more loudly.

'But—'

'*No!*' she shouted. Meggie's ears rang with the reverberations.

'Hadil, why don't you want to go to Hawkenlye Abbey?' she asked gently.

Hadil's eyes flew open. 'They are kind, and they are skilful, I have no doubt. But they pray, and their God is with them always, and they are not of my faith.'

'Isn't he your God too?' Meggie asked.

But Hadil's only response was to close her eyes once more.

Meggie looked up at Faruq. 'What do you think?'

He straightened up, walked a few paces away and beckoned to her. 'If we take her back to the nuns,' he said very quietly once she stood beside him, 'she'll only try to get away again.'

'She'll find it hard to ride with that damaged arm,' Meggie observed.

Faruq gave a sort of snort. 'If you think that'll hold her back, you don't know my mother.'

Meggie nodded. She was thinking that, even if somehow they managed to shut Hadil up in the abbey so that escape became a physical impossibility (and it would be all but impossible to persuade Abbess Caliste to agree to *that*), that wasn't the only important consideration: far more crucial was Hadil's state of mind. To imprison her against her will would be very bad for her, in virtually every way Meggie could think of.

There was, however, another possibility.

Later, when they had all had a bite to eat and Meggie had bound up Hadil's arm as best she could, they were ready to set out. After considerable thought, they had decided that Meggie should ride Auban again, with Hadil sitting in front of her, and Faruq remain mounted on his black gelding; the grey mare, limping quite badly, would follow on a leading rein. Auban was sturdy and his pace was smooth and comfortable; furthermore, as Meggie assured Faruq

79

several times, he wasn't the sort of horse to shy at shadows and be spooked by sudden sounds in the undergrowth. Short of making poor Hadil walk, he was the best they were going to do.

Between them, they got Hadil mounted. The pain made her bite her lips so hard that they bled. Meggie, suffering with her, knew better than to flood her with sympathy; the woman had clearly made up her mind not to cry out, and so Meggie supported her in silence. Only when they were once more on the move, retracing their steps back towards the abbey, did she say quietly in Hadil's ear, 'The pain will lessen soon. It was a pity we had to move you, but unavoidable.'

Hadil nodded. After a pause, she said, 'Already it is more manageable, and I am able to release my lip from the clench of my teeth.' She gave a very short laugh, quickly curtailed.

'I will make you comfortable once we reach our destination,' Meggie said. 'I shall prepare a drink that will both help you sleep and ease the pain.'

'A miracle worker, then,' Hadil remarked wryly.

'A herbalist,' Meggie corrected. 'And, before you ask, no, we're not going to Hawkenlye Abbey.'

'I see.' Even pain and distress couldn't remove the note of satisfaction from Hadil's voice.

'Not that you deserve such consideration, mind,' Meggie couldn't help adding. 'You brought this entirely on yourself by creeping out and running off on your own.'

To her surprise, Hadil nodded again. 'I know,' she said meekly. Meggie thought she'd finished but, after a moment, she went on, 'I realize you

80

think I'm a foolish old woman who has caused a lot of trouble and anxiety and who really ought to know better.' Meggie, who quite agreed, refrained from saying so. 'All I can say in my own defence,' Hadil concluded in a suddenly sharp, hissed whisper, 'is that you have no idea what is at stake.'

From then on, she didn't utter another word.

When they reached the House in the Woods, Meggie realized straight away that there had recently been a big crowd of people there. The courtyard still bore signs of many horses, although Will was doing his best to clear up, and the grass either side of the path up to the house was flattened and crushed by the passage of booted feet.

Ninian must have heard her talking to Will, for he came hurrying out to greet her.

She cut short his questions. 'Is Helewise here?'

'No, she's gone to the Sanctuary.' He came to stand closer. 'We had a band of visitors, last night,' he went on in a low voice. His eyes flicked to Hadil, then back to Meggie. 'Some of the forest bowmen, and they may well return tonight. Helewise, I think, prefers a quieter location, and I reckon she'll stay at the Sanctuary. For now,' he added.

Until this is all over and Father comes back, Meggie thought silently. For a moment, eyes on Ninian's, she knew he was thinking exactly the same.

'I have a patient for her!' she said. She'd spoken too brightly, but she sensed Ninian understood

81

the reason. She found it so hard to think of Josse out on the road somewhere, and she was quite sure it was the same for Ninian. 'In fact, the tranquillity of the Sanctuary would be the very best place, so we'll head on there straight away.'

'Of course,' Ninian said. He glanced at Faruq, sitting on his black horse just inside the courtyard gates. He hadn't said a word. 'If you're all going,' he added, 'you'll be needing some more supplies, so please tell Helewise I'll send some over in the morning.'

'I will, and thank you.' Before he could say anything else, she gave him a smile, turned Auban and set out on the track to the Sanctuary.

Helewise was alone at the Sanctuary. The day had brought its usual quota of visitors, especially around noon, when empty bellies rumbled with hunger. Now, with time to spare – she doubted if anyone else would turn up today – she was busy washing bowls, sorting the pots and little bottles of herbal preparations and the sachets of dried herbs for the remedies taken in the form of hot drinks, and about to fetch more water from the stream. *I need some more firewood, too*, she thought. There was plenty to draw on, but the main supply was a short distance from the clearing around the Sanctuary.

She heard a noise. A horse . . . two, no, three horses, approaching from the depths of the forest.

She straightened up.

It was not that she was afraid, or even particularly apprehensive. But she was a woman, alone, and the nearest friendly soul was quite a long way away; well out of range of a shout or a scream for help.

'Stop that,' she commanded herself aloud.

A thick-set horse with an auburn coat, a long creamy mane and a friendly expression came into the clearing. Astride it sat, or rather slumped, a veiled woman in a dark gown and a brilliantly coloured shawl, and behind her – holding her up, in fact, as Helewise quickly realized – was Meggie. There was another horse behind the chestnut, ridden by a black-haired young man with surprisingly light eyes who was leading a grey, but Helewise barely spared him a glance.

'This woman's name is Hadil,' Meggie called out, 'and she has hurt her right arm. It may be broken but I'm not sure. She's in a great deal of pain. She also suffered quite a bad blow to her forehead, also on the right side.'

Helewise nodded her understanding. She went to the stocky horse's left side, holding out her arms to receive the semi-conscious woman. Then suddenly someone else was beside her, strong arms helping to take the woman's weight as Meggie eased her out of the saddle. 'That's Faruq,' Meggie said. 'He's Hadil's son.'

As soon as it was safe to let go of Hadil, Meggie leapt down, and between them the three of them bore Hadil into the Sanctuary. There was a bed made up ready beside the hearth, and gently they laid Hadil on it. Helewise drew up the covers, tucking her in up to the waist. Then, meeting Meggie's eyes, she said quietly, 'Best to see to the arm now?'

'Yes,' Meggie said firmly. 'She fainted, I think, some way back, so with any luck we can treat the injury before she recovers consciousness.'

Helewise heard the young man give a soft sound of distress. Turning to him, she said, 'Could you help, do you think?' It would be far better, she thought, to give him something to do.

'Of course!' he said instantly. 'Anything!'

'I was just about to fetch more water, from the stream over there.' She indicated. 'The pails are beside the door. When you've done so, please could you fill that pot—' she pointed again – 'and suspend it over the fire to heat up? Then more firewood, from the pile along the track over there, because we'll need to keep your mother warm.'

He was up and away before he'd even given himself time to answer.

Meggie had already pushed the woman's clothing back from the injured arm and was now running her hands up and down it, feeling for damage. 'I believe I can feel a break,' she said quietly. 'What do you think?'

Trying to probe along the bones of the forearm without causing the patient even more pain, Helewise found what Meggie had found. 'Yes,' she said. 'Just there.'

Meggie was on her feet, searching along the Sanctuary's tidy shelves. 'The splints are at the far end, lowest shelf,' Helewise said.

The next part was the worst. They had to straighten the damaged bone and align it with the one that ran beside it; if they failed, their patient would end up with a crooked, weak arm that would

84

not be very much use to her. The process, however, could not be done painlessly.

Hadil awoke from her faint, screamed very loudly for several heartbeats, and then as quickly subsided. She had passed out.

Now Meggie and Helewise worked as swiftly as they could. Meggie reset the bone, Helewise verified that it was as good as they could make it, then they applied splints, padding and bandaging. Meggie placed the arm diagonally across Hadil's chest and bound it in place. They settled her against several pillows and covered her with as many blankets as they could find, for pain and shock had made her shiver with cold.

Silence fell.

From the doorway, Faruq said tremulously, 'Is she all right?'

Helewise got up, her heart wrung with pity. She wondered how long he'd been standing there. Poor young man, to hear his mother cry out so! 'She will be all right now,' she said, taking hold of his hand and then, for that didn't seem to be enough, enfolding him in a hug. 'Meggie has seen to her poor arm,' she went on, holding him tightly, her voice calm and soothing, 'and presently, when she wakes, she shall have a drink that will make her sleep and help with her discomfort.'

For a few moments he had accepted her sympathy. Then, as dignity reasserted itself, he disengaged himself. He looked at her and she noticed how he stood up straighter, squaring his strong shoulders. He said, 'My thanks to you, my lady, for all that you have done to help her,' and gave her a low and graceful bow.

'I'm not "my lady", I'm just Helewise,' she said with a smile. 'This is the Sanctuary, and that's what we do here. Help people, that is. Now,' she went on briskly, for he seemed to be struggling to control his emotion, 'what about using some of that wood you just fetched to build up the fire?'

Meggie prepared a herbal infusion for Hadil, setting out chamomile, valerian, linden flowers and a pinch of the poppy that she reserved for severe pain. Hadil's face was grey, and the manner in which she kept shifting on the straw mattress told Meggie that, however she sat or lay, she couldn't get comfortable.

Helewise made a thick broth of vegetables, barley and some pieces of bacon, and there were chunks of bread to dip in the rich liquor. Meggie persuaded Hadil to eat a few mouthfuls, and encouraged her to drink some water. But then, too soon – for Meggie knew she'd barely eaten all day – she pushed Meggie's hand holding the wooden spoon away, turning her face into her pillows.

'Sleep?' Meggie asked softly.

Hadil's eyes flew to her, an expression on her face that suggested she'd just been offered the keys to paradise. 'Oh, yes,' she whispered.

Meggie strained the infusion into a small pottery cup. It was cool now, and Hadil gulped it down, making a face at the bitterness. 'I'm not going to ask what's in it to make it taste so terrible,' she said, managing a very small smile.

Meggie was impressed by her courage. 'Best

not to know,' she replied lightly. Then, leaning close, she added, 'But I do know what I'm doing, I promise.'

Hadil watched her for a short while. Then, with a sigh, she let her eyes close. Meggie sat beside her for some time. When she was quite sure her patient was asleep, she got up, stretched, and announced she was going out to make sure the horses were secure for the night.

Faruq leaped to his feet. 'I will do that,' he said gravely. 'You have earned your rest.'

'Thank you, but I need some fresh air,' Meggie said. 'Also, I think I . . .' hastily she corrected herself, 'I think we ought to look at your mother's mare.'

'I have already done so,' he said. 'I think it is not a serious injury, and requires little more than rest.'

'She can rest here, as can her mistress,' Helewise said calmly. She glanced at Meggie. 'It's a pity Geoffroi isn't here, for he'd no doubt have the right poultice prepared and slapped on in an instant.'

'My brother,' Meggie explained to Faruq. 'He's gone to . . . er, he's away, with my father.'

'Then there is nothing to do now but make sure they will not wander off,' Faruq said. 'This I will do.'

'They won't,' Helewise said softly as they heard his receding footfalls outside. 'Geoffroi made that little stockade for me, and he doesn't make fences that fall down under a little pressure.'

Meggie smiled. 'I know,' she agreed. 'I think, however, that Faruq wants to do something; in return for us helping his mother, I mean.'

Helewise looked at her affectionately. 'I think you are right,' she said. 'Don't worry! In the morning, I shall find plenty of tasks he can help us with.'

Some fifty miles to the north-east, Josse and his small party were also settling down for the night. As Meggie had surmised, they had indeed crossed the estuary that day, taking ship late in the afternoon from the Hoo peninsula over to the Essex shore. They had been ferried by a small craft whose sole purpose was the transporting of human, horse and other cargo, and Josse told himself that nobody had taken any notice of three more passengers. He, Yves and Geoffroi wore good wool cloaks, but they were old and well worn. They were also sufficiently voluminous to cover both their garments and the weapons they carried. Little could be done to disguise the fine quality of their horses, however; Josse had made sure the three of them and their mounts went on board the ferry last and stood right at the stern for the crossing, in the hope that they would go largely unnoticed.

It was difficult to judge the mood among the people, for so well had he and Geoffroi planned their route so far that they hadn't encountered many. *What is everyone else doing?* Josse wondered. *Does Prince Louis still hold London? Have more rebel barons gone to join him, or has his failure to push on and gain some significant victories persuaded men that they're better off with the King?*

That, he reflected with a smile, was the less

welcome side of having encountered few other travellers: they'd met nobody from whom to acquire news.

Now he and the others were deep in the peaceful Essex countryside, some eight or ten miles away from the area's southern coast. Geoffroi had scouted ahead and found a ramshackle barn on the edge of an overgrown field. He'd chased out quite a lot of rats, scooped out a shallow pit and made a fire, and now, with the horses untacked and hobbled outside, already fed and watered, he was setting out food for their supper.

'Where did you find this lad, Josse?' Yves asked, leaning back comfortably by the fire, propped against his saddle and watching his nephew work.

'Oh, he just blew in one fine day,' Josse replied nonchalantly. 'Not bad, is he? I reckon I might keep him around.'

Geoffroi stirred his savoury stew, smiling. He didn't bother to comment.

When they had eaten, and Geoffroi had washed and packed away his pots and cooking implements, they wound themselves in their blankets and prepared for sleep. Josse felt a nudge in his ribs and, looking to his left, saw Yves's hand emerging from his bedroll. It held a small silver flask. He jiggled it, obviously inviting Josse to take it. 'Calvados,' he whispered. 'It'll help you sleep.'

Josse grasped it, and took a mouthful. Delicious. 'Thank you,' he whispered back.

Sleep, he thought, settling down. It was late, he

was tired, and he knew he should rest and restore some of his strength for the next day.

But it wasn't easy, when he really had no idea what the next day was going to bring.

At the Sanctuary, Meggie woke in the morning to find her patient a little feverish. She examined her, and found no obvious cause. There was no overlooked flesh wound that was beginning to suppurate, no symptoms of any disease that might be developing.

'It may be the after-effect of the blow to her head,' she said quietly to Helewise, who crouched beside her. 'I'll prepare a febrifuge, and we should bathe her forehead with cold water. Oh, and keep her warm.'

She picked up one of the larger wooden bowls and went outside to the stream, bending down to wash her hands and face and then fill her bowl. The water was so cold that the actions made her hands ache. She had always suspected that the little stream was spring-fed, from a source somewhere nearby, for its water was always sparkling fresh and extremely cold. It was likely, she thought, that it still bore the effects of its long sojourn deep within the earth.

Someone called her name, and she came back to herself.

'Good morning, Faruq,' she said. 'Did you—'

He nodded a cursory response to her greeting, then, interrupting, said, 'How soon can you be ready to leave?'

'*Leave?*'

'Yes!' He looked surprised that she was protesting. 'Where are we going?'

He turned away, and she had the impression he was controlling his irritation. 'We have to go to the Queen,' he said tightly. 'You told me you knew where she'd be.'

Meggie tried to collect her thoughts. 'Yes, indeed I did, but it was only because your mother had set off to find her, and we had to go after her!' She realized that she hadn't even thought about what might or might not happen next.

He seemed to understand. 'I am sorry,' he said quickly. 'I thought you would – I mean, we still have to carry out our mission. We must *warn* her. My mother and I—'

'Your mother will stay exactly where she is.' It was Meggie's turn to interrupt. 'Her arm is grossly swollen and she should keep it immobile, for the next few days at least. Riding would be agony, as well as perilous, as she would only have the use of one hand. Besides, this morning she is feverish.' Silently she cursed; she'd been going to break the worrying news to him more gently. 'Only a little,' she reassured him, 'and I know how to help her.'

'You will have to tell that other woman, then, for you won't be here,' he said firmly. She shot him an angry look, for she didn't like being told what to do. Realizing his error, he said, 'Meggie, I apologize, and it is not for me to give you orders. But *please!* I cannot tell you how vital this is, but, believe me, we *must go!*'

Meggie was torn by indecision. Already uneasy

91

because her beloved father had ridden off into uncertainty and in all likelihood danger, she had thought to pass the days – weeks? – of his absence by working as hard as she could with the nuns of the Hawkenlye infirmary or, as it had transpired, looking after Hadil here at the Sanctuary and assisting Helewise in her many daily tasks.

Both options, she admitted to herself, were designed to take her mind off worrying about Josse.

Might not a ride far off westwards with this exotic, desperate stranger and his mysterious mission achieve the same end? And he was certainly desperate; any idiot could have seen that. What *was* this danger to the Queen? Meggie guessed it must be something to do with the invading French prince and the rebel barons. Perhaps there was some plot to abduct Queen Isabella and use her to force the King's hand.

If that were true, though, how had Faruq and his mother come to know about it? And how was it, moreover, that it had been left up to them to warn the Queen or, more probably, warn the captain of whatever bodyguard King John had detailed to keep her safe?

It all seemed very unlikely.

Faruq was watching her, his face impassive but his blue-green eyes intent.

And, to her vague surprise, Meggie heard herself say, 'Very well, then. Go and prepare our horses, fill the water bottles and sort out your kit. I'll talk to Helewise about your mother's care and pack up some food.'

* * *

92

Before they finally left the forest, Meggie left Faruq holding the horses and hurried off down the narrow path to her hut. She'd told him she needed to fetch some personal things, which was perfectly true. She kept a change of under-linen and a thick travelling cloak in the hut, so fortunately she'd avoided having to go to the cottage by the forge. She didn't really think Jehan would be there, but she was relieved not to take even the small chance of encountering him.

She didn't know what she would have said to him, and that made her heart hurt.

The other reason for calling in at the hut was to fetch something she kept hidden there. She already had the Eye of Jerusalem, safely tucked away inside her gown. Now, it was a gift from someone else she loved that she wished to collect.

It was a sword, given to her by Jehan. He'd made it in his original forge back in the Breton forest. It was quite small; only a little longer than a man's hunting knife. The blade was slim, and it had a very slight curve. The hilt was bound in purple leather, of a very fine quality, and the colour had been chosen to complement a subtle sheen of violet in the dull, grey steel of the blade.

It was a killing weapon – she kept it viciously sharp – but, nevertheless, beautiful.

Jehan had told her as he presented it to her that all fine swords should have a name. Because he was a Breton, and because of where her sword had been created, she had called it Limestra. It was the Breton word for 'purple'.

She slid it back in the scabbard and, raising

her gown, fastened the scabbard's belt around her waist. Once she'd let the folds of her skirt fall again, the sword was invisible.

She secured the hut's door and hurried back to Faruq.

Six

Some forty miles to the north-west, Jehan's secret journey continued.

Jehan was increasingly worried at the thought that this was going to be a very different exercise from the last time he'd set out after the man who had murdered Arthur of Brittany. Then, he'd been one of a band of young men – boys, some of them – who'd had little or no military experience, were poorly armed, undisciplined and without any very definite plan; the only things they'd had in abundance were courage and the blind fervour of a just cause.

Now, he had the unsettling feeling that he had joined up with a band who were all a great deal more professional than he was, which, he admitted to himself, wouldn't be difficult, since his experience of fighting was so limited as to be almost non-existent. Under the leadership of Yann Duguesclin, it was an army of solemn and determined men who knew exactly what they were doing; who followed orders instantly and without question; who, in short, very often made him feel like a silly and incompetent boy.

It hadn't been so apparent to begin with, when with the seven others he had ridden north from the Great Forest and crossed the Medway valley. He had expected they would join similar small bands and head for London; in fact, he was quite sure someone had told him so. Perhaps it had been Joséph, the man he knew from when they'd all come over to England for the original mission. Whoever it was, it appeared now that it had been deliberate misinformation; he wondered if they'd kept the truth from him because they didn't yet trust him. It would be typical, if so. Because they hadn't done that at all. Instead, they had veered westwards when still some ten or fifteen miles south of the capital, and ridden along the ancient, dry tracks on the top of the North Downs, still keeping to out-of-the-way paths and making simple camp under the sky each night. Then one morning they hadn't set out as usual but stayed where they were. Watchmen had been set. An air of expectancy had grown; men whispered behind their hands, stopping abruptly when the leader's eye fell on them. And, a day and a half later, Jehan understood what they'd been waiting for: another band joined them, and together they set off northwards. The pattern repeated itself as stealthily they worked their way north-east, repeatedly meeting up with other groups, the army growing larger until currently – and it seemed that this was the full sum of the Breton rebels – it numbered some sixty or seventy men. Now – by Jehan's reckoning, putting together the few bits of information he'd managed to glean from hurried, muttered remarks – they were somewhere to the north-west of London, and had turned north-east.

And it was still Yann Duguesclin who led them.

If Jehan had thought they were tightly disciplined before, it was as nothing compared to how Duguesclin ruled his men. Previously, soft-voiced conversations as they rode along, or anything other than strictly necessary remarks in camp at night, had been met with a scowl, a hissed 'Shut your mouth!' and occasionally a cuff round the back of the head. Now, such offences – together with a great many more – had a fixed punishment. Depending on what you did, you could expect to pay a penalty ranging in severity from a fine or the cutting of your ration to a flogging.

Not that there were many transgressors. Virtually to a man, Jehan's fellow soldiers were as dedicated as their leader and, their hearts and minds firmly focused on one end, they obeyed without demur or even resentment.

Sometimes Jehan had to work hard to convince himself he was doing the right thing.

He had to fight his own nature quite a lot of the time. In his own mind he was a man of standing. A blacksmith was a valued member of his community, and Jehan was used to being treated with consideration; with respect, even. Now, when almost every man who rode with him was far more experienced than him and, he was sure, had a far better idea of where they were going and what they'd do when they got there, he felt like a boy whose condescending elders deliberately kept the truth from him for his own good. Despite his best efforts, it nagged and picked at him.

In camp one night, his resentment finally got the better of him. One of the hard-faced, silent men who habitually rode close to Yann Duguesclin had set off on a brief sortie to spy out the land ahead and, on his return, had gone into a huddle with Yann and some of the older men. Jehan had gone to see what they were muttering about, and one of the senior men had scowled at him. 'Unless you know how to shoe a horse, fuck off and get back to your duties!' he hissed.

Jehan stood his ground. 'I do,' he said.

The man spun round again. 'You still here?' He fixed cold, angry eyes on Jehan. 'What did I just say?'

'I heard you.' Jehan knew the danger but he couldn't stop himself. 'I'm offering to help, you—' He clamped his jaws tight on the word that had almost escaped. 'I'm offering to help you,' he said. 'I'm a blacksmith.'

Such were the expectations, in that rebel army of fierce, fanatical professionals dedicated to their cause, that he only narrowly escaped punishment for not having told them sooner.

Josse, Yves and Geoffroi were making steady progress through the southern half of East Anglia. Josse, delighting in the company of his brother and his son, was enjoying himself so much that on occasion he forgot what they were doing there. One evening, as they settled into camp in a pine forest, the ground cushioned by a thousand

97

years of fallen pine needles and promising a comfortable night, Geoffroi interrupted Josse and Yves's laughter and provided an unwelcome reminder.

Yves had been recalling how, when he and Josse had been boys, they had constructed what they'd grandly called a cart, although it had been little more than a piece of wood with wheels fixed to it. They'd had the bright idea of Josse towing Yves on it, and Josse had mounted his pony and kicked him to a brisk trot. They had misunderstood the nature of ropes and of towing; as the rope suddenly snapped taut, the platform gave an almighty lurch and Yves, clutching the handle they'd fixed for him to cling on to, was hurled forward and fell flat on his face. Josse, horrified at the blood pouring from his little brother's nose, had hurriedly taken him home where one of the older grooms – a kindly man with sons of his own – had mopped him up. On being told how the mishap had occurred, he told them, once he'd finished laughing, that they should have paid out the rope first and, with it stretched between them, Josse ought to have steadily increased his speed with Yves accelerating at the same rate behind him.

'And then, d'you remember, Josse, he . . .' Yves paused to wipe his eyes.

It was then that Geoffroi took his opportunity. He said quietly, 'Father, how do we know where to go?'

Josse, still chuckling, turned to him. 'Hm? What's that, son?'

'How do we know where to go?' Geoffroi repeated.

Josse stared at him. He glanced at Yves. 'Don't look at me,' his brother muttered, trying to hide a grin.

'Ah,' Josse said. 'Er . . .' He stopped to think. Then he went on, 'The King was heading for Lincoln when he wrote to me.'

'Yes, but that was some time ago,' Geoffroi pointed out. 'Is he still there now?'

'*I* don't know!' Josse exclaimed, chuckling. Then – for he realized he was being no help at all and that his son was really worried – he thought some more and said calmly, 'We need to find others loyal to the King, for, now we are that much closer to what must be his position, his movements will be known.'

'How do we tell King's men from rebels?' Geoffroi asked.

Yves met Josse's eye. His expression said all too plainly, *How are you going to answer that, then?*

'I shall set out in the morning and make contact with troops loyal to the King,' he said.

'But how—' Geoffroi began.

Josse silenced him with a look. 'Give me a little credit for many years' experience, son,' he said gently.

Later, as they settled down to sleep in the silent pine forest, warm under blankets and cloaks, he wondered just how much use that experience was going to be.

In the morning, before doubt and a certain lack of confidence could undermine his resolve, Josse left his brother and his son packing away all

99

signs of their simple camp and set out to find the answers they required. Their overnight camp had been isolated, and he rode for some two or three miles with few signs of human habitation. He skirted a patch of ancient woodland, which reminded him of the forest surrounding his home, and spotted in the distance a solitary man taking a stout old sow towards the trees, presumably to forage on the rich diet of acorns. Josse called out a greeting, and the man stopped. 'Where's the nearest village?' Josse called out.

The man waved a hand down the track and then, before Josse could ask anything else, turned and hurried away, prodding his pig's stout backside with his stick to make her run.

Josse nudged Alfred with his heels and rode on.

Presently the fringes of the little settlement came into view. A row of single-storey houses, small and simple but apparently in good repair; a bigger house, and a tavern beside a pond; a forge, busy even at this early hour. There was a noise in the still air . . . Josse paused, trying to decide what it was. A sort of humming, and the occasional clash of metal on metal; was it connected with the work of the smithy?

He rode on around a bend and suddenly he understood. Before him, stretched right across a large field whose hedgerows had been severely damaged and whose grass was in places churned into muddy tracks, was a small army. Tents had been erected, camp fires still burned, and a smell of cooking hung like an almost tangible cloud. Approaching cautiously, Josse revised his first astonished and alarmed impression: the men numbered perhaps only forty or fifty. Not an army, then, but a smallish detachment.

Best of all, for Josse's purpose, the standard flying over the largest tent was that of a lord loyal to King John. Or at any rate, Josse thought with a wry smile, he had been the last time Josse had heard tell.

He dismounted and, leading Alfred, approached the young man standing beside the huge gap ripped in the undergrowth that was presumably the entrance to the camp.

'Good morning,' he said with a smile. 'Who's in charge here?'

'Who wants to know?' the young soldier replied challengingly. His hand had gone to his sword hilt.

Josse identified himself. 'You won't know the name,' he added, 'but I'm a King's man and I'm on my way to join him.'

The soldier eyed him suspiciously. 'I've only your word for that.'

Josse reached inside his tunic. 'I have a letter bearing the King's seal, addressed to me.' He held it up, but not close enough for the soldier to take it. The seal, however, seemed to impress him. 'Wait here,' he said curtly. Then, looking at Alfred, 'You can take your horse over there—' he pointed to a long row of water troughs beside the horse lines – 'and let him have a drink.'

'Thank you.'

A short time later, a short, stout figure in surcoat and mail came trotting up to Josse. He waved a hand, a smile creasing his plump face.

'Knew I recognized the name,' he panted as soon as he was within earshot. 'I'm Matthew de Compton, and you and I once tried to drink each other under the table.'

Josse reached out to take the man's proffered hands. 'I won, as I recall,' he replied.

Matthew de Compton gave him a suspicious look. 'Maybe. It was a very long time ago.'

'Aye, when Henry was King and we were green lads.' He and Matthew smiled at each other, and Josse felt the warmth of happy memory sweep through him. 'Still a King's man, I see,' he said, lowering his voice.

Matthew de Compton sighed. 'Yes, that I am, although . . .' He broke off.

Josse nodded. 'Aye.' There really was no need to say more.

'You're heading off to join him?' Matthew said.

'I am, for he sent me a summons.' Once again, Josse reached for the letter.

Matthew stopped him. 'No need, for I have seen other copies of the same appeal.' He grinned at Josse. 'I'm sure you didn't think you were the only one.'

'Of course not.' Josse decided to keep to himself those few words that the King had added in his own hand.

'Do you bring many with you?' Matthew demanded.

'No, we're but three.'

Matthew suppressed a smile. 'Ah, well, all mighty warriors, no doubt.'

'Have you up-to-date news?' Josse asked. 'Do

102

you know where he is? Last I'd heard, he was on his way north to Lincoln.'

'We receive reports daily,' Matthew said with a slight swagger. 'We've a good system of messengers operating, and, with relays of horses set up at many way stations, they can cover the ground swiftly and thus keep us all informed. The latest news is that King John has left Lincoln, sent the rebels holding the castle fleeing for their lives, fired everything flammable and killed anyone foolish enough to stand against him.' He paused, shooting a glance at Josse. 'But he missed his chance to apprehend the Scottish King,' he added softly. 'They say he's beside himself.'

Josse nodded. It was understandable, for if John could have apprehended and curtailed Alexander, one threat would have been removed. 'So where's he bound now?'

'He's come storming all the way down the Lincolnshire coast,' Matthew said, a wide smile of satisfaction on his face, 'and he's in no mood to be merciful. He's got the local barons worried, that's for sure, because those lands are almost universally rebel-held, and King John's made sure not to leave a barn standing or anything edible in the fields. Burnings and destruction are the order – he's even set fire to the bloody hedgerows – and the abbeys haven't escaped either, since he's commanded them to be gutted.' Apparently noticing Josse's questioning look, he added quietly, 'He's wild with fury, is the King. He's got it into his head that the abbeys are full of food, and meat, and harvested grain, hidden away in the hope that he'll leave the holy houses alone. It may be so, it may not, but it seems he's not prepared to take the risk.'

Against his will, Josse thought of Hawkenlye. Would John have done the same, if he'd been fighting the rebels in the south-east rather than in the east? He had an image of the beautiful old buildings, gutted, on fire. And for nothing, for there was no more hidden store of food and grain at Hawkenlye than there was likely to be in Lincolnshire.

He has his reasons, he thought loyally. *It's not for the likes of us to question him.*

But nevertheless, the images wouldn't go away.

Matthew was still talking, and Josse made himself concentrate. 'If you're hoping to find him, best bet is to go on to Lynn,' he was saying. 'Bishop's Lynn, I suppose I should say. He received word in Lincoln, back at the start of October, that there was a big shipment of supplies on its way there, and he wants to be in port to arrange for the goods to be distributed to his northern castles.' He leaned closer and added confidentially, 'Seems he's anticipating another attack from the northern rebels, now that he's convinced himself they're in allegiance with Alexander of Scotland, and he needs his defences to be well prepared and sufficiently well supplied to withstand a siege, if needs be.'

Josse nodded. 'He really thinks an attack from the north is likely?'

Matthew shrugged. 'If it comes, we'll be ready,' he said confidently. 'The news is all good!' He nudged Josse in the ribs, quite hard, as if determined to cheer him up. 'Dover Castle still holds firm, and they're saying now it's impenetrable!'

'My wife's grandson is there,' Josse said softly, thinking of Ralf. Thinking, too, of Helewise.

Matthew nodded approvingly. 'Good for him,' he said. 'You'll be proud of him, no doubt. It's a vital job they're doing down there, since we must at all costs hold on to Dover.'

'I'm sure he's doing his best,' Josse murmured, but he didn't think Matthew heard.

'They're a feisty lot down there in Kent,' he was saying, admiration warming his voice. 'They're saying the resistance to Prince Louis and his half-hearted invasion is strengthening all the time, no doubt buoyed up by the Frenchie's failure to take Dover.' Once again, he leaned closer. 'Prince Louis's men are deserting in their hundreds,' he whispered, 'either slipping off back to France or, in the case of native English support, going over to the King's side.'

Josse was sceptical about 'in their hundreds', which seemed a little optimistic. It was, however, very encouraging to hear that Dominic and his fellow defenders were doing so well, and, indeed, that the band of rebels in the Great Forest was acquiring a fine reputation and a few new recruits. He felt a glow of pride for the men and the women of his home.

Matthew was grinning. 'They'll see sense sooner or later, these rebels, the whole cursed lot of them,' he said confidently. 'Oh, I grant you times have been hard, and the King's had his doubters and critics . . .' That, Josse reflected, was putting it mildly. 'But when all's said and done, King John is ours and that Prince Louis isn't.'

Josse didn't think it was the moment to go into the highly complex history of the relationship between the Crowns of England and France. Anyway, what was the point? It boiled down to precisely what Matthew had just said: King John was theirs and Prince Louis wasn't.

'Get on the road to Lynn,' Matthew was urging him. 'That's where you'll find him!'

Meggie and Faruq were making good progress, covering from perhaps thirty to as many as almost forty miles a day. The October weather was warm, sunny and dry, so that sleeping out under the stars was no great hardship. As long as the rain held off, Meggie reckoned they would reach their destination in another couple of days. She had travelled the route westwards with her mother in the past and, to her relieved satisfaction, soon realized that her memory of the lesser paths and tracks remained accurate. Joanna and her people had preferred to move around the land on unfrequented roads; since these were often also the most direct, Meggie reckoned that she and Faruq were lessening their journey by many miles.

Faruq, it seemed to her, was torn between confiding in her as to what this mysterious mission really involved, and keeping faith with the vow of secrecy he had made to his mother. So far, Meggie had discovered little more than she'd known when they left Hawkenlye: Faruq and his mother believed the Queen to be in terrible danger, and somehow – still Meggie had no clue as to *how* – they were convinced that this was in some way their family's fault and it was their duty to protect her. What Faruq thought he could do that couldn't be done far better by whatever forces the King had detailed to safeguard his Queen, Meggie just couldn't begin to work out.

There was, it appeared, little option but to ride on and hope for clarification.

Queen Isabella was cross, frustrated, weary of the walls of the castle and bored to tears. She would, she thought, not for the first time, very much like to present her long list of complaints and dissatisfactions to her husband, preferably accompanied by a hurled object or two and her own angry fist.

She stretched out on the silk coverlet, the soft mattress yielding as she shifted position. She gazed around the walls, the huge, skilfully dressed stones of which they were built evident only around the doorways; for the purposes of both insulation and decoration, everywhere else they were concealed with hangings. In some places, these took the form of heavy curtains, lined and interlined, trimmed with decorative borders; elsewhere there were vivid tapestries, usually depicting lively hunting scenes and frequently featuring some animal being ripped to pieces with a lot of severed limbs and spurting blood. John liked hunting scenes. The floorboards were oak, varnished and burnished to a dark, golden shine and covered by thick rugs. As well as the vast bed on which Isabella lay – piled with pillows, with extra blankets and a glossy fur pelt folded ready in case she was chilly – there were other, smaller truckle beds that pulled out from beneath the master bed for the servants who attended her by night. Even they had a more than adequate complement of covers. Around the walls were various chests containing her garments and the King's, as well as enough personal possessions to equip an average-sized village. King John was renowned for being a perpetual traveller, restless if he stayed in one place for more than a couple of days, and he never went anywhere without a full household of equipment.

Although she was reluctant to concede that anything about her present location was acceptable, Isabella had to admit – but only to herself – that the accommodation was very comfortable and, even by John's high standards, luxurious. Ever since he had made Corfe Castle one of his regional treasuries a few years ago, he'd poured money into improving it. Isabella stroked a hand heavy with rings across the smooth scarlet and blue silk of the bedcover. She smiled at the memory of her fiery husband, driven to fury at the penny-pinching, coin-counting ways of the Exchequer, as yet again he wasn't given the funds he demanded the very instant he'd demanded them: 'I'll fortify a series of my castles out in the regions,' he'd yelled, 'and keep funds in every last one – then we'll see who's prepared to stand in my way when I'm required to spend money on the defence of my realm!'

He had done more than strengthen the castle's fortifications: he had also turned the private, residential quarters of his favourite dwelling into the perfect domestic retreat, and the Gloriette, which had been constructed to the east of the keep, was a sophisticated, high-quality dwelling more than suitable for a king and his queen. It was an area within the safety of more than one circle of walls, with a curtain wall and a ditch separating it from the main bailey, and the narrow access gates were manned at all times. A contingent of heavily armed and well-trained soldiers was garrisoned within the walls, and one of the longest-serving and most trusted of the King's personal bodyguard led them.

Isabella knew she was in the safe confines of Corfe Castle for her own protection. It was a time of peril, and the abduction of those closest to kings was a tried and tested method of putting pressure on them. Isabella had no wish to be the captive of the rebel barons or, even less, of Prince Louis. She would probably be treated with courtesy and consideration, but she would be their prisoner and everyone would know it. There would be no escaping the humiliation. Here, locked up in her husband's castle with no hope whatsoever of leaving until he said she could, they could at least pretend that she was there for her sake and not the King's.

But she knew different, as she suspected did most people. The present conflict had given John the excuse to imprison her and he'd leapt at the chance. It sometimes seemed to her that this was his latest, and in some ways most ruthless, move in the endless game they played with each other.

She hadn't been too displeased when the men of power in her family had told her she was to marry John of England, and not the man she'd always believed would be her husband. Hugh de Lusignan was neither as powerful nor as rich as John; two facts that had weighed quite heavily in persuading the young Isabella that the surprising change of plan for her wasn't all bad. And, although at first she had been horrified at the reality of her thirty-four-year-old husband (she'd only recently passed from girlhood into womanhood, and he was old enough to be her father), the dismay hadn't lasted. Admittedly he hadn't been much to look at. He wasn't tall, and even then his heavy, muscular body was becoming stout, and the thick, unruly hair was coarse and at times looked decidedly ginger (where it wasn't going grey), clashing rather unappealingly with the flushed, red cheeks. But, almost from the start, something about him had called out to her.

She found it all but impossible to say what it could have been; she had concluded, after much thought, that what had attracted her back then (and, despite everything that had happened between them, still did now, despite her furious attempts to resist) was his humour. He'd always had the ability to make her laugh. The escalating arguments, the fights, the hurling of objects, the urge to hit, punch, bite, wound, had so often been halted in their tracks by some wry comment of his that had appealed to her sense of the ridiculous and, even at the height of her rage, made her burst out laughing. Then, oh, then, how swiftly fury had changed to passion, and they would tumble into bed and make love in the ways that he had taught her, each bringing the other to such a pinnacle of ecstasy that everything else would be driven from her mind.

She'd known he had lovers. It had hurt like a deep knife-cut to begin with, and in her pain and her jealousy she had wanted to kill him. But since she couldn't, she'd had her revenge in a more subtle way and taken lovers of her own. He knew; of course he knew. The knowledge of each other's infidelities had somehow worked to add further piquancy to their lust, however; once, when he'd found out about her dalliance with an extremely handsome but particularly bone-headed young man who had little to commend him but his family's wealth, John had held her down in the huge bed and, as he brought her to the sort of world-eclipsing climax that she'd known in her early days as his wife, hissed in her ear, 'Does *he* do that? Can *he* bring you joy like I can?'

And she'd had to admit that he couldn't. Nobody could, although she'd kept that bit to herself.

She'd heard the whispered rumour that he'd executed one of her lovers and had the corpse suspended above her bed. It wasn't true – which was a pity, really, since it was a good story – but she wouldn't have put it past him.

With a sigh, she got up from the soft bed and stretched. She straightened her gown – she had selected the crimson silk today, and its deep,

111

glowing colour pleased her as much today as when she had first set eyes on the beautiful fabric – and, moving over to the oak-framed looking glass, rubbed at its silvery surface with her sleeve. Turning it so that the light fell on her face, she studied herself. She would soon be thirty, but everybody told her she didn't look her age. They were sycophants, of course, the lot of them, and even if she'd lost her teeth, sported crows' feet, grown warts with hairs coming out of them and her rich, fair hair had turned to a scraggly white rat's nest, they would have said she was still the beautiful girl she'd been when the crown was put on her head.

She leaned closer to the reflecting glass. Her face was a long oval, her skin smooth and pale. Her features were regular and well placed, her hazel eyes slightly hooded, the small, straight nose perfectly set above the generous and well-shaped mouth. She bit her lips, bringing the blood to colour them. The shade, she was well aware, was a soft, flattering echo of the colour of her gown. She knew she didn't look like a girl, though; her eyes had seen far too much, and no girl had that calculating knowledge in her glance.

Knowledge. She sighed again. She had never been able to ignore an unpleasant fact once it had been proved to be true, even when that would have been the more comfortable option. Moreover, although she had told lies to many people – to almost everyone, come to think of it – the one person she didn't lie to was herself. She could no longer persuade herself that her life was

112

tolerable, and that meant she'd had to take certain steps, the first of which had been to work out the precise reasons behind the escalating discontent and unhappiness.

The problem had been where to start.

In the early years of the marriage, John had treated her like a child. Well, that was fair enough, since she'd been little more than one. Was that where the corruption had set in? Was it then that the habit of making her decisions for her, of working out what was best for her, of ordering her wardrobe, her personal routine, her comings and goings and every other detail of her days – and always, *always*, decided because of what was best for *him*, never for her – had set in? Probably it was. And it had been a habit that was, or so it seemed, unbreakable.

The queens who had preceded her had been permitted so much more freedom and liberty than John had ever allowed her. So much more money, too; for he'd never given her access to the revenues from her own inheritance, and he had kept from her the Queen's Gold that was hers by right and long custom. He allowed her no voice in anything but the most trivial of domestic matters; as regards political decisions, she had as much influence as his favourite hound. She was totally dependent on him: he could pen her up here in Corfe Castle – a luxurious prison, perhaps, but a prison nevertheless – and there was absolutely nothing she could do about it.

And now there was this new thought, which had arisen from the deep recesses of her mind and given her no peace. Unable to suppress it, she had been driven to make a decision. It had been hard – so very hard – but she had realized she had no choice.

Not that it had made it any easier . . .

She turned away from the glass, suddenly unable to look into her own eyes.

Anyway, it made no difference now, for he was long gone, and by now would be far away. She'd obeyed the impulse, and there was no way she could undo what she had done even if she wanted to. She sighed. In all likelihood, she told herself, it would all come to naught and her misgivings – if that was what they were – were for nothing.

She felt herself relax.

Time would tell. If anything did happen, nobody would even begin to imagine she was involved.

She smiled.

Seven

At the Sanctuary, Helewise bent anxiously over her patient. Hadil's fever had not abated, despite Helewise's administration of several of the sovereign remedies. She had made an infusion of elder and yarrow to induce sweating, and kept one of sweet-smelling chamomile always ready. She had spent hours gently sponging Hadil's face, neck, chest, arms and hands with fresh, cool spring water. Still the woman burned, her skin dry and tight, and she moaned as she threw herself from side to side in the narrow bed.

Sometimes she spoke in a language Helewise didn't understand, but now and again she whispered a few words in the common tongue. Once, in the darkest pre-dawn hours, she suddenly sat up and said with perfect clarity, 'We must locate the very last of it, for it is so very dangerous and it must leave the world . . .' The unseeing eyes had lit upon Helewise, crouched beside the bed, desperate to put a flame to more than the single candle that burned all night like a sanctuary lamp, but frightened to leave her patient even for an instant. 'It is evil, tainted, heavy with sin,' Hadil insisted, her face filled with horror. There was a terrible sense of urgency about her and, pushing Helewise aside, she tried to get out of bed. Gently Helewise took hold of her shoulders and pushed her back against the pillows, tucking the blankets around her. 'Stay here, Hadil,' she said softly. 'I will take care of you. You are far too weak to leave your bed.'

Hadil seemed to accept that and, for a while, lay back as if exhausted. But then, as Helewise was about to fetch fresh water to bathe her once more, abruptly – and making Helewise jump with shock – she began to shout in a voice so loud and strong that it almost hurt.

'*Why will you not help me?*' she roared.

'I—' Helewise began.

'You promised you would do whatever I asked and yet now, when I need you most and all I am doing is trying to make you fulfil your oath, *you will not do as I command!* Ach, but I despair of you, for you are just like all the rest!'

Helewise realized she was addressing her son.

'He is not here, Hadil,' she said softly. 'He has gone to—'

But Hadil wasn't listening; did not, probably, even know where she was, who she was with, or that Faruq wasn't there.

'Why will you not help me?' Hadil wept.

Helewise took hold of the hot, flailing hands in her own cool ones. The gesture – the very touch – seemed to calm the woman a little.

'He can't help you, Hadil, for he is not here,' she said. 'You cannot stand, let alone mount a horse and travel the roads all the way to wherever it is you were bound.'

Now Hadil turned to look at her, right into her eyes, and Helewise had the feeling that perhaps, at last, she understood. 'He will come back?' she asked pitifully.

'Of course he will,' Helewise assured her.

She stayed where she was, holding the hot hands, occasionally removing the soft cloth on Hadil's brow to rinse it in cool water and replace it. After a while, she felt her patient relax. Soon the deep breathing and the steady snoring told her Hadil was asleep.

Helewise took the opportunity and crept away to her own bed. The Sanctuary was only one small room and she would not be far away if her patient suddenly cried out for her.

Before she gave in to fatigue, Helewise prayed for Faruq and Meggie. She asked the Almighty Father in whose loving solicitude she had

116

absolute faith to watch over them, keep them safe and, above all, bring them home again. *For I have promised his mother that Faruq will come back to her*, she reminded God, *and I beg your help so that I will not be proved a liar.* Then, as she always did, she went on to pray for her family, and for all the many other people she loved and cared about, ending, as ever, with Josse.

I don't know where he is, dear Lord, she prayed, *but I entrust him to your care.*

Then, a faint smile on her face, she fell asleep.

She was awakened by the quiet little noises of somebody moving about the Sanctuary and trying not to wake the occupants. Opening her eyes, she saw the tall, stooped figure of the strange woman who had once been the Hawkenlye herbalist and now lived in solitude in the forest.

Sensing eyes upon her, Tiphaine turned round. 'Good morning, my lady,' she said, making the reverence that she had performed daily when both women had lived a different life and Helewise had been her superior.

'It's just Helewise now,' Helewise muttered, pushing back the blankets and sitting up. 'How many times must I tell you?'

Tiphaine handed her a welcome drink; hot, aromatic, with the promise of bringing invigoration and optimism to one who hadn't had enough sleep. Tiphaine's morning infusions were legendary and they never failed. She grinned. 'It could be a thousand times,' she said in answer to Helewise's question, 'and it'd make not a scrap of difference.'

She crouched down on the floor as Helewise sipped at her drink. Helewise looked across at Hadil, still sleeping, and Tiphaine followed the direction of her eyes. 'Who's that?' she asked quietly. Helewise told her. 'And what ails her?'

Helewise shrugged. 'I suspect it is mainly exhaustion, for it appears she and her son had travelled a very long way before she collapsed. She took a fall from her horse and broke her arm, and in addition she had a nasty blow to the head.' Tiphaine nodded, all her attention on Helewise. 'I think, however, that the overall source of her disquiet is anxiety,' Helewise went on. 'It seems that she and Faruq – that's the son – came to England to fulfil some dangerous mission, and she is finding it very hard to find any peace all the time she doesn't know if Faruq is succeeding or not.'

'He's gone off with Meggie, you said?'

'Yes, and it's no use asking me where, as I have absolutely no idea.'

Tiphaine smiled. 'Then I won't bother.' With one strong, graceful movement, she got up. 'Best thing I can do is examine the patient and see if I can come up with anything you haven't thought of.' She stopped in the middle of moving over to Hadil's bed. 'That is, I'm quite sure there won't be anything,' she went on in a very different tone, almost obsequious, 'because you—'

Helewise burst out laughing. 'Tiphaine, stop it!' she said. 'You no longer have to treat me as your superior, and the timely reminder that you know far, far more about herbs and remedies and the best treatment for virtually any ailment

118

or condition under the sun won't have me trembling in outraged fury, I assure you.'

Tiphaine studied her in silence for a moment. Turning away, she said calmly, 'I'd better have a look at her, then.'

She was some time studying the sleeping woman. Eventually, straightening up, she said, 'There's a few things we could try.' She paused. 'Like me to stay, would you?'

And, on a grateful and relieved sigh, Helewise said, 'Yes.'

Meggie and Faruq were nearing their destination. They had ridden in silence for some time. Meggie, noticing Faruq's deep frown, had been reluctant to interrupt whatever worrying thoughts preoccupied him. She had, moreover, quite enough anxieties of her own.

But as Corfe Castle came into view, high on its headland and ringed by its strong, well-maintained walls, she sensed him jerk out of his reverie and, turning, saw his frown deepen as he stared ahead. 'Is that it?' he asked, and she could hear the disappointment in his voice.

'Yes.'

'But it's—'

'Impenetrable? Yes, of course it is; what did you expect?' She heard the echo of her voice and realized she'd spoken too critically. 'King John made it one of his regional treasuries a few years ago,' she went on in a gentler tone. 'He strengthened the castle massively then, and made sure it's perpetually guarded, because he keeps money at the ready so that he doesn't have to beg for it from the Exchequer and explain endlessly why he wants it.'

Faruq nodded. 'Very wise,' he remarked. Then, flashing her a look: 'How do *you* know? Is it common knowledge?'

Stung at the implication that she would only know if it was, she said, 'I have no idea if it's commonly known or not. *I* know because my father told me.'

And Josse, she guessed but didn't add, had probably acquired his knowledge from Leofgar. While it was true that Helewise's son was now in sympathy with the rebel barons, it hadn't always been so. Leofgar – married to a difficult woman who had tired of country life and wanted more sophistication, more importance, more wealth, more everything (Meggie didn't much like Rohaise) – had encouraged her husband to penetrate the outer royal circles, and by so doing become aware of what went on in the King's court.

'And you're sure that the Queen is here?' Faruq demanded.

Meggie shrugged. 'Possibly. Probably,' she amended.

Isabella, living there either as a prisoner, according to John's enemies, or for her own safety, according to his loyal supporters, couldn't really be anywhere more secure, Meggie reflected. According to Josse, John had put a trusted constable, Peter de Mauley, in charge of Corfe Castle; in addition, Queen Isabella also had her own personal protection detail under the command of Terric the Teuton, another man whose loyalty to the King was absolute.

Faruq had let his horse slow to a stop and now he sat in the saddle, looking up at the castle in dismay. 'We'll never be allowed in,' he said in an almost inaudible whisper. 'Oh, why ever did I come?'

Meggie shot him a scathing look. Now was no time to give up, she thought crossly, for they hadn't even tried yet.

She said bracingly, trying to mask her irritation, 'You – we – have come here to help. You want to warn the Queen and those who guard her safety, you say.'

She had not meant it to sound like a question, but it did. He turned a furious face to her and hissed, '*I do!* Of course I do!'

'Yes, all right, I believe you,' she said. 'Well, we must tell them so. We'll say that we have information that there may be a danger to the Queen—' *as if they don't already know that*, she added silently, beginning to have doubts of her own – 'and that we've come to reveal what we know in the hope that it, whatever it is, can thus be averted.' She looked at him questioningly, but if she had hoped he might now, at this last moment, give in and tell her why they were there and what this was all about, she was to be disappointed.

He gave a curt nod, put his heels to his horse's sides and rode on.

Queen Isabella, bored of her sumptuous quarters, bored of the rich food and fine wine, bored of the simpering women who attended her and their constant, sycophantic remarks (*My lady is*

121

so beautiful! My lady's hair is like spun silk! My lady's most gorgeous and costly gowns are barely fit for one so perfect as she!), bored of the male attention and admiration that was her life's breath, flung out of her chamber and banged the door behind her as hard as she could, causing the heavy, solid oak to crash against the frame with such force that she imagined the walls shook.

Ha! she thought. *Take that, serfs, servants, slaves. I wish your heads had been in the way and your stupid skulls were now crushed like eggs!*

She made her way along the chilly, ill-lit passage – there was only one thin, slit-like opening; yet another of the many drawbacks of living in a fortress – and the leather soles of her little slippers echoed off the stone walls. Where was everybody? She stopped suddenly, listening. Silence – no sound of voices . . .

Yes, there was. From somewhere far below, someone – more than one person – was arguing.

Arguments and quarrels always drew her. Lifting her long, heavy skirts, she hurried to the spiral stair, leapt nimbly down it and came to the inner hall. Crossing it at a run – there was no one to observe the undignified scurrying – she went under the low arch and, slowing her pace now, glided down the wide and elegant stone steps leading to the enclosed courtyard that opened outside the huge, iron-bound doors to the King's private quarters.

Half a dozen steps from the bottom – height lent dignity and importance – she stopped. Resting one elegant, bejewelled hand on the rope that ran down the wall beside the stairs, smoothing the glorious gown, lowering and drawing back her shoulders so that her breasts stood out, extending her neck and raising her chin, she waited for the people in the courtyard to look up, notice her and perform their obeisance.

Peter de Mauley stood with his back to her, hands on his hips, sword at his side and dagger in his belt. Flanking him on each side were two of the bodyguards. In a doorway across the yard stood Terric, Isabella's personal protector. He was watchful, his expression carefully neutral, and obviously biding his time.

In front of Peter de Mauley stood two people, a man and a woman. The man was bare-headed, and his thick, black hair had an almost blueish sheen. He was young – about twenty, perhaps a little older – and he stood with the assurance of one born to privilege, his back straight, his clear eyes firmly on those of his interlocutor. His tunic was well cut and fitted him as if it had been made for him, and the light travelling cloak he wore over it – the hood down and the generous folds thrown back over his shoulders – was of a sufficient quality to protect its wearer from all weathers.

So much for the man. Now Isabella turned her attention to the woman.

She too was young; maybe a few years older than her companion, but not many. She was dressed in a simple gown in a nondescript brownish-grey shade; the sort of colour that didn't show the dirt of travel. But the fabric was good; narrowing her eyes, Isabella studied it

123

more closely. It had the soft sheen of the finest wool . . . Hmm. The woman wasn't a peasant or a pauper either. She too, Isabella noted, wore a travelling cloak, also thrown back.

Belatedly Isabella realized that nobody had noticed her.

They were all too intent on their conversation to look up.

It stung, as anything that undermined her self-importance always did.

She was on the very point of issuing some sharp command or reproof when – almost as if she'd *known*, although that was surely impossible – the young woman looked up and met Isabella's eyes.

In an instant Isabella took in a broad, deep forehead under soft, wavy brown hair, wound in a practical, unfussy style that nevertheless managed to enhance the woman's attraction. Her face narrowed to a firm chin below a wide mouth. But Isabella was drawn, irresistibly, unavoidably, to the eyes.

They were brown – a very rich brown – but lit as if from within by bright, golden lights; like the clear, lively water of a peaty forest stream, Isabella thought, at the moment when the sun brings it to life . . .

Isabella liked a fine, descriptive phrase.

She narrowed her gaze and prepared a suitably crushing comment.

But then the young woman smiled.

Their eyes locked together, sparkling brown to hazel, and just for a heartbeat Isabella felt a surge of power pulse against her. She wasn't afraid, for she detected even in the instant she felt it that it was no threat. It was more as if she had been languishing, tired, dispirited, dejected, and someone had just given her a fine, crystal glass of the best chilled white wine . . .

Then, before she could dwell on this strange phenomenon any further, it had gone. Vanished, as if it had never been, and Isabella forgot all about it.

She went on down the imposing steps until she was at ground level. She walked calmly across the courtyard until she stood just behind Peter de Mauley. Then, in a voice that all who knew her later remarked was quite uncharacteristic of her, she said courteously, 'And who, may I ask, are these visitors? Might I know their names?'

Peter de Mauley and the two bodyguards spun round, already bowing deeply even as they did so. The young man, too, touched a hand to his brow and lowered his head. The woman with the bright eyes dipped in a graceful curtsy.

She was still smiling.

Meggie had been aware of the tall, slim, elegant figure in the beautiful silk gown as she slowly descended the steps and came to a halt, posing, waiting for those below to notice her and give her the recognition – adulation – she considered her due.

From the first instant that the Queen had come into view, Meggie had been sending out tentative mental sensors and, even before that powerful moment when their eyes had met, she had already begun to form a picture. Isabella was irritable, restless, resentful, impatient, bored. That would have been evident to a novice in the art of studying people and Meggie, experienced healer that she was, was far from that. The lines that drew the beautiful face downwards; the little cleft of a frown between the dark, arched, perfect eyebrows; the slight slump of the narrow shoulders; they all told their tale, for those prepared to read it.

But Meggie had seen a great deal more.

In a series of images – flash, flash, flash, somewhere behind her eyes and in some secret, mysterious place deep in her mind – she'd seen the Queen with the King. Seen that stocky, sturdy, irascible, unreasonable man of power and the wife he had at first adored, then doubted, then mistrusted and finally driven to . . . To what? It was as if a heavy curtain had fallen, so that Meggie had not seen the most recent scenes. She pushed harder, and just for an instant she saw another picture: in this one, the Queen, tense, watchful, was alone in a dark room and intent on some task she did not wish anyone else to know about. A task that brought with it terrible danger to—

It was as if a heavy door had slammed in Meggie's face.

Isabella, she guessed, had sensed her interest and somehow shut her out.

She is more powerful than I suspected, Meggie thought, maintaining her smile despite her shock. *Although I do not believe she is aware of it.*

She committed the last image to memory, for she knew she must recall it.

So this, she thought, was his wife; this was the woman married to that strangely appealing man with the bright blue eyes whom Meggie had met in a forest clearing and who had once offered to teach her swordsmanship. Automatically her hand reached down for her sword, but of course it wasn't in its usual place in its sheath at her side. The guards at the outer gates had been very reluctant to admit her and Faruq at all, and there had been no chance of progressing even a step inside the keep until they had surrendered their weapons – left with the horses – and been thoroughly searched.

With Isabella's descent into the courtyard, more guards had materialized, moving with quiet efficiency to stand encircling the Queen.

The Queen folded her arms across her slim body and tapped a foot. 'Well?' she prompted.

Peter de Mauley gave her another deep bow. 'My apologies, my lady Queen. The woman is called Meggie and the man's name is Faruq.' He paused, shooting a narrowed-eyed glance at the visitors. 'They say – well, *he* says he's come to warn you that you could be in danger. He says that—'

'Of course I'm in danger,' Isabella interrupted, her tone scathing. She seemed to have abandoned politeness. 'My husband, the lord King, is fighting for his realm – fighting for his life, I dare say – and I am kept here in this desolate, blighted castle *for my own safety*.' The last four words were spat out with such venom that Meggie could almost imagine it, smoking in the air and scorching the ground as it landed. 'The rebels, the French prince, roving bands of foreign mercenaries who are probably also out for his blood and wouldn't mind a drop or two of mine – dear God, what's a bit more danger here or there?'

Peter de Mauley bravely held his ground in the face of her furious tirade, standing quite still, hands clasped in front of him, head bowed. When she had finished, he said quietly, 'If my lady is content to allow me to make some enquiries, it will be my honour to do so.'

Perhaps, Meggie mused, watching the Queen closely, that was how you dealt with queens. For, as if de Mauley had known quite well what Isabella's reaction would be, she seemed to be calming down. A sudden noise not unlike the frantic cooing of a flock of agitated doves interrupting her intense observation, and, raising her eyes, Meggie watched as a group of some seven or eight ladies-in-waiting came fluttering down the steps. As if to serve as a foil for the Queen's dramatic and eye-catching crimson gown, all of them were dressed in soft shades of grey and beige. Most of them were at least a decade older than their mistress; the majority were comely but plump. Together with the generous petticoats fluffing out the wide skirts, they looked like doves as well as sounding like them. At a subtle nod from de Mauley, the one leading the advance came trotting over to the Queen.

'My lady, will you not come back to your quarters and rest awhile?' she said timidly, her voice high-pitched with nerves. 'It is warm out here in the courtyard and we would not want the sun to burn my lady's fair cheek, would we?'

Slowly Isabella turned to the woman. She was about to make some hurtful, cruel remark – Meggie thought she could almost see the words forming in the Queen's mind – but then abruptly she slumped a little. 'No, we wouldn't,' she said softly. 'Very well, then . . .' She paused, staring down at the woman – Isabella was at least half a head taller – '. . . Marjorie? Matilda? Whatever your name is. Very well.'

She turned and began to walk away, the waiting woman tripping along at her side and the others falling into place behind. The guards watched as the little procession approached the steps, some already melting away into the shadows of the dark room from which they had emerged.

Gradually, gently, Meggie began to retract the sensors she had been extending towards the Queen. The process was almost complete when, her foot already on the first step, Isabella turned and stared right at her. 'I suppose I should thank you, you and the dark-haired fellow,' she said grudgingly. She glanced at Peter de Mauley. 'See to it that they get some food once you're done with them,' she commanded. 'They look as if they need it.'

She began to walk slowly up the steps. But then once more she stopped and looked down at Meggie. 'Be thankful you live in the freedom of out there,' she said, waving her arm towards the steeply sloping fields beyond the walls. The long sleeve of her gown blew in the breeze like a crimson banner.

129

Then, her face briefly falling in an expression Meggie couldn't read, she went on up the steps, under a low archway and out of sight.

As Peter de Mauley led her and Faruq off into the small guardroom that appeared to be his own private domain, Meggie was at first too busy thinking about Queen Isabella and that strange, powerful image of looming peril to pay attention. It was only when the two voices began to sound angry that she pulled herself back into the moment.

'She's not going to be poisoned, I tell you!' Peter de Mauley was saying crossly. Meggie was quite sure it wasn't for the first time. 'Her food is prepared under very close scrutiny and at least two people taste every item of food and drink before it is put before her.'

Faruq, Meggie thought, looked like a man who was trying to convince someone of a vital, crucial point while not being allowed to explain fully what that point was. *It's not only I who is not hearing the full story*, then, she thought with a wry smile.

'But . . .' Faruq began. He met her eyes, and his held an appeal that she couldn't answer.

Not wanting to let him down, she said, 'And, of course, the Queen is always attended at her meals, so if there was any danger of her choking, for example, help would be at hand?'

Peter de Mauley looked puzzled, as well he might. 'Well, yes,' he agreed. He was staring quizzically at her, as if to say, *Why on earth should she choke?*

Faruq said suddenly, 'May I be shown the place where food is prepared?'

Meggie was quite sure de Mauley was going to say no. But, watching Faruq closely, suddenly she saw him as the constable must surely be seeing him: a young man, sincere, distressed in his urge – his *need* – to help; his conscience deeply disturbed at the thought that only he could save the Queen from some terrible fate.

And then, as she'd known he would, Peter de Mauley grinned and said, 'Oh, why not?', adding in a mutter, 'What harm can it do?'

With Faruq and Meggie following close at his heels, he led them out of his little room, across the courtyard, under a low arch, along a network of branching passages and up a long flight of steps that emerged into what was clearly the castle's kitchen quarters.

Meggie's first reaction was amazement at the sheer amounts of food and drink contained on the shelves, the boards, hanging from the beams supporting the roof and stacked in barrels and crates on the floor. A stab of fury flooded her – swiftly she suppressed it – at the thought of all this for one woman, her ladies-in-waiting and a modest garrison of troops, when the vast majority of the population had little idea of where the next meal would come from.

She took several deep breaths and returned her focus to Faruq.

He seemed to be circling the huge room, stopping here and there to inspect and sometimes pick up whatever had caught his eye. But, she realized, he was being very clever: if he was

131

checking just the one commodity – the meat, perhaps, or the barrels of beer, or the shelves groaning with costly and beautifully made platters, cups and knives – he was disguising the fact. Watching closely, in only a brief time she saw him sniff at, feel all over with his fingers and even surreptitiously lick objects as diverse as a crust of bread, the end of a smooth, round goat's cheese, a knife, the dregs in a wine jug, an elegant glass goblet containing water, a side of bacon, one of a batch of newly baked cakes and a wooden platter.

Finally, after what seemed like a long time, he raised his eyes to Meggie and shook his head. Peter de Mauley, who had clearly seen the gesture, said with indulgent patience, 'Satisfied now, young man?' He gave Meggie an exasperated smile.

Faruq, head down, strode over to the arch under which they had entered. Leaning close to Meggie, de Mauley said softly, 'I knew he wouldn't find anything.' Straightening, a faint look of pride on his face, he said, 'We have to take good care of her. The very best care, in fact. Otherwise . . .' He didn't finish his observation.

There was no need to say what he and his garrison might expect if they let their guard down and allowed any harm to befall the Queen.

Indeed, Meggie reflected as she followed Peter de Mauley along the twisting and turning route back to the courtyard – already worried about a brand-new concern of her own – it didn't really bear thinking about.

Ahead of them, Faruq suddenly stopped.

132

Preoccupied, Meggie barely took in the expression on his face. But then, running back to de Mauley, he asked him a question; an urgent question, by the tone of the muttered words, although Meggie couldn't make out what he was saying. Forcing her own anxiety to the back of her mind, she hurried towards the two men, but Faruq saw her coming and drew Peter de Mauley away. Now he was demanding something, holding de Mauley by his sleeve, his face close to the older man's, light eyes narrowed and intent. De Mauley said something – a few curt words – and Faruq spoke again, desperate now. De Mauley, shaking off the grasping, clinging fingers, added something else, pointing away over the high castle walls towards the north-east.

Then Faruq moved. He began to run as hard as he could, calling back to Meggie, '*Come on! We have wasted so much time and now we must fly like hawks!*'

She looked at Peter de Mauley, who stood watching Faruq's retreating back. If she had hoped for some clue as to what had just happened, she was to be disappointed, for de Mauley's expression had closed into a disapproving frown and, even as she stared at him, he spun round and strode back inside the inner keep.

Meggie ran after Faruq.

As they reached the horses and Faruq hurried to mount, she yelled, '*What's happened? What did you just find out?*'

'*Hurry!*' he cried. 'Get on your horse!'

She stayed exactly where she was.

He seemed to understand that she would

not move without some explanation. Casting a despairing look into the sky and muttering a curse in his own tongue, he met her angry eyes. 'I came here to seek something,' he said, speaking very fast in a low voice. 'It is evil and very, very dangerous, this object, and, because I believed it was the Queen who was in such peril from it, I expected to find it in her vicinity, but *it is not here!*' He gave a sound that was a cross between a sob and a moan. 'But if what I fear is right, we must follow it because now—'

Meggie was already up on Auban's back, kicking him to a trot then a canter, for she didn't need to hear any more. She heard Faruq thundering along behind her.

Faruq had believed that this perilous object, whatever it was, threatened the Queen, but he was wrong. What he had just said was combining powerfully with her instinct and those worrying impressions that had come into her mind as she stared at the Queen, and – for the moment, anyway – she knew all she needed to know.

It wasn't Isabella who was in danger.

It was the King.

Eight

Josse, Yves and Geoffroi were a day's journey from Lynn. They hoped to reach the town late the following afternoon, and Josse was very worried that they might arrive only to find the perpetually restless, endlessly peripatetic King had already left.

They should have arrived by now but Yves's horse had picked up a stone and, despite Geoffroi's care and his meticulous tending of the injured foot, they'd been forced to spend a whole day in their camp until Geoffroi deemed the horse fit to travel again.

Yves, observing Josse seething with impatience, tried to comfort him. 'Your lad's the one who knows about horses,' he said, 'and you'd be a fool to override his advice.' Josse gave an injured, indignant sniff; it was a very long time since anyone had called him a fool to his face.

'But we have to get on!' he snapped at Yves. 'It's been far too long since we heard the King was aiming for Lynn, and there's absolutely no guarantee that—'

'Be calm,' Yves interrupted gently. Despite himself, Josse found that he was soothed; it was strange, he reflected, but over the past days it seemed that he and Yves had slipped back into the character of the men – the boys – they had been long ago in their youth. Josse had always been the impatient one; the one who had all the ideas, who urged Yves and the younger ones on to more and more daring exploits, who tried to make them ignore the perils and dared them to follow where he led. Had it not been for Yves and the quiet voice of reason, he had often thought, who knew if all of them would have survived to manhood. It seemed highly unlikely.

Sensing Josse was weakening, Yves said, 'I approve of my nephew, Josse.' He nodded over to where Geoffroi stood beside the injured horse, a frown of concentration on his open, friendly face, one hand feeling for the heat of infection in the horse's foot, one moving gently in a constant, soothing motion on the horse's shoulder. 'And how I admire his touch! It's only a matter of days since he and my old Hector met each other, and usually it's months before Hector puts his trust in someone, if he ever does. Yet there they are, peaceful as you like, and you'd almost think your boy had whispered in Hector's ear and said, *Trust me, I'm here to help and I'll do my best not to hurt you.*'

Josse grinned. 'Knowing Geoffroi, he probably did.'

For want of something to do to fill the long hours of their enforced day's rest, Josse and Yves had left Geoffroi with the horses and explored their surroundings. They had camped on a wide tongue of land that extended into the marshy fenland to the west, where waterways twisted and turned this way and that before collecting and flowing out into the Wash. They were on the edge of what appeared to be an ancient settlement, with the remains of long-abandoned huts and simple, one-roomed dwellings strung out along a track that rounded the curve of the land. Up on the higher ground to the east stood a solitary oak: huge, spreading, magnificent, and, from the width of its massive trunk, hundreds of years old. Down at the fen edge, with the wide expanse of dark water stretching out before them, they had stood staring at what seemed to be a little island, a few yards from the shore. On it there were some large stones; as Yves observed, stone was unusual in the vicinity, and so it looked as if these had been brought here and transported out to the island for some specific purpose.

'You'd almost think they were grave markers,' Josse said softly. The island, and indeed the whole area, was affecting him oddly, and he seemed to sense the presence of phantom people . . . friendly, inquisitive people; he felt no fear.

Practical, reasonable Yves, standing by his side, said, 'They can't be graves out there, Josse. Whoever would have buried their dead out on that little offshore island?'

But Josse, perhaps more sensitive than most men since his years with Joanna, wasn't so sure. Just for an instant, he had thought he'd seen the outline of a figure, crouched over a raised hump of ground on which someone had placed flowers.

It wasn't the moment to mention it to Yves. Josse, smiling, didn't think there was ever a moment for that. His down-to-earth brother had never been one for flights of the imagination. So, turning and beginning the walk back to their camp, he merely said, 'I expect you're right.'

They made steady progress the next day and rode into Lynn as twilight fell. Even from some distance away it was clear that King John was there. The roads leading into the town were thick with horse-drawn carts, ox carts, men on horseback, troops of marching men, local men and women laden with all manner of goods that they thought they had a chance of selling to the

King and his followers, from bread and barrels of beer to leather belts, mending kits and spare stirrups.

Lynn was a thriving, hard-working and growing port, one of the country's wealthiest. The extensive quays and wharves were always lined with vessels: some crossing the seas and oceans; some voyaging up and down the English coast and trading in items such as herring and timber. The richest of the merchants had built their fine houses well above the noise and the filth of the harbour, but the majority of Lynn's population lived and worked in the seething throng of constant arrivals and departures. Shopkeepers and tavern proprietors rubbed along with sailors, captains, prostitutes, priests, thieves, fortune-tellers, acrobats, and young men with the bright eyes of unsullied innocence and untried optimism, drawn to the prestigious port and hoping for a little of what they saw as the easy success of its inhabitants.

Josse was tense and cross even before they arrived. For the last dozen miles he had been beset by an image of reaching Lynn to be told the King had just left and nobody had much of an idea where he was bound. He had constantly tried to force the pace, and Geoffroi's repeated refusals – 'Uncle Yves's horse is still not totally sound, Father, and we will do more harm than good if we make him hurry!' – had finally made Josse lose his temper and yell at him.

Yves the peacemaker had intervened, pointing out gently but firmly to Josse that, for one thing, the three of them wouldn't be much use to the

King if one of them had a lame horse; and, for another, there was no reason whatsoever to assume King John had left Lynn. 'When last we received news a couple of days ago,' he said with calm reason, 'he was on his way to Lynn but still some distance away. It is surely unlikely, even for him, to have got there and already left again.'

'He might have done!' Josse, hurt that his brother seemed to have joined his son in opposition, was angry all over again. 'He's always been like that and—'

But Yves had had enough. 'If you want to gallop on ahead, Josse, do so,' he said with an air of finality. 'Geoffroi and I—' *the ones with a bit of sense* hung unsaid in the air – 'will proceed at our own pace and meet you there.'

'I don't . . .' Josse began furiously.

Yves gave him the look he'd given him when they were lads; the one that said, *You're being stupid and quite unreasonable and I'm not talking to you any more.*

Josse gave an angry, disgruntled *hrrumph* and the three of them proceeded to Lynn together.

They found a reasonably decent inn that offered good stabling. Geoffroi, having already dismissed two similar establishments, went inside to check and returned to say this one was passable. Josse and Yves waited in the narrow, cobbled street outside, standing right at the edge to avoid the channel of filth running down the gentle slope, and Josse still jittery with impatience.

Finally, the horses having settled to Geoffroi's satisfaction, at last they set out to find the King.

It was a mindlessly simple task, for they simply followed the crowd. A big, expensively dressed and loud-mouthed man striding beside Josse told him – with the pride of a man whose beloved King was honouring his own home town with a visit – that King John was being entertained by one of Lynn's most prominent citizens, a recently ennobled ex-sea captain who now owned a fleet of sleek, well-built ships and who, it was rumoured, had brought in the majority of the supplies that had just arrived with which the King intended to resupply his northern castles.

Surreptitiously trying to brush off the mud of travel from his cloak hem as they strode along, Josse – taller than almost every other man there, with the exception of his brother and his son – peered over heads and tried to spy out their destination. Soon it became obvious: they were approaching a wide-fronted house set apart from the main thoroughfares, its stout timbers well maintained and its daub freshly lime-washed, perhaps in expectation of the King's visit. Solid oak gates leading on to a large courtyard stood partly open, guarded by several well-armed men. The door to the house was firmly shut.

Edging his way through the crowd, reaching inside his tunic for his letter, Josse went up to one of the guards. 'I have a summons,' he yelled, his mouth close to the man's ear to make himself heard.

The guard, perhaps accustomed to seeing such documents, had a quick look and nodded. He turned to one of his companions and gestured towards the gates into the yard, which the man

140

hastened to open a little wider. 'I have two more with me,' Josse shouted, pointing at Yves and Geoffroi, right behind him. The guard nodded again, and swiftly the three of them were bundled through the gates, which were banged closed behind them. The crowd, apparently angry at the ease with which these strangers had been admitted, were pushing forward, demanding similar favourable treatment, but the guards were having none of it. As a man in the King's livery hurried forward to usher Josse and his party inside the house, Josse heard a loud crash. Spinning round, he saw that soldiers inside the yard had dropped a huge iron bar into its supports on the gates and on the stout stone walls either side; nobody else was coming into the courtyard unless the guards said so.

Josse had imagined that his letter – with its personal addition in the King's own hand – would smooth his path straight into John's presence. He was wrong. He, Yves and Geoffroi stood for what seemed like hours in a long queue, shuffling forward by almost imperceptible steps, taunted and tantalized by the sounds and smells of what was obviously a splendidly sumptuous feast going on in the wide hall they appeared to be aiming for. The cooks had clearly begun to roast the meat some time ago, and rich, mouth-watering aromas floated out to them on the hot, over-breathed air. Josse heard Geoffroi's stomach give a loud rumble.

They edged inside the great hall. There were long tables lining it from end to end, most of them already occupied with men and women

141

dressed in their best. The bright colours of their fine wools and silks, and of their splendid array of jewellery, danced and shimmered in the light of hundreds of candles. Serving men and women paced up and down between the rows, platters and baskets in their strong arms, and the pot boys, heavy jugs in each hand, were so much in demand that some of them were actually running.

On a raised cloth-covered dais at the far end sat five men, a pair on each side of the central figure, whose throne-like chair was elevated slightly. Josse had barely a glance to spare for the four wealthy merchants or barons of Lynn, one of whom must surely be the host of this huge and unimaginably costly feast. His eyes were drawn – as, he reflected, men and women's eyes always were – to King John.

He was bare-headed, the thick reddish hair – streaked with silver now – brushed back from the broad forehead and shining in the light of lamp and candle flame. His face was flushed, grease and gravy on his chin. He was clearly enjoying himself – as Josse watched, the man to his right, pointing with his mug to one of the comeliest of the serving girls, leant over to whisper something in his ear, and John burst out laughing, wiping a hand across his mouth as a bit of roast meat fell out.

The King wore red: scarlet red, costly red, a shimmering silk surcoat over padded tunic and clean white chemise. He liked clean clothes next to his skin, and bathed whenever he got the chance. His broad, thick-palmed, short-fingered hands were decorated with several rings: a ruby and an emerald, a couple of diamonds, a pearl surrounded with what looked like garnets. As Josse took the last few steps that would take him before his King, he watched John pick up his goblet – a beautiful gold cup, glistening with precious stones of deep blue and brilliant green – and drain it, putting it down with a thump and burping loudly. Josse thought disloyally: *He is dressed in garments and jewels whose cost would feed a family for a year or more, yet he has the manners of a half-witted stable boy.*

But then King John's eyes turned to him – those incredible blue eyes – and, seeing who it was, his large, sweat-shiny, grease-splattered face broke into a genuine smile of delight.

'*Josse d'Acquin!*' yelled the King. 'I was beginning to think you'd never get here.' Then, unseating the man on his left by the simple means of tipping up his chair (the King, Josse observed, had lost none of his strength, for the man was fat-bellied and broad and the chair solid and heavy), he beckoned to Josse to come up and take the man's place.

Josse looked at Yves, right behind him. 'There's only one seat,' he muttered.

Yves grinned. 'It's for you, my brother. Don't worry,' he added, 'Geoffroi and I will find somewhere.' Then, the grin widening, he said, 'Enjoy yourself!'

Josse, all too aware of his well-worn tunic and his dirty boots, discomfited by the furious scowl of the fat man whose place he was about to take, wasn't at all sure that *enjoy* was the right word.

* * *

As food and drink were brought and placed before him, Josse paid close attention to the King, trying to detect his mood. On the face of it, John was optimistic, ebullient even, slapping Josse on the back and repeatedly crowing that rebels were deserting their cause all the time, flocking to him and clamouring to be readmitted to his favour. All the same, Josse sensed that he was uneasy about something. *I cannot ask,* Josse thought worriedly, *for he has just told me how well matters progress and I dare not say anything to suggest I doubt him.*

And then, his florid face serious suddenly, the King leaned closer to Josse and said quietly, 'Of course, I should have arrived here in Lynn earlier, but we had a bad time coming round the Wash.' He frowned, a look almost of puzzlement creasing his brows. Then, the expression turning to one of irritation swiftly mounting to anger, he went on, 'You hire an expert who's meant to know all about the tides and the currents, and yet when he's put to the test the fucking idiot knows barely more than the lad who empties my piss-pot. D'you know, Josse, I had to tell *him*, my so-called local man who knew everything, that we shouldn't take a long procession of mounted men, men on foot, and ox- and horse-drawn wagons across an inlet when the tide was coming *in*?' John shook his head. 'I don't know; there's something about those waters . . . There's so much mist, and you can't see what's around you, and then when it clears you find you've set off in one direction and you ought to have gone in another. It's as if . . . as if there are spirits out there in the

144

fog and they don't like you. They mean you harm. I'm not sure I trust the Wash. I'm not sure I don't hate it.'

At a total loss as to how best to reply, Josse heard himself mumble, 'The region can be tricky for those not used to it, my lord, and how prudent, if I may say so, to have engaged a local man.'

John stared at him, eyes narrowed, a calculating expression on his face. For a frightening moment, Josse thought he was in for the explosive and vitriolic response that his inane remark deserved. But then John smiled, reached for his golden cup and, clashing it against Josse's, said cheerfully, 'Drink that down, Josse. You were late on parade and have a deal of catching up to do.'

But it was worrying, Josse thought later, as John's attention turned elsewhere, to hear the King speak like this. Sitting beside him, able for a few moments to study him without his noticing, Josse could see the exhaustion behind the extravagant bonhomie. *The King is now forty-nine*, Josse thought, *and I don't suppose he has stopped charging round the country for months. He may be jubilantly optimistic now, but how quickly that could change. And, besides, there is the strange shadow that I perceive over him . . .*

But then the King turned back to face him and said loudly, 'What d'you think of Dover, then, eh, Josse? Still my troops hold out against that rat Louis, and all of them, from lords to scullery lads, set the courageous and indomitable example that all the rest of my army are following! We will drink to their bravery and resolve!' Again

145

he clashed his cup against Josse's, then drank deeply until he had drained it.

'My wife's grandson is there,' Josse said.

John slapped him on the back, so hard that Josse winced. 'Good man!' he yelled. He raised a hand, and the ever-attentive pot boy hurried up and refilled his beautiful cup. He leaned across to Josse as the lad poured and, enveloping Josse in alcohol fumes, said, 'I love this cup, y'know. It's solid gold and those are sapp—' he hiccupped – 'sapphires and em-emeralds. Present from my dear mother, God rest her brave, stalwart, warrior's soul, and I told myself it was a sign that she loved me.' The lad had filled the gorgeous cup to the brim and now stood hesitant. John nodded at Josse's mug – a lesser item of pewter, well shaped but undecorated except for an engraved border of vine leaves – and the lad slopped in wine till it overflowed on to the white cloth. Not that it mattered, Josse thought muzzily, since the pristine linen was already stained with drops and blotches of pretty much everything the King had consumed.

John stood up and roared for silence. After only a short while, even those far gone in drunkenness realized they should stop their chatter and laughter, usually because a marginally more sober neighbour had dug an elbow in their ribs. When everyone was quiet and the eyes of all in the vast hall were turned his way, John raised his goblet.

'We must *all* drink a toast,' he yelled with a lopsided smile. 'To my loyal men who hold my castle at Dover – long may they triumph, forever

146

may they throw the copses . . . cop-*corpses* of the invader into the sea! *Dover!'*

There was a huge noise of wooden benches being pushed across stone flags as, with varying amounts of difficulty, the congregation rose to its feet, hands clutched on cups, mugs and goblets and raising them to slack, wine-stained lips, and then came the deafening chorus: *'DOVER!'*

The King sank down abruptly on his cushioned throne, and, awkward now at being still on their feet, slowly everyone else resumed their seats. For some time there was virtual silence in the hall. Nobody seemed to know if it was all right to talk again. Then, slowly and steadily, the mutter of voices started up, and soon the volume was as loud as it had been before.

And the eating, the chatter, the laughter, the ribald jokes, the grasping hands that sought the round breasts of the serving girls and the firm buttocks of the pot boys, the fumblings in corners and, above all, the drinking, went on for much of the remainder of the night.

Meggie couldn't recall a time in her entire life when she had felt so tired. She and Faruq had been riding as hard as they could for what felt like forever, although it was in fact only four days; five, if you counted what had remained of the first day after they'd left Corfe Castle, when they had ridden for hours long into the night. As she tried to make herself comfortable on the pine-needle bed of the forest in which they had stopped to sleep and eat, yet again she went through what she suspected, what she had managed to find out, what she guessed. It still didn't add up to much.

As together they had sped away from Corfe Castle, her mind had been so full of fear and anxiety that it had hurt. She was desperate to ask Faruq questions – so many questions – but, to begin with, all she could concentrate on was covering the ground as fast as they could.

When they were about five miles from the castle, riding at a swift canter, he called out to her. 'We must ride north-east,' he panted. 'Do you know how to do that?'

'Yes.' Of course she did. She would have smiled but it wasn't a smiling moment. They were approaching a place where the road divided. One branch went straight on – eastwards; it was the road by which they had arrived – and the other veered off half-left. She raised her arm and indicated. With a curt nod, Faruq increased the pace.

Meggie was close behind. She tried to distract her mind from her fear by thinking about how she could be so sure she was sending them the right way.

She was Joanna's child; a descendant, through her mother's blood, of the Forest People. They never asked for directions. They had no use for diagrams scratched in the dust with bits of twig. They were like animals; they navigated by methods that Meggie suspected were available to all men and women, although most of them – the vast majority – had forgotten.

When Faruq had said north-east, she'd known without even thinking about it which way that was. *How did I do it?* she wondered. *By the sun's position? By the lie of the land? By the unconscious realization that if we came from the east, and it was that way* – she thought back to the junction of the two roads – *then north-east must be this way?*

She didn't know.

They rode on. Her anxiety didn't let her mind rest. Other than her occasional instructions when they came to intersections, they didn't speak. She guessed that, like her, Faruq had nothing to say and no breath with which to say it. While there was still enough light, sometimes she risked short cuts over open ground; once, along the edge of a ploughed field; once through a copse of birch trees, their horses' hooves scuffing and rustling the fallen leaves. When possible, she took them along the little roads and the quiet tracks. She knew without either of them saying so that this was a journey to be made in secret. It was better not to be seen. Especially at a time like this, when a foreign prince had landed in England and half the King's barons had rushed to support him.

They covered a lot of ground that first night. At first, it had been Auban – steady, comfortable, easy-paced Auban – who had held them back, for he hadn't the speed of Faruq's beautiful, fine-boned, fast and light-footed black gelding. Meggie had sensed Faruq's impatience and once or twice been tempted to snap, *Go on alone if you think I'm keeping you back. See how far you get!* Aware of Faruq's increasing distress, she didn't. But, as the night went on, it was the black

149

gelding that tired. The fine head on the graceful neck began to droop, the small feet began to drag; taking pity on the proud young man who rode the exhausted animal, Meggie broke a long silence and said, 'Enough, Faruq. We'll stop now, tend to our horses and we'll sleep awhile.'

'But . . .' He was frowning, furious with her.

'*Enough*,' she said again, already slipping off Auban's back. Swiftly she untacked him, throwing the saddle and her pack down on the soft ground – she had halted them on the mossy bank of a fast-flowing stream under the shelter of a stand of alders – and then led the ginger-coloured horse to the water, where he bent his head and drank deeply. She hobbled him – there was probably no need, as he, like the black gelding, was worn out and wouldn't wander far – then made herself comfortable, her back against an alder trunk. Swiftly she extracted bread and cheese from her pack and, barely pausing to wipe her hands, tore into it.

After a short while, Faruq sat down beside her.

And, finally, it was time to talk.

'Faruq, I know why we're going,' she said quietly.

He shot her an alarmed glance, bread and cheese arrested halfway to his mouth. 'But that's not possible! You can't have heard what Peter de Mauley told me, for you were too far away. You—'

'I *do* know,' she interrupted firmly. 'Look, Faruq, it's no good sitting there glaring at me. Listen to what I'm trying to tell you, will you?'

After a moment, he gave a curt nod.

'Thank you,' she said, wondering if he'd pick up the ironic tone. 'I showed you the way to Corfe Castle because you told me that you and your mother believed there was some threat to Queen Isabella.'

'Not believed, knew,' he corrected her sharply.

'Very well.' She held back the obvious comment. 'However, when we met the Queen – looking very bored but perfectly fit and well – and we saw with our own eyes how securely she was guarded, we were forced to accept how unthinkable it was that anyone wishing her harm could get anywhere near her.'

'But the danger wasn't—'

Again she interrupted. 'We actually managed to inspect the kitchens, and even you must have been reassured that neither morsel of food nor sip of wine or water entered the Queen's mouth unless it had been tested on someone else. We had to accept the only conclusion: Queen Isabella is perfectly safe; as safe as – no, much, much safer than – anyone else in the land.'

Very slowly he nodded.

'And then you pinned Peter de Mauley to the wall and fired all those frantic questions at him,' she went on. 'He answered you as briefly as he could, probably realizing that to do so was the best way to see the back of the madman – that's you, by the way – and his companion. Then you yelled at me to hurry up because we had to flee away north-east.'

'Yes,' he said softly. 'Yes. It was no longer there, this evil, tainted thing that I have to find. And, because some inspiration came to me so

151

that I knew what I must find out from Peter de Mauley, I believe I know where to find it. It is—'

'It's with the King,' she finished for him.

His light eyes, wide with shock, met hers.

'We are riding north-east,' she said. She had some idea of the lie of the land and she could see, somehow, inside her head, where her home was, where London lay, and what there was to the north-east. And, remembering word for word what her father had said regarding his own destination, she knew what – or rather *who* – was there.

As if that was not enough, there had been that sudden, terrible realization as she had stood in the courtyard of Corfe Castle. The instant of seeming to see into the Queen's mind; the understanding, as Faruq had urged her to hurry away, that it was not Isabella whom the peril threatened but John.

Faruq was still staring at her. 'Yes,' he whispered. 'I think – no, I *know* – that it is.'

'What *is* this evil object? Can't you tell me?' she pleaded. 'Some dreadful poison? A fatal potion disguised as a flagon of wine?'

'No, not a potion or a poison,' he said. He lowered his eyes. 'I wish I could tell you, for your guesses are shrewd and not so far from the mark, but I cannot.'

'But we—'

'Meggie, please do not attempt to persuade me, for trying to decide what is right – to honour my solemn oath of secrecy or to reveal the truth to you when you have done so very much to earn my trust – tears me *apart!*'

The last word was almost a sob.

'Very well.' She made herself relax. 'But, as I believe I said to you before, if you change your mind and decide you need an ally to confide in, I'm here.'

That late afternoon, evening and night had set the pattern for the days that followed. They would sleep till late afternoon, safe in some out-of-the-way spot, then rise, pack up, erase all traces of their presence and set off again. It was October now and past the equinox, and already the nights were drawing in. This worked to their advantage, and they made the very most of the lengthening hours of darkness. With Meggie's unerring guiding hand, they travelled fast.

Now, as she lay on her pine-needle bed, comfortable and warm, her appetite reasonably well sated, she knew she should try to sleep. She still didn't know precisely why Faruq had to make this journey – this difficult, exhausting, tension-filled journey – but she knew why she did, and she guessed it amounted to the same thing. Filled with a deep-seated worry that there was danger – not just the danger of battle, of assault by the rebel barons or by some advance party of the French prince's, but a danger she didn't begin to understand – she knew she had to find the King.

The next day they almost came to grief. Riding at dusk, the night's ride only just begun, they should have been alert. But, somehow, both of them managed to miss the fact that the little track they were on was about to join a wider, much

153

more frequented road, and on that road was a troop of well-armed, finely mounted men.

Just in time Meggie, in the lead, drew up Auban so sharply that he almost threw her in protest. She managed to stay in the saddle, twisting round, mouthing frantically to Faruq, 'Back! *Back!*'

He understood. Thankful to her soul for a bright, perceptive companion, Meggie slid off Auban's back and led him in Faruq's wake, along the path they'd just travelled, deep, deep into the thick forest where they'd slept the daylight hours away.

They tethered the horses and crept back to stare down at the road. The troop of soldiers was still passing by: they were riding two abreast and there must have been getting on for a hundred of them. Meggie stared at the banners. Were they King John's men, hurrying to lend their might to his army? Or were they rebels, travelling the same way but with the opposite intent? She didn't know.

When the last pair had passed and the dust was settling, they went back to fetch the horses. 'Faruq, listen,' she said.

He glanced at her. 'We had a narrow escape, yes?'

'Yes.' She grimaced. 'That's what I need to talk to you about, because we might not be so lucky next time.'

He stopped dead. 'We will not stop,' he said sharply. 'We cannot, for I—'

She put her hand on his arm. It was rigid with tension. 'That wasn't what I was going to say.' He relaxed slightly. 'We need a reason for heading into the fighting zone,' she said. He stared at her. 'Faruq, here we are, the pair of us, racing across England to find King John, and we need a very good excuse because most people who aren't either soldiers or out of their minds will be fleeing in the opposite direction.'

She had his attention now.

She remembered her father's summons; nobody ignored a demand from the King.

'I suggest we say we're healers,' she went on, more confidently than she felt. 'I am one anyway, so it's no pretence, and we'll say you're my pupil.' He frowned. 'My assistant,' she amended.

She could hear the protest before he made it.

'Look, Faruq,' she said before he had a chance, 'I know you're a man and used to being the one in charge, but I doubt very much you know as much about healing as I do, so if we're challenged and have to convince someone, you won't be as good at it as I will.'

Slowly he nodded. 'That is sense. Very well.'

'We shall say that I've been sent for because—' she thought hard – 'because they're worried about an outbreak of some sickness and they need healers to get the troops better and back on their feet,' she improvised.

He looked at her doubtfully. 'You think we'll be believed?'

'Oh, why not?' she replied recklessly. 'Anyway,' she added as they untied the horses' reins and mounted up, 'it's the best I can think of.'

He nodded again, then led the way off down the path.

* * *

155

East Anglia. Marching feet, the thump of hooves, the ring of metal on harness, the clink of sword in scabbard. Jehan, too, was riding north-east. His Bretons under Yann Duguesclin were crossing the wetlands, and even their fast progress had slowed down.

Jehan was deeply troubled. Despite Duguesclin's iron control, rumours flew among his Breton band. There was whispered talk of his plans. He was going to select a small band of spies, men breathed to each other as they huddled in quiet corners, and send them, disguised, to infiltrate the King's army. They would report back and in this way he would know when and where to strike. He would judge the perfect moment to send in the killers, and the plan would not – could not – fail.

The men seemed to have a faith in Yann Duguesclin amounting to worship. It was as if he was holy.

Jehan could no longer ignore his misgivings. Away from Meggie, oh, how far away, he was missing her; missing the life they were making together. He had tried so hard to suppress his doubts, but he was habitually honest with himself and he had all but given up. He made himself face the fact: this vengeance on a man who may or may not have killed a Breton prince seemed an act of folly.

Do I even care? he asked himself. *Did I ever, really, believe all this was so vitally important? Important enough to chuck everything else away?*

But whether he did or not was swiftly growing

irrelevant. He was here, in Yann Duguesclin's army, and Duguesclin had no doubts whatsoever. He had his plan, he believed in it utterly, and he would forge ahead until its end was achieved. The latest rumour was that he had already selected his killers, and there were three of them: hard, lean men with impassive, expressionless faces; expertly trained, so it was said, in their art. There would be no going back, for them or any of the Bretons, once the plan had been implemented.

The long column had drawn to a halt. They were crossing a narrow stream and the order had come to water the horses.

A runner came panting along. He caught sight of Jehan. 'He wants you,' he said curtly. There was no need to say who wanted him. 'Follow me.'

Jehan stood before Yann Duguesclin.

'I want someone good with horses,' Duguesclin said softly. 'They tell me I need the blacksmith.'

Jehan didn't know what to say and so kept silent.

Duguesclin nodded towards a trio of men standing a little way off, their horses in the stream beside them. 'You'd better start riding with them straight away,' he said. 'The sooner you grow familiar with them and their mounts, the more use you'll be.'

He turned and strode away.

Jehan, his heart knocking painfully in his chest, went to fetch his bay gelding.

Nine

Josse awoke with a sand-dry mouth and the embarrassing awareness that he'd been snoring. Loudly, probably, for the previous night's eating and heavy drinking would have led to very deep sleep. He raised his head from the mean and smelly pillow. The shutters were still firmly closed across the three or four high, small windows – nobody in the big sleeping room had made any effort to open any of them, although fresh air would have been extremely welcome – and he could only just make out the long, broad shape of his brother, lying next to him. The space where Geoffroi had slept was now empty, and Geoffroi's blanket was rolled and neatly tied.

Perhaps, Josse thought hopefully, Geoffroi was out foraging for breakfast and something to drink. A bucketful of water wouldn't have gone amiss.

The three of them had taken lodgings in the same establishment that Geoffroi had deemed good enough for their horses. Josse smiled. His son had clearly taken more care in selecting accommodation in accordance with the horses' comfort than that of his father and uncle. Still, the place wasn't too bad. It was very crowded, but that probably applied to everywhere in Lynn

158

just then. Bringing their own blankets had, however, been a wise move.

He waited for a little longer but, when Geoffroi did not appear, got up, pulled on his boots and reached for his cloak. He roused Yves, already stirring, and the two of them were just emerging from the latrines when Geoffroi came hurrying up. 'We're to go back to the hall where we feasted last night,' he said. 'There's food and drink set out, apparently, and we'd better hurry if we're not to find it's all gone – they're falling on it like raptors.'

In the hall, they joined the queue and found themselves swept along through a wide arch and into another, smaller hall, where meats and bread had been set out. Most of the men had been at the feast. Many, Josse noticed, were roughly his age, and had probably been summoned by the King for the same reason. He recognized a few faces from the distant days of his youth and young manhood, although, with the unreliable memory that comes to all men as they start to grow old, he found that no amount of effort could bring back their names . . . He reassured himself that his former companions would undoubtedly suffer the same affliction, however, and put it out of his mind.

Looking back through the arch, Josse could see King John seated at the heavy oak table on its dais at the far end of the main hall. Two men, a lad and a couple of comely young women were waiting on him, proffering various jugs and dishes. With increasing impatience and rising temper, John waved them all away.

Josse studied him. He didn't look very well. Whispers were chasing each other round the high hall, and it seemed everyone was aware of the King's symptoms. He had been sick, he had a crushing headache, he'd voided his bowels at least twice. Other symptoms, such as the yellow whites of the eyes and the greyish pallor of the usually ruddy face, Josse could see for himself. The King was clearly suffering from an almighty hangover and, given the astonishing amounts of alcohol that he'd consumed the previous evening, it was hardly surprising.

Josse felt a lurch of sympathy. He'd never known when to stop, he reflected. Despite the very early age at which John had started to acquire a taste for wine, ale, cider – pretty much anything alcoholic, in fact – he had never learned the fundamental laws of consequence. How many times, Josse mused, had he watched John suffer like this? Too many to count . . .

Yves and Geoffroi had pushed their way to the boards where food and drink had been laid out and, using their height and width advantage shamelessly, had managed to pile three platters with an assortment of the proffered fare. Now they made their way to a half-empty table towards the back of the hall, and Josse was about to join them on the bench when one of the men attending on the King came hurrying up.

'You're to come with me,' he said. He jerked his head in the King's direction. 'It's an order.'

With some reluctance, Josse followed him through the crowd and up the steps to the raised table where King John sat. He stared up as Josse

160

approached. 'Sit down, my friend,' he said in a hoarse voice. Josse had a vague memory that the night had ended with some singing; probably quite a lot. He obeyed the command. John studied him, and Josse was just deciding that he had no idea at all which of the old faithful he was when the King leaned closer and, amid a fume of hot breath that smelt unpleasantly of fermented fruit, said quietly, 'How is your daughter?'

Other men also have daughters, Josse told himself firmly. *It's probably just a lucky guess.* Nevertheless, as he told the King briefly that Meggie was well and would be honoured to be remembered, he couldn't prevent the warm glow that suffused him.

'She does you credit, Josse,' John said. 'You must . . .'

But his eyes had caught movement at the back of the hall, and, as Josse turned to look, he saw a rider – hot, sweaty, dusty, and with an expression of the gravest apprehension – shoving his way through the throng towards the King.

'What news?' John demanded as the man, reaching him, fell on his knees on the filthy floor. 'Oh, get up, you fool,' he added impatiently, 'I can't hear what you're muttering down there.'

The man stood, straightened his clothes, leaned forward and, on tiptoe, put his face up close to the King's. Now he looked as if he was on the point of breaking down, his exhausted face falling into lines of abject distress.

Josse heard the hissing of his whispered words. He couldn't make out all of them but one was enough: Dover.

161

He knew already that it wasn't good news, for he had seen the messenger's expression. He was, he reflected in a strange moment during which he seemed to stand apart from the hall and turn into an observer, probably only the second of that vast company to have that realization.

But, only a few heartbeats later, everyone knew.

For the King stood up, so violently that he overturned his big, heavy chair and sent it flying off the dais to land with a deafening crash on the stone floor behind him. And, in a voice so loud, so filled with anguish that it hurt to hear it, he bellowed, 'Hubert de Burgh has failed!'

Almost every man there knew who Hubert de Burgh was, and the few who didn't were swiftly enlightened by those standing nearest. There was a moment of silence, and then the uproar began.

Josse edged closer to the King, who was staring down at the parchment that the messenger had just given him. Josse could hear his frantic, muttered words; see the blue eyes in their yellowed whites scanning the few lines of writing, as if desperate to find he'd been mistaken.

Then he turned and stared straight at Josse. 'He can no longer hold out against the besiegers,' he said dully. 'He asks my permission to surrender the castle to Prince Louis.'

Just for a few moments, Josse really believed the King was going to see sense; to yield to the inevitable, give the necessary orders and send the messenger straight back to Dover, perhaps even with a word or two of thanks to de Burgh and his garrison for having fought so well for so long.

But this was King John. And, very soon, Josse acknowledged his own foolishness.

The King boiled over like a tightly lidded pot on a hot stove. His incandescent fury roared up through him in a red tide and, the foam gathering at the corners of his mouth, and gouts of spittle flying like hailstones, he screamed, '*No surrender! NO SURRENDER!* He'll hold the castle and the garrison will fight to the very last man!'

There was a great roar as at least half, and probably two-thirds, of the company caught his fervour. But quite a lot of men were looking sick and ashen. They were the older men, the veterans of battles and sieges, the ones who knew that holding out was sometimes pointless, and that fighting to the very last man was wasteful, agonizing and ultimately quite futile.

And now Josse felt a rising fury of his own. The men at Dover had given all they had, and the dear Lord alone knew what conditions had been like; what privations had been endured, how much pain and suffering – how many deaths – had been witnessed.

Helewise's young grandson Ralf was there. Was he still alive? If so, if somehow he had managed to survive, was he now to have his life thrown away by the King's careless and uncaring hand, purely because John was too angry to see sense?

No. He wasn't.

It was reckless and extremely dangerous, but in that instant Josse didn't care. He shot to his feet and spun to face the King, so close that they were almost chest to chest. He said, his words clear and cold and only for the King's ears: 'That, my lord King, is madness.'

John stopped his rant. He seemed to freeze, his face as still as if he'd suddenly been paralysed.

'They have fought for you so bravely,' Josse plunged on, too furious to stop. 'Undoubtedly they would die for you, but is it right to let them?'

The King did not move.

I probably have only moments to live, Josse thought. He was quite surprised to discover it didn't really bother him very much.

But then John seemed to collapse into himself. He felt around behind him for his chair. Swiftly Josse substituted another, less grand one. As if the King was suddenly boneless, he sank into it.

He rested his elbows on the table, then dropped his face into his hands. After some time, he said, his voice muffled, 'Oh, what's the point?'

Nobody else in the vast hall seemed to know what had happened. Some were still happily celebrating – although precisely what, Josse couldn't work out – and some sat bewildered, pale, as if wondering what the surrender of Dover Castle – fortress, rallying cry, symbol of holding out, holding on – might mean.

Then John raised his wrecked face, turned to the nearest hovering attendant and barked, 'Fetch a scribe.'

The scribe must surely have been lurking nearby, for almost instantly he was at the King's side. And Josse, standing just behind him, heard John's instructions: in a weary voice and a tone of deepest reluctance, he dictated the message

164

informing Hubert de Burgh that his King agreed to the surrender.

Josse's passionate, furious distress had gone. Now, his eyes on the King as John stared after the scribe, who had already raced over to where the messenger was hastily stuffing down bread and cheese and gulping a mug of ale, he was filled with pity. It had always been the same, through all the long years since Josse had known John. He'd been an undisciplined, wilful, resentful child, intelligent enough to know that neither of his parents liked him much, and sensitive enough that it caused pain. He would have worked out for himself that, as eighth and youngest child and third surviving legitimate son, he didn't matter very much to anyone. Perhaps it was that which had forged his fierce, combative, self-interested, self-absorbed character. Most people probably would have said they loathed him.

But Josse had never been of their number. He had often asked himself why, although he'd never come up with much of an answer.

Now, prompted by memory, prompted by an affection that began too many years ago to count, he stepped closer to the King, bent down and said very softly, 'I am sorry, my lord King.'

John turned to look at him. 'For what, Josse? For this devastating news from Dover, or for bawling at me as if I were a child again?'

Josse was just trying to scrape together some sort of an answer when the King spoke again, and now his voice was gentler. 'The one is hardly your fault, although I thank you for your commiserations. The second . . .' To Josse's surprise and relief, a brief grin creased the haggard face. 'Ah, Josse, you were right, and it was brave of you to bring me to my senses.'

'My lord, I would not presume to—'

'Oh, Josse, shut up,' said the King without rancour.

Josse waited to see if he would say more, but John appeared to be deep in thought. Surreptitiously, Josse drew up another chair and sat down, careful to position himself a little way away but close enough to answer if questioned.

After a moment, the King said, 'We leave tomorrow.' He waved an arm over the assembled crowd, most of them, the drama over, busy tucking into the food while they had the chance. Seasoned soldiers for the most part, Josse reflected, they knew better than to pass up the opportunity to eat, drink and rest.

'Aye, my lord,' Josse ventured, when the King didn't continue. 'Er . . . do you wish me to spread the word?'

John was gazing round the hall, studying the faces. 'I am fortunate, am I not,' he said softly, 'to have old friends? To have so many good knights who, receiving my summons, hastened to come to me.'

'A man acquires the friends he deserves,' Josse said.

The King smiled. 'Yes, Josse, that's why I'm mildly surprised at how many turned up.'

There wasn't a diplomatic answer to that, so Josse didn't try to find one.

Then John said, 'I expect you'd like to know where we're going.'

'Well, yes, my lord King.'

Suddenly John squared his shoulders and sat up straight. His colour, Josse observed, was a little improved, and the bright blue eyes looked more alert. 'We'll ride north, heading first for Lincoln, and we'll travel there round the Wash via Wisbech and stop at Spalding,' he said decisively. 'We shall spend a night with the monks at Swineshead Abbey, where I'm told they keep a decent board, although I admit I doubt it. The supplies I'm dispatching to the northern defences are now well on their way, and I shall follow.' Eager now – his moods, Josse thought, had always been mercurial – the King went on, 'The south must look to itself. Dover may have to yield, but it is not the only stronghold. My presence is required on the northern borders, for that—' he pounded the table for emphasis – 'that is where the next attack will come. Mark my words, Josse, Alexander of Scotland and those bastard northern rebels believe they have a strong alliance, and that will make them over-confident.' He nodded as if to emphasize his words. 'They will not, however, find it as simple a matter as they believe it to be, for I shall be there waiting.'

Almost in the same breath, the King bellowed for his body servant and, as the young man hurried up, Josse sensed himself dismissed. He stepped down from the dais and went to join Yves and Geoffroi. He wolfed down the food they had saved for him and, as soon as he had finished, said, 'We're leaving in the morning. Lincoln, then on towards the north.'

167

'Hasn't he just come from Lincoln?' Geoffroi asked.

'Aye, son, he has.' Josse took a draught of ale. *But when would that ever have stopped him?* he thought. John had always been such a restless man, and it seemed to Josse that the desire to be ever on the move, hurrying on to the next place, the next task, as if staying in one place was somehow indicative of a king – a man – who was a failure, had increased recently. It was said that for virtually the whole of the past month, John had been travelling up to thirty miles a day. It was a hard, relentless routine for a man who was nearly fifty years old. No wonder he looked ill.

Josse realized that Geoffroi and Yves were waiting for him to elaborate on the brief answer. 'He intends to travel north to support his loyal barons against Alexander,' he said.

Geoffroi nodded. He asked one or two questions, mainly concerned with practicalities, and Josse answered. His attention, however, was on Yves, for his brother was looking worried.

'What's the matter?' Josse asked him, when Geoffroi went off to check on the horses.

Yves didn't answer immediately. But then, taking his eyes off whatever he'd been staring at, he said, 'It's probably nothing.'

Josse grinned. 'Why not share it with me anyway?'

'There's a young man I've noticed. Well, not much more than a lad, really. He was sitting there, not far from the high table.' He pointed. 'Oh, he's gone now,' he added quickly as Josse

168

looked around. 'He's not one of the companions summoned by the King, and, as far as I can tell, not one of their attendants.'

'Is that why you were watching him?' Josse queried. 'Because you think he's an outsider?'

Slowly Yves shook his head. 'No, not exactly. That's part of it, I suppose, although there are others here who have only newly joined us and none of them concern me.'

Josse waited. His brother would speak in his own time, and there was no point in hurrying him.

'I know what it was,' Yves said presently. 'It was the way he was watching the King. Not so much when he was shouting with rage about de Burgh and Dover, but later, when he leaned across and spoke to you.'

When he told me where we'll be going tomorrow, Josse thought. 'And then he got up and left?'

'Yes. Almost instantly, as if, having heard what he needed to hear, he didn't have to stay.'

'Why would that information be important?' Josse said. 'No doubt we'll all be told, sooner or later.'

'Perhaps *sooner* is relevant?' Yves suggested. 'Perhaps somebody wants advanced warning of the King's movements?'

'Perhaps,' Josse said. 'But he couldn't have heard!' he protested. 'The King spoke quietly and, even sitting immediately beneath the high table, surely your young man wouldn't have made out the words?'

'No, you wouldn't think so, would you?' Yves

agreed. 'Yet I would almost swear that he followed what the King was saying.' Leaning closer, dropping his voice, he said, 'Josse, we had a deaf man at Acquin. Stone deaf from late childhood, couldn't hear a sound. He had some sickness, some infant malady, and that was the result.'

'I don't recall—'

'No, it was after your time. But, Josse, *he* could understand what you said to him if he could see your face; your lips, I suppose. He wasn't always very accurate, but it was enough to get by.'

'And you think that's what your young man was doing?'

Yves nodded. 'I do. He was watching the King so closely, you see. His attitude as he strained to see put me in mind of Deaf Paul, straight away.'

Josse's thoughts raced. Was it likely? Was it possible? Had someone quietly slipped into the throng around the King a man who could interpret whispered confidences, even when far too far distant to hear them?

It was both possible and, given the vast numbers of the King's enemies, quite likely. With a sigh – for had they not enough to worry about without this? – he turned his full attention to Yves and said, 'You'd better describe him to me.'

Even as he listened – fifteen, sixteen or thereabouts; mid-brown hair worn to the shoulders; keen, light-coloured eyes in a narrow face; slim build, not very tall, dark tunic and hose under a hooded grey cloak, bare-headed – he was already

170

wondering whose ears were the best to receive the information that they probably had at least one spy in the company.

Jehan was increasingly disillusioned. Having finally admitted to himself that it had been a mistake to join Yann Duguesclin's private army, he didn't know what to do. He had to accept, though, that they were unlikely to let him go home.

He was riding with the three assassins now, tending their horses, fetching and carrying for them when they were in camp. Already he was wary of them and, if he was honest, he had to admit that *wary* really ought to be *terrified*. It wasn't that they treated him badly or cruelly; for the most part they ignored him and they barely spoke. It was just that they seem to exude an almost visible air of menace.

'Home.' He repeated the word softly, under his breath. Perhaps it was the distance that enhanced the pleasure – the joy – of that simple life of hard work, the primitive but well-constructed and sparklingly clean little dwelling in the forest glade, the ever-present company of a loved and loving woman. *You weren't so keen on it when you were there*, he reminded himself. *And don't fool yourself into believing Meggie was always there with you, because you know it's not true.*

Meggie. He thought about her so much. When he felt the need to keep his spirits up, he wove a pleasant picture of how it would be when he returned to the charcoal burner's camp; how she'd be there, welcoming him with love;

171

how both of them, after that joyful reunion, would say how much they regretted having allowed distance to grow between them and resolve to do better. Perhaps he'd ask her to be his wife and, her eyes bright with tears, she would accept . . .

The last, he had to admit, was probably unlikely.

He knew it was by no means certain that he *would* return. His initial apprehension was steadily growing into certainty, and he guessed, from what the whispered rumours said Yann Duguesclin planned to do, there was a fair chance that quite a lot of the band would be injured, even killed.

He tried not to think about what lay ahead, but it was more difficult each day. On the morning that the young deaf mute came racing back to camp, his strange voice – like some bird's cry – echoing with excited anxiety as he sought out Duguesclin, Jehan was hit with the sudden certainty that something terrible was going to happen.

He withdrew into himself, and in his mind set his steps into the tranquil glade where he worked the forge. Where he and Meggie had built their home. The images brought comfort. He sent up a brief, heartfelt prayer, asking God for the grace of just a little more time with Meggie. *If I am injured, Lord, if in the end I have to die*, he pleaded, *please grant me leave to tell her that I felt her presence as I tried to gather my fortitude and my courage for what I know is ahead. Give me, I pray, just a moment, to tell her that she was here with me, and that she was, as ever, a solace.*

172

He finished his prayer. Then, calm now, he went to join the group waiting outside Yann Duguesclin's rough and basic tent to hear what they were going to be ordered to do.

They could all hear the weird sounds that were the deaf boy's only means of speech. 'How in the good Lord's name does he understand?' one of the older men muttered.

'They've been together a long time,' another replied. 'The deaf lad makes signs, see, with his hands. Makes pictures, and somehow Yann picks up his meaning.'

His hands. Jehan pictured the deaf boy's hands. Long-fingered, graceful; eloquent, if hands could be said to be eloquent. The deaf lad's could. It was strange, he mused, how they all called him the deaf lad, or the deaf mute. Didn't the boy have a name? Presumably Yann Duguesclin knew it, but if so, he didn't share it with his loyal followers. That was typical, Jehan thought in a moment of sudden, deep revulsion. Yann appeared to prize secrecy above almost everything else, and his insistence on not explaining, on not telling them what they were to do until the last moment, on not revealing any man's identity other than by what his job was, so that they were Cook, Horse-master, Forager, and, in his own case, simply Blacksmith or, more usually, Smith. Would it hurt to allow the small intimacy of knowing a man's name?

A wave of profound disgust rose in him, primarily against his enigmatic leader but also – for he was ever more determined to be honest with himself – against his own stupidity in being so eager for adventure and for something *different*, out of the daily routine, that he had hurried to join the Bretons without really stopping to think.

There was a sound of movement. Voices were raised in brief acclaim, as if something had just been decided to general satisfaction. Then Yann Duguesclin threw back the tattered flap of his tent and emerged, his senior officers behind him and the deaf lad following. He waited until every pair of eyes was on him, then he told them what they were going to do.

And Jehan, recognizing at last and far too late the trap he had set for himself, and how unlikely it was that he would emerge from it alive, felt a moment's profound sorrow.

Then, resigned, he raised his head and joined in the cheers.

Ten

At the Sanctuary on the edge of the Great Wealden Forest, Helewise stood in the open doorway staring out into the darkness of the surrounding trees. It was late; after midnight, she was sure, and there was barely a sound on the cold air. Tiphaine was out there somewhere. She had been in the Sanctuary constantly, tending the sick woman, taking turns with Helewise to sit by Hadil's bedside to hold her down when the violent fits took hold of her and trying to soothe her.

Apart from the extreme distress the poor woman was enduring, as were the two women who were caring for her, thrashing about like a trapped animal threatened to do further harm to the broken arm.

Tiphaine had finally come up with a concoction that seemed to work – either that or the patient had finally exhausted herself – and Hadil had been sleeping since dusk. Helewise, aware of Tiphaine's growing restlessness, had suggested gently that she take herself off into the forest for a while. Tiphaine, of course, had refused: 'I cannot leave you here alone with her, my lady. What if she should wake and throw another of those screaming fits?'

'If she does, I shall administer more of whatever remedy you gave her earlier,' Helewise said calmly.

'But she's strong, despite that arm. It's been taking the two of us to control her.'

'I believe that, with her fever slowly subsiding, there is little likelihood of further fits.'

'But . . .'

With a smile, Helewise watched Tiphaine's stern face contort as she tried to come up with further objections. She reached out and put a soothing hand on Tiphaine's arm. 'Go,' she said firmly. 'I shall be perfectly all right. You need . . .' She had been about to say, *You need to get out into the open air for a while, since too long cooped up within the four walls of a small room makes you as jumpy as a fox in a box.*

It had always been so, in all the long years of the women's acquaintance. In the Hawkenlye

175

Abbey days, Helewise had known perfectly well when, and for how long, her herbalist slipped away into the Great Forest. The convenient excuse had been that she needed to gather leaves, flowers, roots and fungi for her herbal preparations, but Helewise had always been aware that was only a part of the reason for Tiphaine's absences. Dutiful and as obedient as her nature allowed, Tiphaine had never returned empty-handed, but she had needed to restore herself with the quiet energy of the vast, living forest in the same way that others needed air and water.

Helewise had watched with private amusement as Tiphaine struggled with herself. Then, abruptly yielding to the greater force, she strode out through the door with a muttered, 'Back soon', and was gone.

That had been hours ago. Not that Helewise was worried. Tiphaine was at home in the forest as others were in a familiar, beloved and long-occupied cottage.

With reluctance, she turned her back on the night and went back inside the little room, drawing the door closed. There was a single lamp burning, and by its soft light she went over to look at her patient. Hadil was deeply asleep, making a soft sound on each out-breath. Putting a gentle hand on her forehead, Helewise judged that the fever had reduced still further. With a nod of satisfaction, she went over to her own bed, lay down and was soon asleep.

She can see figures in the mist . . . It's a thick mist and there is the smell of water. Sea water, for there is saltiness in it. But there is also the rank, throat-catching stink of rotting vegetation, of the fringe waters of some wild marshland. At first all is quiet, as if the mist has muffled every sound. But then there is the jingle of harness, the puffing breath of hard-working horses, a shout of frustration.

She can see figures. Three mounted men – big men – riding in the mist, their horses' feet splashing in the water. There is a cry of panic, the shrill neighing of a terrified horse.

The mist swirls as if it is alive. Sometimes it is so thick it's like a white wall. Sometimes it blows away in tatters, like streaming pennants on a wind that can't be heard or felt.

And then suddenly a tunnel seems to open up within the blinding whiteness and she can see straight down it. There are the three figures again – they are big men, oddly similar. There is a sudden whistling sound. A hard thump, a cry of agony, a big red patch spreading on the breast of a tunic. A figure falls to the watery ground with a splash.

Help him; get him up, he'll drown! she hears herself cry.

There is someone else watching: someone she knows, although she can't think who he is or why she should recognize him . . . what is *he* doing there?

And in a voice that rings like a deep, mournful bell, he says, *It is too late. He is dead.*

Helewise woke with a cry of dread. The cry was still echoing as, profoundly distressed, she wrestled herself out of deep sleep and sat up.

The cry came again. 'Please. *Please!*'

It wasn't she who had cried out. It was Hadil.

Still fighting the horror of the nightmare, Helewise got up. She lit a second lamp and, one in either hand, hurried over to Hadil's bed. She knelt beside the sick woman, putting the lamps on a narrow shelf, out of the reach of a flailing arm. 'Are you in pain?' she asked softly, her hand on Hadil's forehead.

'Your hand is cool,' Hadil said. 'No, not pain – well, my arm is sore, but no more than before.'

'Are you thirsty?'

'Thirsty . . . yes.'

Helewise poured water from an earthenware jug into a cup and held it to Hadil's lips. Hadil drank a few sips, then lay back on the pillows.

Helewise waited. After a while, Hadil said, 'It was only a dream, you know.'

'A . . . *what?*'

Hadil smiled. 'You were moaning in your sleep. Restless. Twisting and turning. Then you were crying, and I thought it was kind to wake you.'

'Thank you,' said Helewise gravely. 'It was not a pleasant dream.' She shook her head, trying to disperse the persistent images. Then: 'Do you think you could sleep again? It is not yet dawn.'

Hadil sighed. 'I will try.'

'Call me if you want me.'

Hadil nodded.

Time passed. Helewise was afraid to sleep again; what if the dream came back? *I am worried about him*, she thought. *That is why my dreaming mind makes these pictures.*

Sleep did not come.

And so, when Hadil began muttering, Helewise heard every word.

'. . . should have left it alone, ought to have destroyed it . . . they *knew* it was evil, a curse out of antiquity, and that nothing good could come from something so tainted . . .' There was a pause. It lengthened, and Helewise thought Hadil had entered a deeper sleep. But suddenly she cried out, '*Father!* Oh, Father, you were her grandson, the first male to inherit the responsibility! Why did you not end it? Why did you leave this final horror for my son and me?'

There was such anguish in her voice, such weariness and grief, that instinctively Helewise hurried over to her. Fully expecting to find Hadil asleep, she was shocked to see that her eyes were open.

'Do not distress yourself so,' Helewise said soothingly. 'I will prepare an infusion, and we shall hope that . . .'

Then she realized that, despite the open eyes, Hadil was not truly awake. What was it? Helewise wondered, anxiety swiftly rising. Was she in a trance? Was another of the frightening fits about to take her over?

She searched her memory for everything she'd ever been taught about dealing with patients in such states. *Listen to them*, dear old Sister Euphemia used to say. *Respond as if what they are saying is perfectly sensible and lucid. Above all, do not let them see that the unnaturalness of it is worrying you.*

And so, with the calm, kindly, comforting

179

presence of the long-dead infirmarer's shade beside her, Helewise sat on Hadil's bed, took her hand and said, in her usual tone, 'I'm sure your father did his best. He would not want you to suffer so.'

Hadil turned to her, wide-eyed. 'Yes, yes, Father was a good man and, even as a boy, he tried to do the right thing. That's what my grandmother told me, and she did not lie. But Father was too kind! Gentle, like his mother and his grandmother, and that was why he did not do what he should have done.'

As the low, urgent voice went on, Helewise, bemused, tried to make sense of what Hadil was saying. She didn't think this was the rambling of delirium. For one thing, Hadil's fever was much reduced. For another, there seemed to be logic, of a sort, in her words.

Hadil seemed to be saying that something bad – *evil* – had somehow come into her family's possession. She spoke of her father, his mother, his grandmother. So that was – Helewise counted – three generations back. What was this thing? And where had the family found it? For it sounded, she reflected, as if it had been found, and perhaps by accident, rather than being acquired, or received as a gift.

'Did he find it at home?' she asked. She had no idea how Hadil would respond, or even if it was the right place to begin.

'At *home?*' Hadil echoed. 'No, no, not at home!' Her voice was scathing, as if to say, *How could you possibly think that?*

'He dug it up – he must have done, it's what my grandmother used to tell me. Then, when they set on him and killed him, they took it. They should have left it on his body! But they were greedy, her father and her brother. They stood there, *his* body and the body of my father's brother's son lying dead at their feet, and they took it from him. They *knew* he was evil!' Her voice had risen to a shout. 'They ought to have realized that nothing good could come from robbing him. Oh, *oh*, and now we are here, my son and I, and we have come so far, so very far, and although my kinfolk have tried so hard, down through all the years, still it is not ended!' She stopped, panting. Slowly her breathing returned to normal. Her eyelids drooped, and Helewise thought she was drowsy.

'Sleep, Hadil,' she said very softly. 'Go to sleep.'

Hadil turned on her side, settling herself. For a little while there was silence. Then, just as Helewise was creeping away to her own bed, Hadil said, quietly and poignantly, 'I wish I could go home.'

Almost afraid to ask, for Hadil had been so very secretive and the question might rouse her fury, Helewise drew a breath. Then, casually, as if it wasn't really very important, she said, 'And where is home?'

Hadil, in the middle of a huge yawn, didn't at first answer. Helewise wondered if she'd heard the question. But then, sleepily, uncaringly, Hadil murmured, 'Jerusalem.'

* * *

181

Meggie and Faruq were riding as fast as they could, pushing the horses and themselves to the limits of their strength, racing to catch up with the King's party. Some factors were in their favour: the weather stayed dry; the tracks and roads were in reasonably good condition after the summer and early autumn; the land was neither hilly nor marshy, and they didn't often have to cut through forest or thick undergrowth; the horses, although of very different breeds, were both fit, strong and, most importantly, used to covering many miles in a day. Nevertheless, the journey seemed endless and, as day after day passed, Meggie began to wonder if they would ever reach their destination.

Other than that they were bound for East Anglia, she didn't really know what that destination was.

They had passed Cambridge the previous night, going round it to the west at a distance, and on smaller tracks that had kept them from the notice and the unwelcome attention of those who might have been using the main roads during the hours of darkness. Now they were almost at the end of the night's ride, going north-north-east, and the increasing frequency of marshy ground told her that they were in the fenland. That realization led to another: they were in East Anglia now and that vague description of their destination was no longer enough. Somehow they must find out the King's present position.

Then, before they found him – she felt sure they would – there was something else she must find out.

It seems most likely that Faruq wishes to save the King from harm, she thought, *because that was his intention when he believed the threat endangered the Queen.*

But what if she was wrong?

I cannot help Faruq to harm the King.

She knew that, and it made no difference if it was right or wrong. It followed, then, that somehow she was going to have to ask him.

She drew rein and waited until Faruq came level with her. 'There's no point going much further until we've asked someone where the King and his party are,' she said.

He understood instantly. 'And he might be in any part of this region.'

'Yes.'

He looked at her, half-questioningly, half-amused. 'You have already told me your idea, about saying you are a healer.'

She nodded. 'Yes. I'll say we've been summoned to help in an outbreak of fever. We'll say camp fever, I think, because that's pretty common among armies.'

'You *know* about this fever?' He sounded disbelieving.

He's wondering how a forest healer like me can have such sophisticated knowledge, she thought. She resisted the strong temptation to explain, to tell him of the wide experience she'd gained working in the Hawkenlye infirmary; how Sister Liese had invited her to help nurse a couple of sick soldiers making their way up from the coast towards London, both feverish, with red spots on their torsos and their arms, explaining

183

how the crowded and insanitary conditions of an army in camp led to the widespread presence of lice, whose blood-sucking activities, by some strange and unimaginable process, spread disease from man to man. The soldiers were lucky, for they came under the care of the Hawkenlye nuns and survived.

She simply said, 'Yes.'

He watched her, not speaking, for a moment. Then he said, 'And I am to be your assistant.'

To her relief, he hadn't made it sound like a question. Perhaps, she reflected with a wry smile, he had managed to swallow his masculine pride at the very idea of being the assistant to a mere woman, and now understood the wisdom of it. Perhaps the fact that she knew about such exotic maladies as camp fever had finally convinced him.

But, again, she just said, 'Yes.'

He was frowning. 'So, tomorrow we shall ride in the daytime, I think?' Following his thoughts, she nodded. 'In the day, yes,' he went on, 'for we need to encounter others. And, when we come across someone who is knowledgeable about the progress of the King, we shall ask where to find him. Should this person be suspicious, we shall explain our purpose and that will reassure him.' He looked enquiringly at her. 'This is correct?'

She suppressed a smile. Put like that, it sounded simplistic and slightly absurd, but, in essence, he had it right. 'It is.'

She put her heels to Auban's sides, and they rode on. She had one more idea, although she hoped she wouldn't need it. She had decided, anyway, not to tell Faruq. It was almost guaranteed, she thought, to make him give her that sceptical, doubting, undermining look of his, and she had enough to worry about without that.

They stopped soon after dawn for a few hours' rest, hobbling the horses beside a narrow little stream that flowed its quiet and gentle way towards some larger watercourse. There was still plenty of grass, and Meggie fell asleep to the sound of large equine teeth tearing off clumps of it.

They found what they had hoped to find the next morning. No longer avoiding the towns and the settlements, they rode along a straight causeway into the small town of March, standing on slightly elevated ground above the surrounding marshland. In an open square among close-huddled dwellings, a farmer stood beside his cart selling bread, vegetables and cheese. Meggie bought two loaves and a soft, garlic-scented cheese, and was mounting up again when, with a great clatter of hooves and the smell of men who had been in the saddle for too long, a band of about twenty riders came into the square. They were soldiers, without a doubt: well armed, some clad in surcoats over mail, one bearing a banner with a recognizably royal device.

Not pausing to think – not wanting to give herself time to think – Meggie went up to the man at the head of the group.

He looked down at her from his horse's back, grinning. 'You've left us some, I hope?' He nodded at the provisions in her hands.

'Oh, yes,' she said with an answering smile. 'Try the garlicky cheese – the farmer gave me a morsel to try and it's delicious.'

'Thank you, I shall.'

He turned, perhaps about to issue instructions, but she stopped him. 'Please, can you tell me where to find the King?'

His expression changed in a flash. He had looked friendly, relaxed, clearly enjoying the mild flirtation with a pretty woman. Now, though, suspicion darkened his face. 'And why do you want to know?'

She steeled herself. This had to sound right.

'I've been sent for. Me and my assistant.' She jerked her head towards Faruq, still mounted on the black gelding and holding Auban's reins. 'I'm a healer, see, and they're worrying in case fever breaks out in the camp. They want me near, to treat men before it spreads.'

Now his expression had changed again. Like all soldiers, he feared the dreaded fever. She saw him cross himself, heard his swift, muttered prayer. 'Can you treat it?' he said, not much above a whisper.

'I can make men wash, and launder their clothes, and, for those already sick, make sure they keep drinking good, clean water. I have potions, too.' She patted her leather satchel.

He studied her for several anxious moments. But then, as if he knew she was telling the truth – which indeed, when speaking of the fever, she had been doing – he gave a curt nod. 'He's been at Lynn these past couple of days. Now he's on the move again and word is he's going north.'

She needed more than that. 'Where will they stay next?'

He shrugged. 'I can't say for sure.' He gazed up and to the right, eyes narrowed in the bright morning light. 'South from Lynn, round the base of the Wash at Wisbech, then north to Spalding . . .' Now his gaze was on her again. 'He'll likely stop overnight at one of those places, but which one will depend on how fast they move. Tough going, round the Wash,' he commented. 'Too many streams and rivers all making their way to the sea, and unless you're a Fensman born and bred, you don't know from one day to the next what the tide'll be doing.' He paused, apparently thinking. 'Make for Spalding,' he said eventually. 'That way.' He pointed and, following the direction of his hand, Meggie made out the same causeway by which they'd arrived, stretching away beyond the little town.

She turned to go, thanking him. Then, hurrying now, she mounted Auban and moved off.

She was aware of the soldier's eyes on her as she and Faruq kicked their horses to a trot and then, once on the firm, elevated causeway, a canter.

He'd been suspicious; she was quite sure. Best, she decided, to be far away before he made up his mind to come after them.

Eleven

11 October 1216

Josse had been out and about since early on. His sleep had been uneasy. Vaguely distressing dreams had visited him, so that when he finally gave up and decided to abandon his bed and see what was happening outside, it had been a relief. And, as early as soon after dawn, there had been plenty to observe. He had followed his nose to the kitchens, helped himself to freshly baked bread thickly spread with butter, and a mug of small beer, then gone outside into the inn yard, where he had found himself a comfortable perch at the top of steps leading up to a hay loft and settled down to watch.

The biggest of the great wagons, drawn by teams of oxen, were already being prepared for departure. Their pace was slow, and if there was to be a chance of their arriving at the next destination by this evening, they had to make an early start, well ahead of the rest of the long train. Josse munched on his bread, smiling as he saw a fat, red-faced servant, unaware that Josse was watching, help himself from one of the ale barrels he was loading. Now the first wagon was pulling away, rolling towards the wide entrance to the huge inn yard; the man driving the oxen, apparently checking on directions, paused to exchange words with a tall, broad man in the livery of a senior servant. 'You head for Wisbech, then you're following the better road further inland,' the liveried man said impatiently. 'You've been told enough times! The heavy carts and pack animals aren't to be risked on the tracks running close to the shore.'

The driver muttered something about it being a long way round, but the liveried man interrupted. 'Those are your orders. Follow them.'

He turned on his heel and strode away, missing the vulgar gesture the driver made to his departing back.

There was a sudden confusion of noise: men's voices raised in shouts; the crack of horse- and ox-whips; a series of slow, creaking sounds as the vast wagons slowly moved away, oxen straining with the effort. The huge ox carts were followed by horse-drawn wagons and then by the strongest and largest of the packhorses, laden with panniers. So absorbed had Josse been in watching the busy activity that, until he glanced up to see the position of the sun, he hadn't realized how much time had passed.

The early morning had been still, with swirls of mist hanging in the grey sky. Now, with the sun strengthening as it climbed, the moisture had largely burned away and the day was clear and bright. 'A fine morning for a journey,' Josse said aloud.

Just for an instant, one of the troubling images from his dreams flashed into his mind. But, before he could study it, he saw Geoffroi come hurrying into the yard, calling for him, and the image went away. He descended the steps, went to join Geoffroi, and the two of them went on to the stables to prepare their horses for the day's ride.

Josse sat on Alfred's broad back, eyes roaming around the throng of men, both mounted and on foot, in the wide courtyard in front of one of Lynn's finest houses. It was the house where the King had been staying, and he had sent word to summon Josse and others of his trusted companions to await him there. It seemed he wanted to have his old friends close; what was it, Josse wondered, that he feared?

The owner of the house emerged through the heavy oak door and stood on the steps, eyes busy, darting this way and that as he took in the activity, and an expression on his face suggesting he wasn't going to let any slapdash preparation get past *him*. He had been host to his King! For two precious days, King John had been an honoured guest under his roof. Josse didn't think anybody among the man's kin, friends or casual acquaintances would ever be allowed to forget it.

Suddenly there was a commotion from within the house: loud voices, some laughter, some ribald exchanges, the sound of many feet clattering on the stone flags of the great hall. Some liveried servants emerged, one of them frowning, as if inspecting the scene and the people in it to see if they matched some pre-ordained standard. Evidently they did, for the man stood aside, bowed low and waved an arm as if to say, *Behold!*

And King John stepped out through the doorway into the sunshine.

The King, clearly, was his usual impatient self. He was jittery with the habitual restlessness, never having learned the lesson that experienced men with their regular work to do were best left to get on with it, and that constant, irritably bellowed questions such as, 'How much longer are you going to be?' and 'Can't you do that more quickly?' did more harm than good.

Josse watched King John with sympathy. He didn't look as bad as he had the previous morning. Josse had noticed that, last night, John hadn't drunk nearly so much. He had, in fact, been subdued; perhaps even depressed. He'd sat up on the dais, moodily staring into the distance, clutching his beautiful gold goblet with the blue and green jewels close to his breast, as if wary of someone trying to wrest it from him, and answering remarks tentatively addressed to him with a surly growl.

The surrender of Dover Castle had obviously hit him very hard. More, surely, than it should have done, for John was used to the vicissitudes of a long campaign, and must know that gains and losses occurred with regular frequency. It was a blow, naturally, but still Josse would have expected the King's optimism to be reasserting itself by now . . .

His musings were interrupted by Geoffroi, nudging his horse up to Josse's side. 'We should be moving out soon,' he said. 'The last pair of packhorses has been lined up on the road leading out of town, and they're just loading a few horse-drawn carts.' He grinned. 'I didn't know kings travelled with so much baggage, Father! I just saw a portable chapel being hoisted on to one of the carts, and there was a priest in attendance yelling at the men to be careful of the holy relics and to treat them with due reverence, not hurl them about like a bag of carrots.' He leaned closer, dropping his voice. 'I reckon these light wagons must be reserved for the King's personal valuables, judging by the number of heavily armed guards.'

'Aye, it's always said of him that he likes to keep his most precious jewels close,' Josse remarked. Idly he wondered if John's gorgeous jewelled gold cup was on the cart, carefully packed in its own box and padded with wool.

There was movement in the line of pack-horses and carts. A command was issued, and men hastened to their appointed places. The first of the two packhorses led off, followed by the other one, and then the three laden carts slowly pulled away. The one which was guarded by the armed men was piled high, and the pair of greys drawing it had a struggle to get it moving. *It's overloaded*, Josse thought. *And they've stacked the luggage too high, so that it's in danger of overbalancing*. He nearly spoke out, but then, appreciating that a repacking operation would mean more delay and that would cause the King to seethe with furious impatience, thought better of it.

He sat watching until the final elements of the King's long baggage train set off along the road.

Geoffroi was looking at the King, a frown

on his face. 'Doesn't King John lead the way?' he asked.

'No. He'll want to give them a start, but we'll soon overtake them once we set out after them.'

'Then why are we all mounted and ready, if we're not leaving yet?' Geoffroi demanded.

Josse smiled. 'Don't question the ways of kings, son. They are a rule unto themselves.'

A good hour later and probably more, at last King John set out from Lynn. The road out of the town ran south-west, roughly following the coast of the Wash. The land was marshy and often consisted not of solid, continuous firm ground but of a series of small islands, separated either by fordable ditches and streams or else linked by wooden bridges. It was, Josse thought, very diffi-cult to determine where the coastline actually was. Locals said it was constantly changing and, now that Josse was riding along it and could see for himself, he understood.

The King, it seemed, was well aware of the dangers of travelling in this difficult terrain, having taken the precaution of engaging local men to advise him. Riding between Yves and Geoffroi, only a few ranks behind the King and his intimate circle, Josse saw John frequently exchange remarks with the two guides who rode with him. As always, he was in a hurry, and more than once Josse heard him dismiss a suggestion because it threatened to slow his progress.

They came to the south-easternmost point of the Wash, rounded it and set off north-west. They skirted the town of Wisbech, the castle visible in outline on top of its rise. Josse had been hearing various mutterings about stopping to eat, and, indeed, a big crowd of the town's inhabitants had come out to greet the procession, many offering food and drink. Josse's optimism rose; they had been on the road for more than two hours and covered perhaps a dozen miles and he was feeling hungry. But the King, acknowledging the cheers and shouts with an impatiently waving hand, did not stop.

The long procession rode on.

The King's party overtook the light wagons and the packhorses a few miles beyond Wisbech. But if John had held any hopes of hurrying on ahead and reaching Spalding well in advance of his baggage, they were to be disappointed, for all at once they were on the smaller, lesser-used, far more perilous tracks that ran close to the Wash, and abruptly the terrain changed. The packhorses and the carts slowed down, but so too did the mounted men. Here the land was broken up by numerous waterways, some large, some little more than a trickle, which emptied their contents into the sea. The ground was often uncertain. At one point Josse heard a cry of fear from somewhere behind him, and loud splashing. There was the shrill, sharp neigh of a terrified horse. Geoffroi, always unable to bear the thought of any animal suffering, swiftly turned his horse and hurried back down the line. After some time, he came cantering up to resume his place beside Josse and Yves.

'What happened?' Yves asked.

'A chestnut mare went too close to the margins of the firm ground,' Geoffroi replied tersely. 'Another rider was pushing up from behind and, it seems, his larger horse shoved the mare off the track.'

'Is she all right?' Josse said.

'She's frightened and she's trembling violently, and the arsehole – sorry, Uncle – riding her has no consideration for her well-being. But, aye, she's all right, if you mean by that she's not drowned.'

Josse, picking up his son's fury, wisely said no more. Life in the company of the King and his entourage was tough, he reflected, on a young man who cared as passionately as Geoffroi did for all those of God's creatures at the mercy of uncaring men.

It was well past noon now. Since it appeared that the King was intending to press on, his sense of urgency too great to allow a stop for refreshments, Josse and his companions copied what many of the other men were doing, and, extracting bread, cheese and meat from their saddle bags, ate as they rode.

The morning had started fair, with a warm sun shining out of a clear blue sky and a gentle south-westerly wind. A wind that blew from the land, Josse reflected, keeping the air dry. They couldn't really have asked for a better day for riding.

He could smell the fresh, salty tang of the sea. It was very close now, a wide, silvery-green mass over to the right, beyond the expanse of marshy foreshore. The sunshine caught sparkling lights on the rumpled water, and if he strained his ears above the noise of the men and the horses, he fancied he could hear the regular flop of small waves breaking on the shore. Perhaps, he thought vaguely, the tide was coming in.

He noticed, not for the first time, that Yves was uneasy. He was repeatedly staring round at the men surrounding the King, studying them with a frown. 'Are you looking for your spy?' Josse asked quietly.

'Aye, I am,' Yves muttered. 'I thought I saw him this morning, before we set out, but now I'm not so sure – there's no sign of him, or not that I can see.'

Josse forbore to say that the man wouldn't be much of a spy if he allowed others to observe his movements. Instead he said mildly, 'If your guess is correct – and I'm not saying it isn't – then, once he found out where we're bound for today, he didn't really need to stay around.'

But Yves was still frowning anxiously. 'You're probably right. But I wish I knew why I feel so worried.' He glanced at Josse. 'I feel all but certain there's danger ahead.'

Slowly Josse nodded. 'I would say that you were letting your imagination run away with you – only I feel the same.'

Then the wind changed.

The breeze, strengthening now, was coming from the sea. More quickly than Josse could have imagined possible, a sea fret came rolling in from the east, and where a moment ago they had been riding along in sunshine, with good visibility and no danger of allowing their horses to stray too close to the perilous marshes, suddenly everything was different.

They had just come to a stream. It was quite wide, its banks dissipating into the surrounding marshy ground as its mouth opened out into the sea, although it didn't appear to be deep; at least, it wasn't when they first approached. But it had arrested their progress. Up at the head of the train, a few rows in front of where Josse, Yves and Geoffroi rode, the King and his senior attendants were talking to the local guides. Quite soon they were not so much talking as arguing. The King, as ever, wanted to hurry on across the stream and be on his way. The elder of the two guides – a weathered man of late middle age with deep-set grey eyes and a skin tanned by sun and sea – was advising caution.

'Tide turned quite a while ago,' he said calmly. 'With this mist we can't see what the sea's doing, but I don't much like the conditions, what I can make out of them.'

'Explain,' said the King tersely.

The man paused, obviously thinking. 'Water's higher than it should be at this time,' he said eventually. He fixed the King with his grey stare, apparently undaunted at being in conversation with his monarch. 'I'm thinking perhaps something's piling up the sea out there.' He nodded towards the Wash.

The King tapped his crop against his boot, the gesture swift with irritated impatience. 'What do you mean?' he demanded.

The man paused once more, then said, 'You get the onshore wind, see. Out of the east, like this here.' He raised a hand in a cupping gesture, as if testing the air. 'Now there's strange currents swirling out there at the base of the Wash. They're unpredictable.' He paused, gazing out to where the sea could be heard but no longer seen. 'Sometimes – and my bones tell me this is one such time – the wind and the current combine with the tide, and the water rushing in up these streams and little rivers comes with an unusual force.'

The King urged his horse forward so that he stood on the near bank of the stream. 'The water does not look deep,' he said. His tone, Josse thought, was carefully neutral.

'Maybe not. But, like I said, the tide's coming in.'

The guide gave the impression that he thought that was the end of the argument.

But the King said, 'How long until it goes out again?'

The guide narrowed his eyes. 'Won't be before dusk. And, if I'm right and there's a surge of water coming in, it'll be later.'

The King sat silent for some time. Watching him closely, Josse sensed he was deeply uneasy. *He is spooked by this place*, he ₊thought . *He mistrusts the marshes, the rank smell, the silvery fog off the sea insinuating itself through the air.* But just then, a ray of soft, golden sunshine speared down through the mist, diving down between the billows of cloud and piercing the ground almost at the feet of the King's horse.

The King's expression changed. His mouth stretching into a triumphant smile, he roared, 'An omen! God is with us!' Then, nudging his horse further into the water, he said with an air of utter finality, 'We go on.'

There was a low murmur among the attendants. The younger guide, anguish on his face, spoke to the older man in a low voice, the words indistinguishable but urgency clear in his very tone. The older guide nodded.

'My lord King,' he called, 'we do not advise this. There is a wide band of quicksand in midstream, slightly closer to the far bank, and, in this mist and with the water coming in so fast, it's not going to be easy to spot it.'

Without turning round, the King called out coldly, 'Then the pair of you should keep your eyes open and be particularly vigilant.' Then, raising his right arm, he shouted, *'On!'*

The men in the first rank behind him plunged into the water. There was a great noise of shouting, and a confusion of angling for position as they hurried to follow the King. Josse cried out above the uproar, *'Wait!* For the dear Lord's sake, wait! See if he has found the safe way!'

Some of the men, appreciating the good sense of this, reined in. Others – perhaps they were more devoted or sycophantic; perhaps they were more foolhardy; perhaps they simply didn't hear – forged on. The mist was swirling more densely, and sometimes Josse could barely make out Geoffroi and Yves, positioned right beside him. Then abruptly he and Alfred were nudged out of the way as the first of the wagons bearing the King's personal treasures came creaking and groaning up towards the stream bank, coming to a halt on the edge of the water.

There was a lot of splashing and some cursing. An anonymous voice said incredulously, 'We're crossing over? *Here?*'

Nobody seemed to know what they ought to be doing.

A freak gust of wind blew a hole in the mist and, just for a moment, Josse could see the scene before him: the King was safe on the far bank, already urging his horse up on to the higher ground. He turned round once, briefly watched as two pairs of mounted men came lurching up the slope behind him, then, as if satisfied that all was well, put spurs to his horse and rode away.

All the leading ranks of men were over now. The two packhorses followed. The second one, not liking the feel of the stream-bed beneath his big hooves, baulked and stopped dead. The man in charge urged him on, speaking gentle, soothing words, and with a loud sucking noise, the horse extracted its feet from the mud into which he was already starting to sink and plunged on.

The light carts went next. Josse watched as the first of them made the crossing. There was a brief delay – the men had considerable difficulty getting the trembling, white-eyed horses to pull the heavy load up the far bank – and then the second one followed. The pair of greys were both sweating, big patches darkening their pale coats, and one let out a shrill neigh of fear.

Aghast, Josse noticed that the water lapping the horses' legs and the wheels of the cart was reaching a noticeably higher level this time.

'We must go, immediately,' he called out to Yves and Geoffroi. 'I don't know what's happening out there, but the pace of the tide has suddenly accelerated.' He turned Alfred's head sharply to the left. 'We'll cross upstream,' he said, 'because the water should be shallower there, and we won't get tangled up with the last cart.'

He had tried to keep his tone calm and unworried. He didn't think he'd succeeded. Geoffroi gave him a frightened look. Yves, an anxious frown creasing his brow, began to say something and then stopped. 'You're right,' he muttered. 'We must hurry.' Then, the edge of panic in his voice, 'Oh, for the good Lord's sake, *hurry!*'

Josse knew he should have taken it slowly. Should have made a very careful approach, searching out the best place and staring intently ahead to spot the treacherous band of quicksand. Should have edged forward across the stream step by careful step, steadily, patiently.

But terror overcame him. He urged Alfred down into the water, spurring him, shouting encouragement, giving the big horse his head and leaning forward in the saddle, pushing, pushing on until the horse was heaving himself out of the water and clambering up the far bank. Yves followed close behind. But Geoffroi, struggling to reassure his frightened brown mare and urge her on for the last few yards to safety, had come to a halt. Crying out in alarm, he leapt off the mare's back, landing with a loud splash in water that reached almost to his armpits. Josse cried out, horrified at how fast the water was rising and how powerfully it pushed. Geoffroi, strong young man that he

was, could only just keep his feet. He put gentle
hands on the mare's brow and nose and, even
over the shouting and the roaring of the water,
Josse heard the calm, reassuring words. The mare
heard them too; with a whinny of distress, she
pulled herself free of the water and the perilous,
sucking mud and erupted up the bank, Geoffroi,
struggling to stay on his feet, beside her.

*We have made it. Thank God, oh, thank God,
we are all safe*, Josse thought, relief flooding
through him. He peered ahead through the mist,
trying to count the riders, the packhorses and
the carts. The King and the leading horsemen
were out of sight now, lost in the white swirl.
There were the two packhorses, there were the
carts.

No. There were only two carts.

He said aloud, 'Where's the overloaded one?'

Suddenly the wind rose, turning in a heartbeat
from a gentle breeze to a whirlwind that shrieked
like a demon. A cry of horrified fear. A horse,
neighing in pain and terror, a second one joining
in, the ghastly sound coming again and again
until abruptly it stopped. A tremendous splash
that seemed to go on for ever. And the water;
rushing, pouring, bubbling, so that it seemed it
would rise up, burst the banks of the stream and
engulf them.

Josse, his brother and his son turned as one
back to the stream bank. The water was surging
in now, no longer smooth, clear and sparkling,
the colour of the sea, but brown, turbulent and
cloudy, each powerful wave tipped with creamy
foam.

And, only a few short paces from safety, the overloaded cart that had been so closely guarded lay on its side. The high-piled contents were already disappearing under the water and, as Josse watched, the last of the stout restraining bands snapped with a loud twang. Three of the guards were attempting to rescue the crates, boxes and bags, ducking below the water for moments at a time but, again and again, coming up gasping for air and empty-handed. There was no sign of either the fourth man or the horses.

Then one of the guards, who had splashed and blundered his way on to what appeared to be the sanctuary of a shallow sandbank not far from the middle of the stream, began to scream.

'I'm being drawn under!' he yelled, eyes wide and white with panic. 'Help me! Fetch sticks, branches! *Help me!*'

They did their best. Josse, Geoffroi and Yves linked arms and Josse tried to advance into the water. The desperate man's companions did the same. Other men sought branches, but trees were rare on those watery margins between the sea and the land and there were none to be found.

Still the tide roared inland. The water was deep now, and its increased volume had made the stream almost twice as wide. The men on the bank stood no chance of reaching the drowning man. He was struggling as if possessed, but they could see – in an awful, freak glimpse of a terrible sight they would much rather not have been shown – that he was rapidly sinking into the quicksand.

And the water went on rising.

They watched as it reached his chest. His throat. His chin. The dreadful pressure of the shifting sands that were sucking him down to his death was making his face swell, his eyes pop. The water, mixed with sloppy, choking, deadly sand, poured into his open, screaming mouth.

His screams were cut off. He made a sort of snort through his nostrils, then his nose, too, was under water.

The men who had known him looked away. One was muttering a prayer. One of them – not much more than a boy – was crying softly. Josse wanted to stop watching; wanted to turn his gaze on to anything but those awful, bulbous, agonized eyes.

But the man had fixed his attention on to him. In a strange moment when he seemed to be outside himself, Josse thought he heard the dying man's soul cry out to him. *Stay with me till the end*, it said.

Josse stood perfectly still, eyes intent, not allowing himself to waver. The water and the sucking, relentless sand came up to the man's lower eyelids, and he began a furious blinking. Then the eyes, too, were submerged. Then the forehead, then the head, hatless, hoodless, the longish hair floating on the surface like weed.

The struggling stopped.

The water rose higher.

The man had vanished.

A soft, moaning gasp broke out among the watching men. For what seemed a long time nobody spoke. Then a youthful voice said tentatively, 'What do we do about the King's baggage cart?'

Somebody – an older man – said fiercely, 'Fuck the King's baggage cart.'

It was an eloquent comment, Josse thought.

But, all the same, someone was going to have to break the news to him.

They caught up with King John. One of the senior officers told him what had happened. Instantly the King spun round, turning his horse back the way he had just come.

'We must organize the recovery of my baggage,' he shouted. 'Straight away, before everything gets swept away. You, my guides, where have you got to?' He stared round, eyes wild.

The guides approached him.

The elder one, an unreadable expression on his face, said, 'It won't do any good.'

'Bollocks!' shouted the King. 'My treasures are stowed in wooden crates, carefully packed, and wood floats! It's just a matter of time, but we need to be there, ready and waiting, when the crates bob up and reappear.' The guide said nothing. His face purpling dangerously, the King yelled, *'Get back to the stream!'*

But the guide bravely stood his ground. 'Wood floats in water, aye, my lord King,' he said calmly. 'But we're not talking about water. We're talking about quicksand. The body of that poor man may reappear – it quite often happens – but the weight of your crates and boxes will work against them.' Slowly he

205

shook his head. 'Your Grace has, I fear, seen the last of them.'

King John threw his head back, opened his mouth widely and let out a great cry of anguish.

Despite the guide's warning words – which turned out to be quite right – the King commanded ten men to return to the stream and wait till the water fell again, whereupon they were instructed to do whatever they could to recover the lost baggage. It was as if, Josse reflected, watching John closely, he simply couldn't accept that his treasures had gone for ever. *Oh, my poor King,* he thought with compassion. *See the truth when it is presented to you, and give this up. Do not risk any more lives, for already men are muttering that this journey is cursed.*

He wished he could find the courage to speak the words aloud. But the King was in a strange mood: dark, angry, unpredictable. It was wisest, Josse had to conclude, to keep his distance. And keep his mouth shut.

Twelve

Meggie and Faruq were hurrying to cover the long miles from March to Spalding. She was possessed now with such urgency that at first she refused utterly to stop and rest, and in the end Faruq had to take hold of Auban's reins and physically bring him to a halt.

'The horses are nearing the end of their strength, and so are we!' he cried, his face creased in distress. 'We have gone against our usual, cautious custom and ridden all the hours of this day, and our luck has held so far, for nobody has apprehended us or even questioned us. But we must not chance to luck any more!' He paused. When she didn't immediately leap in to yell at him that she didn't care, that they *had* to go on, he added in a more reasonable tone, 'The light will not last much longer. We are tired, bone-sore and hungry, or, at least, I am.' She smiled slightly, for she was too. Seeing the smile, he grinned back. 'So, what about making our camp on that rise over to the left, under the alder trees?'

She nodded. He released his hold on the reins, and she led the way along a narrow little path, across a small brook flowing at the bottom of a ditch and up on to the low hill beside the track, and their night's refuge.

They watered the horses and hobbled them. They set out their bedrolls under the trees, in a shallow dip that would protect them if the wind got up. Meggie made a little fire and heated water for a restorative drink, and then they ate. The supplies were getting low: one more reason to hope they would meet up with the King's party the next day.

Meggie lay awake. She was warm, comfortable, no longer hungry or thirsty, and exhausted. But sleep wouldn't come.

Why not? She tried to think what was keeping

her awake. She went through her plan for tomorrow, and still it seemed the best that she was going to come up with. It was more than likely that sickness, fever and injuries were afflicting the huge army of men travelling with the King, although she prayed that she wouldn't find anything as frightening and dreadful as an outbreak of the camp fever she had mentioned to the soldier at March.

Fever . . .

With a smile, suddenly she knew what the dark, secret and ungovernable part of her mind had been trying to prompt her to do. Now that she knew, she was amazed she hadn't realized straight away. She must, she reflected, be even more worn out than she'd thought.

Trying to move softly and quietly – although to judge from Faruq's snoring, he was deeply asleep – she reached under her blanket and put her hand inside her under-gown. There, inside the neat pocket she had sewn for it, was what she sought. She pulled it out, unwrapped the little piece of soft leather in which she habitually wrapped it and held it up to the light of the still-glowing fire.

The Eye of Jerusalem was a sapphire, the size of the top joint of a man's thumb. It was set within a gold coin, whose edges had been carefully crimped so as to hold the jewel securely. It hung on a fine gold chain. When Meggie set it gently swinging, the brilliant blue lights that flashed from it had been known to hypnotize people. Some said it was enchantment.

She allowed the focus of her eyes to go soft. She relaxed, breathing smoothly and deeply.

Straight away, the images began to appear.

She can see herself. She is bending over a sick patient: a bulky, restless figure lying on a bed. But he is in darkness and she can't see who he is, can't tell if he is known to her or not. But as she watches herself crouching beside him, she feels a sense of closeness. Of affection, perhaps even love.

And then she believes she knows who this man is.

Yes, it's true, then. He *is* in danger. Deep under the spell of her vision, she recalls those fleeting images from Corfe Castle . . .

There is shadow hanging round him, and she suspects he is near to death. Is she, then, too late?

The thought is so painful that deliberately she makes herself concentrate on what sort of treatment she is administering. She has perhaps been using the Eye (there it is, hanging by its chain from her left wrist), so has she been making a fever-reducing potion? He is undoubtedly feverish, for she can feel the sweat on his skin, soaking his clothes and the sheets. Strangely, he doesn't smell. But then he is, she knows, a fastidious man. She can see a drinking vessel on a small table in the corner of the room. She thinks at first it is a humble cup made of coarse clay, but then somewhere a door opens and a beam of light hits it. The cup seems to catch fire.

* * *

With a start and a cry, for the image was so strange, Meggie snapped out of her trance. She kept very still, trying to recapture what she had just seen. The feverish man, dying, perhaps, the cup with flames racing round its rim . . .

Then Faruq said sleepily, 'What's the matter? Did you hear something?'

'No, all is well. Go back to sleep,' she replied.

She looked at him. He was lying back, relaxed and drowsy. 'Is it nearly morning?' he asked.

'Oh, no.' She wasn't as sure as she had sounded, for she never knew, coming out of the trance state, how long it had held her. But, glancing into the east, she saw no sign of the soft illumination that said dawn was near.

His gaze suddenly fixed on the Eye, still in her hand. Noticing, she wondered if she should have hidden it. *But why?* she thought. *Why shouldn't he know I have it?*

Then she realized, for the first time, that she trusted him.

He said quietly, 'What is that?'

And so she told him.

'It's called the Eye of Jerusalem. It was given to my grandfather, my father's father, Geoffroi d'Acquin. He was in Outremer, in the summer of 1148, where he was fighting in the Crusade. He had saved the life of a little boy who turned out to be the grandson of an important figure of the enemy camp, and the Eye was this man's way of expressing his gratitude.'[3]

She held it out to Faruq. He did not try to take

[3] See *The Faithful Dead.*

it from her; he merely looked at it for several moments, then nodded.

'Legend says that the Eye of Jerusalem has magical, healing properties,' she went on. *As both my grandfather and I could testify*, she added silently. Josse's stories about Geoffroi d'Acquin told how he had used his precious gift to save the lives of two companions, even as he made his slow way back home from Outremer, and Meggie herself had plenty of evidence that proved the Eye's worth. 'It is protector and friend to its rightful possessor,' she continued, 'keeping him safe from both known and secret enemies. It can be dipped in water to make a very efficient febrifuge, which will also stop bleeding. Also, it can be dipped in a cup proffered by a stranger to detect the presence of poison.'

He was, she noticed, looking at her very oddly. She misread his expression.

'This must sound quite unbelievable to you,' she said with a smile. 'Magic stones with healing powers, gifts from Turkish potentates to enemy knights, and—'

He too was smiling. 'You misunderstand,' he said. 'It is not its properties that astonish me so, but that you should have such a thing in your possession. I have heard tell of such jewels, you see, although not one that goes by this particular name. They are – well, they are not common, exactly, in the country of my birth, but they do exist.' He smiled again. 'Or so I am told, for, until this moment, in this far-distant land of cool rains and sudden sun, I had never seen one.'

Time seemed to halt, as if she and Faruq had

briefly stepped out of the normal, everyday world. Hardly daring to ask, she echoed in a whisper, 'The country of your birth?'

And softly he replied, 'I come from the place you call Outremer.'

11 October 1216

In the morning, they set off for Spalding. They didn't hurry, for they had only about eight or ten miles to go. They and their horses were rested, and the sun was shining.

By late afternoon, they were on a good, wide and well-maintained road that approached the town from the south. They had been keeping up a good pace, but now, nearing the town, they encountered the tail end of a long baggage train, stretching ahead into the distance. Enormous wagons drawn by pairs of oxen struggled along at the rear, and ahead were horse-drawn wagons and mounted men. The train was well guarded, and Meggie recognized the device of the King on the pennants.

With a private smile of satisfaction, she knew that she and Faruq had succeeded: they had caught up with the King.

Although Faruq had maintained his policy of telling her virtually nothing, she no longer feared that he wished to harm King John. At some point during the days and nights of the journey, she seemed to have discovered that he was a good man.

Would Faruq now take her into his confidence? They had come so far together, and, for her part, she had learned to trust him. It made sense if he could do the same for her; they were surely stronger working as a team.

She glanced at his set face. He looked very young. Sensing her eyes on him, he turned. 'Is this the King's baggage train?' he demanded. She nodded. He gave a sigh of satisfaction. 'Come on, then.' He spurred the black horse.

'Where are we going now?' She urged Auban to follow.

'To find where the King is to lodge, of course!' He looked surprised that she should have asked. 'Then I've got to . . .'

She thought for one moment that he really was about to tell her. But then, with an apologetic smile, he shut his mouth firmly and rode on.

The procession of ox-carts, mounted men and hangers-on seemed endless. Meggie and Faruq found a vantage point from which to observe them filing slowly into the town, although so many other locals had had the same idea – and were already lining the approaches to watch, enlivening the proceedings by cheers, laughter and ribald remarks – that, as latecomers, they didn't manage to get very close. Not close enough, really, to see faces clearly. Meggie, anxious to spot Josse, comforted herself with the knowledge that she would recognize Alfred even if she was too far away to distinguish his rider. Besides, Geoffroi and her uncle Yves were with him, and three big, broad men together ought to be unmistakable.

Faruq must have picked up on her anxiety. He asked kindly, 'Is anything the matter?'

She flashed him a smile. 'No, no. I'm sure there isn't.' He went on looking at her. 'Well, I'm trying to spot my father.'

He looked surprised. 'And you think to find him riding with the King's baggage train?'

She hesitated. Suddenly it struck her as rather unfair that she was irritated with Faruq for not being open with her, when all this time she had kept back one or two quite vital facts from him.

I felt last night, when he saw me with the Eye of Jerusalem, that I really could trust him, she reminded herself.

She took a deep breath and said, 'Well, in fact I do.' And she told him about Josse's long acquaintance with the King and his family; about how the King, badly needing loyal men at a time when his supporters changed into enemies and back again faster than a man could change his hose, had summoned a company of his oldest companions; how dear, loving Josse, so clearly touched by having been one of the ones singled out, hadn't hesitated to hurry to the King's side, taking his brother and his son with him.

When she had finished, Faruq didn't speak for some time. Then, somewhat to her surprise, he took hold of her hand and said, 'Thank you for telling me.'

'It's all right.'

She wondered if he was instantly going to try to make use of this new information. If he would suggest – demand – that, with the power of her

214

father's name, she should somehow clear a path straight to the heart of the King's inner circle.

He didn't. Still holding her hand, he said instead, 'This looks like the heavy baggage, which would have set off at first light in order to reach here before the King. He and his close group will undoubtedly be some distance away still.'

It was kindly meant, for he was in effect saying, *Don't worry*. She thought: *I ought to have worked that out for myself*. But, nevertheless, she was grateful to him. She gave his hand a squeeze, then released it.

The last of the baggage train entered the town, and still the people waited. Time passed. More were flooding out now. As the townsmen and women finished their work for the day, they were hurrying out to line the road, bringing food and drink, turning the welcome into a party.

And all to celebrate the arrival of the King.

'He is popular here,' Faruq said quietly to Meggie, echoing the direction of her thoughts.

'Yes,' she agreed briefly.

She didn't want to talk. She was trying to reassure herself that there was nothing to worry about. That the King and his group had probably been late leaving wherever they had stayed last night: Lynn, she seemed to recall being told.

But still the worm of anxiety tunnelled through her thoughts. The tracks around the Wash were perilous. The weather was liable to change very quickly, and there was the tide, too, to worry about. What if something had happened? What if the King had endangered himself? Josse, she knew only too well, wasn't a man to stand back. He would rush to help, no matter what the danger to himself.

There was someone coming. A horse, hard-ridden, was flying up the road towards the town. The rider, urging him on with heels and with voice, went in through the town gates, already beginning to pull the horse up; even as he slid to the ground, one of the senior officers came hurrying towards him.

Meggie and Faruq didn't have long to wait and wonder. In the strange way that ill news spreads through a crowd like fire through a hay field, very soon people were turning to each other, muttering, exclaiming; pausing only briefly to exchange an opinion with their friends before passing the word on.

'There's been an accident!' a fat, well-dressed townswoman told Meggie and Faruq, her eyes wide with the avid, excited fascination of an uninvolved onlooker in a stranger's misfortune. 'The King's party was rounding the Wash and tried to cross a flooded stream, and a dozen are drowned if not more! They say the King wouldn't wait for low water!'

Meggie's legs suddenly didn't feel like her own. She felt herself sag, and Faruq caught her before she fell. 'It will not be your father,' he said calmly. 'Also, it is in the nature of gossips that they exaggerate, and probably the true figure of the dead is less.'

The fat woman, overhearing, gave an indignant sniff. 'I'm no gossip!' she said crossly. 'And, as for exaggerating, I'm not, I'm only repeating what *he* said!' She jerked her head towards a skinny man standing nearby, the movement so violent and abrupt that she disturbed her elaborately folded and crisply white headdress.

Faruq gave her a polite little bow. 'I apologize, madam,' he said. 'I meant no insult.'

She gave a little shrug, like a hen shaking water off its feathers, then hurried away to spread the news to the rapidly diminishing number of people who hadn't yet heard it.

There was quite a lot of movement now among the throng, and Meggie and Faruq utilized it to get a little nearer the front of the crowd, although the best they could manage was still several rows back. Then they waited.

As the long hours passed, the crowd gradually fell quiet. There was no more laughter and cheering. But, oddly, even more people seemed to be arriving.

It was dark by the time the King's party finally appeared in the distance. Heralded by a cloud of dust (the day had remained dry here), people stopped even the few, over-repeated remarks they had still been exchanging and went utterly silent, everyone straining their ears to hear the horses' hooves on the road.

The first riders came into view: a pair of guards, well armed, with another pair immediately behind. Then a row of four men, none of them young, watchful, their eyes everywhere as they scanned the crowds lining the route. Meggie knew without being told that these were old knights like Josse, summoned as he had been.

They had such a look of him about them that her heart gave a small lurch.

The King came next.

He wore a gorgeous sky-blue cloak over tunic and hose of darker blue. His high boots were of black leather, fine quality but muddy and wet. His hood was thrown back, and on his shoulder-length russet hair, streaked widely now with grey, he wore a gold circlet. He rode a beautiful chestnut gelding, graceful and high-stepping, a star-shaped white mark on its brow, its gingery mane and tail long and luscious. Both horse and man looked the picture of dejection, heads down, eyes on the ground.

Nobody cheered. Nobody spoke.

More armed men followed, and then came a pair of packhorses and two light carts, each drawn by a pair of horses.

As the packhorses went by, one of them, dazed with fatigue, stumbled. The crowd drew an anxious breath, but the horse recovered. As if this had given a signal, suddenly someone cried, 'God protect King John!'

Someone else cheered. There was a burst of clapping, quickly stopped. But then others were taking up the cry, calling out a welcome, invoking God's blessing on the King, cheering, applauding. The noise grew swiftly until it was all but deafening.

Which was why, when Josse, Yves and Geoffroi rode by and Meggie yelled herself hoarse trying to catch their attention, they didn't hear.

Struggling through the crowds, Meggie raced towards the town gates, pushing, shoving, yelling

218

for people to make room, using her elbows when all else failed. Desperate to catch up with her father, she was only vaguely aware of Faruq behind her, his progress hampered by having to lead their two horses.

But they were too slow. By the time they reached the entrance to the town, there was no sign of the three big men. Meggie stood on tiptoe, peering round the shoulder of the man who was barring her way, trying to see where the new arrivals were heading so that she could follow.

The man would not let her through.

'I don't know you,' he said sternly, staring down at her. 'Nor your companion.' His eyes raked Faruq and he frowned. 'Not from hereabouts, I'll warrant.'

Given Faruq's distinctly foreign looks, there seemed no point in denying it. 'No, we're not. But we—'

'It's orders, see,' the man said, slightly more kindly. 'What with the King's enemies being close, and nobody really knowing friend from foe, we're to be very careful over who's let in. Most of the townsfolk we can recognize, but strangers we turn aside. Sorry, lass.'

'But I was summoned!' she cried. 'I'm a healer, and he's my assistant!' She put a hand on Faruq's arm.

'A healer?'

'*Yes!* I was sent for because they fear an outbreak of sickness, with so many men crowded together in the King's service, and—'

'There's no sickness here.' The man spoke

219

decisively, but Meggie saw him surreptitiously cross himself.

'Yes I know, but I was summoned in case there *should* be!' she protested. She was beginning to believe the fiction herself. If it hadn't happened it ought to have done, since it would be a wise precaution. 'What's the use of waiting till I'm needed before getting me here?'

He was staring at her intently. 'Well . . .'

'Oh, *please!*'

She wondered, even as she spoke, whether her very evident desperation would count against her. It wasn't logical, surely, for a healer to be quite so eager to get to her work.

And then the man shook his head. 'I'm sorry, lass, but I can't let you through.' He must have seen her expression, for quickly he added, 'Not tonight, anyway, but I'll check with my superior and maybe he'll say I can admit you in the morning.'

She opened her mouth for one last appeal, but he had already turned away.

Listlessly she followed Faruq away from the town. Trying to raise her spirits, he said encouragingly, 'We'll find somewhere to camp, then we'll try again in the morning.' He peered into her face. 'Oh, Meggie, don't look so desolate! Do you think I do not feel the same? I, too, have an imperative need to be inside the town.' He paused, then, more quietly, said, 'It will be all right, I'm sure.'

But Meggie, who knew that something terrible was about to happen, would not be comforted.

She did not sleep. She lay away for what felt like hours, then gave up and, sliding quietly out of her bedroll, got up and paced to and fro till morning.

Thirteen

Within the town, Josse and his companions had barely had time to settle the horses and cleanse their faces, hands, clothing and boots of the worst of the sweat, dust, and mud, when the summons came from the King. 'He's sending for the old knights,' the messenger said laconically to Josse. 'The others—' he shot a dismissive glance at Yves and Geoffroi – 'can eat at the mess hall, down there on the right.' He waved an arm to indicate.

Yves gave Josse a sympathetic glance. 'Rather you than me,' he said quietly.

'Aye,' Josse agreed heavily. 'He'll be in no mood for revelry and good cheer tonight. He'll probably drink himself into oblivion, and be as ill in the morning as he was back at Lynn.' He scraped at a stubborn stain on his tunic. 'Do I look all right?'

Yves shook his head. He fetched a cloth and, dampening it, sponged at the mark. 'That's the best I can do.' Then he looked into his brother's face. 'Dear old Josse,' he said affectionately. 'You were always the ragged one, weren't you?'

Josse folded him in his arms, and, just for a

moment, the brothers exchanged an embrace. 'Good to have you here,' Josse said gruffly. Then he strode away.

Josse was shown into the King's presence. John had been accommodated in a brash new hall that gave evidence of having been only recently completed. The wood of its beams was green timber, and brought with it a smell of the forest. In one or two places, awkwardly placed hangings suggested that the walls weren't quite finished. But whoever owned the hall had managed to secure the customary dais and long, well-made table for the King's use, and John sat there on a throne-like chair, attendants buzzing round, five or six of the old companions seated nearby. Looking up and spotting Josse, the King beckoned him.

'Drink with me, Josse d'Acquin,' he commanded.

Josse bowed and, drawing up a stool, sat down beside the King and took the proffered pewter cup.

'I await news,' the King said.

There was no need to ask, news of what?

John, it seemed, needed company while he waited. Josse wasn't sure why, since the King didn't say a word during the interminable time that ensued. Perhaps, he concluded, it was simply that John didn't like to drink alone. But then, he realized, the King wasn't really drinking, either. From time to time he would pick at one or two of the dainties on his gold platter, but, each time the serving boy edged forward to offer wine, the King waved him away. Once or twice, he reached for an earthenware mug and took a draught of water. It was, Josse thought, extraordinary behaviour.

Josse noticed that the usual gold cup wasn't in the King's hand. Instead, a silver one stood before him. They'd been right, then, when they had surmised that the lost cart had been the one bearing the King's most treasured personal possessions.

The interminable evening went on. Hours passed.

Suddenly there was a burst of activity in the wide doorway, and the sound of hasty, muttered speech. Then a couple of wet, travel-stained and all but exhausted men were ushered up to the King's dais. Josse recognized them as two of the group that had been sent back to wait by the stream.

The King eyed them wearily. 'I can tell by your very expressions that you do not bring the news I want to hear,' he said tonelessly. 'But tell me, anyway.'

The older of the two men stepped forward, his cap in his hands, and fell on to his knees. 'My lord King, all attempts to recover the treasure failed. We waited until the water fell, and although we paddled into the stream, right up to that sand bar, and we prodded and poked as far as we could reach, we found nothing, and not a sign of the horses and the drowned man.'

'You didn't even retrieve the cart?' The King's tone – of polite interest – must surely be deceptive, Josse thought. These were the worst tidings.

'We expected to see wooden items bobbing

up, indeed we did, my lord,' the man said eagerly. 'But that quicksand doesn't behave like anything else on God's good earth, and what it takes, it keeps.' The man's face fell. 'We lost another man, my lord King,' he added. 'Well, a lad, really, from one of the nearby hamlets. Thought he could help, he did, and insisted on going right out on to that little island. He . . .' The man choked, lowering his head and wiping at his eyes. 'He died, my lord. His mother tried to go and save him, but her husband wouldn't let her. They took it grievously hard.'

Josse, his heart wrung with pity, glanced at the King. But John's face remained expressionless.

After some time, he waved a dismissive hand, and the man got up and crept away.

Josse found it very difficult to read the King's mood that night. It was as if – he struggled to work it out – as if he'd had news of the most agonizing bereavement; as if someone he had deeply loved for untold years had suffered a sudden and shocking death. The King was deathly pale, his cheeks sunken, deep, greyish circles around the blue eyes, dulled now with loss.

But why? Josse asked himself. The King had lost his treasured belongings, aye; his personal chapel and all its accoutrements had been on the cart, as well as several chests of jewels and precious objects. He had other jewels, though, surely, and a small, portable chapel was readily replaced. King John was renowned for the careful precaution of distributing his gold, his jewels and his other treasured belongings in many different locations, all of them as secure and reliable as the deepest, most secret vault. Rumour had it, indeed, that he had a stash at Hawkenlye Abbey, although Josse was pretty sure there was no truth in it.

What was it about this loss that so affected him?

Or was this deep, grieving malaise the symptom of something else?

After what seemed like hours, at last the King turned to Josse.

'I am heartsick, old friend,' he said. 'The wine is good,' – he held up his silver cup – 'but it does not revive and cheer me, and I have no appetite for it.'

Josse didn't know how to answer. 'Perhaps a little food would put new vigour in you?' he suggested tentatively.

'It would, undoubtedly,' the King agreed, 'but I have no stomach for food, either. The more I try to drink, the more queasy I feel.' He frowned down into his wine, as if by failing to provide the usual effect, it had seriously and unaccountably let him down.

Josse forbore to say that queasiness was the inevitable result of wine on an empty stomach.

Still staring at his silver goblet, the King said, 'I've lost my gold cup, Josse d'Acquin. It is gone. It sank down into those devilish, greedy, sucking sands, and it will never come back.' He suppressed a burp, not very well, and Josse smelt the tang of slightly sick-smelling breath. He managed not to lean back.

'I am sorry for that, my lord King,' he said.

'I loved that cup,' the King went on. 'Had it since I was a lad.' *You told me*, Josse thought. *It was a present from Queen Eleanor.* 'My mother gave it to me when she and my shit of a father finally accepted they couldn't keep me shut away in fucking Fontevraud for the rest of my life.' He winced, a hand on his belly. 'It was the first beautiful thing I possessed, and I kept it close to me always, always, through all the years since I was seven . . .' The desolate voice trailed off.

He looks so sad, Josse thought.

'My lord King,' he ventured to say, 'the one you use instead is very beautiful, is it not?'

And indeed it was. To any man not comparing it with one of solid gold given to him in his childhood by his dead mother, it was a glorious object. It was silver, and in the form of a wide, shallow bowl, set upon a graceful stem that rose out of a firm, weighty base. The rim of the cup was set with opals: milk-white opals in which flashes of brilliant blue, pink and green lay hidden, and fiery orange opals which, when they caught the light, almost hurt the eye with their brightness.

John glanced at it, frowning. 'Beautiful? Perhaps.' His frown deepened. Then, with a decisive gesture, he turned it upside down and the contents spilled out on to the table. 'In the absence of my gold cup, it will have to do, and I suppose I shall become accustomed to it.' He turned to Josse with a ferocious scowl. 'But not tonight.' Then he pushed back his chair,

226

summoned his body servants with a snap of his fingers, jumped down off the dais and strode away.

12 October 1216

Meggie and Faruq were waiting outside the town gates early the next morning, determined to be there even as they were opened after the night.

But still they were not to be admitted: there would, indeed, have been little point. The man who had spoken to them the previous evening took the trouble to come out to find them, and he had news for them.

'The King's leaving again today, and all his followers with him,' he said. 'There's a right uproar going on in there—' he jerked his thumb over his shoulder towards the town – 'and no point whatsoever in you joining in.'

'Where are they going?' Meggie asked.

'They're saying he's going north,' the man replied. 'Now I can't swear that's right, but then I've heard nothing to say it's wrong. Anyway, it's the best I can do. If I were you,' he added, 'I'd get on the road quickly, before the heavy wagons start out. If it rains, they'll churn the surface into a sea of mud, and if it stays dry, they'll put up clouds of dust. I should head north-west towards Sleaford, then on to Newark. That's the route he normally follows. Know the way, do you?' Meggie shook her head, so he gave directions.

'Thank you for taking the trouble to tell us all this,' Meggie said.

'Well, the way I see it, you're trying to help, like all healers,' he said. 'Like I said, my advice is to make your way to Sleaford – or maybe Newark would make better sense – and make sure you speak to someone there; convince them of your worth and persuade them to admit you, before the King and his party arrive.'

In the Sanctuary at the edge of the Great Forest, Helewise and Tiphaine watched their patient anxiously. Hadil's condition was not improving. Tiphaine had tried every remedy she could think of, to no avail, and now Hadil was turning her face away when the old herbalist approached with her little cup. Helewise couldn't get her to eat either.

'Leave me alone,' Hadil said, over and over again. 'Let me rest.'

'I'd not only let her rest, I'd encourage it,' Tiphaine muttered to Helewise as they stood in the sunshine just outside the little room, 'if I could only convince myself that rest was helping.'

'But it isn't,' Helewise agreed sadly. 'For when she lies back with her eyes closed, it is not the deep, relaxed sleep that brings healing but a sort of rigidly imposed immobility, as if she is challenging herself to see how long she can keep silent and still.'

Tiphaine nodded. 'She is so profoundly distressed,' she said. Then: 'I wish that son of hers would come back!'

'So do I,' said Helewise. 'And, even more than that, I wish he'd return with the news that he's

228

managed to achieve whatever this mission is that's brought them here.'

A thought struck her: simple, obvious, and instantly comforting. 'Tiphaine, may I ask you to stay with our patient this morning?'

'Yes, my lady,' Tiphaine replied. 'I had planned to set out to gather more supplies, but I can do that later.' Without another word, without so much as an eyebrow raised in query to suggest she was curious about where Helewise might be going, she turned and went back inside the Sanctuary.

And, straight away, taking the familiar path through the forest, Helewise set off.

St Edmund's Chapel stood on an apron of land that projected out of the forest, opposite the gates of Hawkenlye Abbey and under the protecting shade of the great trees. It had been commissioned by Queen Eleanor to commemorate her favourite son. It was said by those who knew, that the image of Saint Edmund in the stained-glass window, mounted on his horse against the brilliant blue of a summer sky, bore a strong resemblance to Richard.

As Helewise approached the simple stone building, already she sensed a lift in her spirits. She pushed open the heavy wooden door and went inside, falling on her knees before the altar. Then she opened her heart to her God and begged for his help.

So profound was her concentration that she didn't hear the door quietly open and close again.

When, after a long time, she opened her eyes and returned to the present place and moment, it was with considerable surprise that she saw Abbess Caliste standing behind her.

Helewise hastened to stand up, making the bow of reverence. 'My lady abbess, forgive me, I didn't hear you come in.'

The abbess moved quickly forward, taking Helewise's hands and raising her from her bow. 'There is no need for apology!' she exclaimed. 'You have as much right here as anyone, my lady Helewise, and what is God's chapel for but prayer?'

Helewise, overcome, merely nodded.

Abbess Caliste was looking intently into her face. 'You are pale,' she said. 'Shall we go and sit on the grassy slope outside? The sun is on it, and we shall be quite warm.'

She led the way out into the clean air and settled herself on the ground, and Helewise sat down beside her. Neither spoke for some time. Helewise, her eyes on the abbey down below them on the edge of the vale, was scanning every detail, remembering how it had been to live her life within the strong, high walls.

Presently Abbess Caliste said, 'Helewise, I sense you are troubled. Your prayers will have undoubtedly brought comfort, but sometimes when we hear God's voice, it points us towards a course of action whose purpose we do not understand. Is now, perhaps, one of those times?'

The concern and the kindness in the soft voice moved Helewise almost to tears. *How well she perceives the distress of others*, she thought,

*and how gently and diplomatically she offers
her help.*

'I am indeed troubled, my lady . . .'

'Helewise,' said the abbess firmly. 'Out here,
where there is no one to hear but God and the
two of us, let us be Helewise and Caliste.'

Helewise smiled. 'Very well. My concern is
for Hadil, who, despite Tiphaine's and my efforts,
does not improve. She is weak, her broken arm
pains her and does not seem to be healing, and
she is still at times delirious with fever. But
Tiphaine suggests – and I agree – that she is
gravely disturbed in her mind, and I am sure it
is this which prevents her recovery.'

'And you wish to help her by encouraging
her to share what is worrying her,' Caliste finished
for her.

'Yes, I do! But, you see, both she and her son are
so very secretive and, although she has revealed
a little of her past, the few things she told me do
not add up to a cohesive whole. Neither she nor
Faruq would explain their presence here, nor what
this vitally important mission is that they must
fulfil, although I fear it concerns some object –
an inheritance, possibly, for so I have construed
from the little she has revealed – that they believe
to be evil. I fear that if I now try to use her very
weakness to make her talk, it will amount to a
betrayal. As if I was utilizing the fact that she is
so ill, and so sad, to force out of her words that,
in her right mind, she would not utter.'

'A dilemma indeed,' Caliste murmured. Then,
after a pause to think, she said, 'You and Tiphaine
agree, you said, that she needs to talk?'

'Yes.'

'And what, if I might ask, did God suggest?'

Helewise smiled at the way Caliste expressed herself; as if God was a benign and wise old uncle sitting in a chair in the corner. 'I think – although I fear I may be telling myself what I heard because it's what I *want* to hear – that he said the most important thing was to help my patient. But that is, I find, a little ambiguous.'

'I see,' said Caliste. 'And what else troubles you, dear Helewise?'

I thought I had kept that fear hidden! Helewise thought. Moved by Caliste's loving perception, she said very quietly, 'I am afraid that Hadil will die before Faruq returns. And—' she held back a sob – 'I don't know how I shall face him if she does.'

Caliste didn't speak at first. She reached out and, taking Helewise's hand in both of hers, simply sat and held it.

'You and Tiphaine are caring for her with skill and devotion; of that I have no doubt,' she said eventually. 'If it is God's will that Hadil dies, there is nothing more to be done.'

'Yes,' Helewise said slowly. Then she burst out, 'But she is so uneasy in her mind!'

'Then . . .' Caliste hesitated. 'But it's not for me to give you advice.'

'Oh, please! Give it!'

Caliste smiled. 'Then I think you should put aside your scruples and trust your instincts. Do all you can to encourage Hadil to talk. As much as she will, until she has revealed what troubles her so.'

232

Helewise turned her face up to the sun, her eyes closed, absorbing the comfort into her skin. She wasn't sure which of the various elements – her long communion with God, Caliste's sensible words, so kindly expressed, the October sunshine and the good air of the forest – had made her suddenly sure of her course. She was just grateful that, at last, she knew what to do.

She and Caliste embraced, and she watched as the slim, upright figure strode back down the slope to the abbey. Then she set out for the Sanctuary.

As soon as she went in, she relieved Tiphaine. After a morning spent within four walls, the old herbalist looked more than ready to get outside. They exchanged a few words – Tiphaine reported that there had been no change in their patient, who hadn't uttered a word and had taken no more than half a cup of spring water – and then she hurried away. *Before I change my mind*, Helewise thought with a grin.

She went back inside.

She prepared a pretty little platter of dainties. Tilly had come out to the Sanctuary while she'd been absent, bringing more supplies, and evidently she'd been baking that morning. Then Helewise heated milk, stirring in a spoonful of honey. She went to sit beside Hadil, on the low bed, and said, with kindly firmness, 'Now, my dear, you shall sit up a little, and I will arrange the pillows to support you. There! Is that comfortable? First I have good, fresh milk, heated and sweetened with honey' – she held the cup to

Hadil's lips and, with no more protest than an irritable glance, Hadil took a sip. 'Good! Now, you must try one of these little cakes. See, they are no more than a mouthful, and so light!' Before Hadil could argue or even turn away, Helewise popped a cake in her mouth.

Hadil, chewing, glanced up at Helewise, and gave a nod of appreciation. 'Very tasty,' she said. Her face working with emotion, she added, 'You've taken good care of me, you and the other one, for all that she always gives the impression she'd rather be outdoors. Her soul is in the forest, that one,' she observed.

'How right you are,' Helewise murmured.

Hadil was watching her, the old eyes steady. 'I will not eat any more, so it's no use trying to make me,' she said quietly. Before Helewise could protest, she went on, 'I am sick, my lady, and it is a malady which began long ago. Years before Faruq and I set out on my last journey. I am dying, and I know it.'

'You were exhausted and injured when you were brought here,' Helewise replied. 'When you are fully rested, and when your arm heals, why not judge then if death does indeed approach?'

But Hadil shook her head. 'I have been resting these many days, and I am worse.'

There wasn't really any arguing with that. But nevertheless Helewise tried. 'I believe that in addition to your bodily woes, you are deeply troubled in your mind,' she said. 'You began to speak of your past, and to hint at what has brought you so far from home. Would it not help to tell me more?'

234

Hadil watched her gravely. 'Perhaps. But we are sworn to secrecy. Each one who, in his or her turn, learns the full story keeps it safe within their head, only passing it on when they are dying.'

'So . . . You are the present keeper, and Faruq will inherit it from you?'

Hadil nodded. 'Yes. He knows something of the tale, for I had to explain to him why we must travel so far. Besides,' she sighed heavily, 'he has observed others of his kin set off on similar missions, and he is not unintelligent. He is more capable than most of extracting the whole story from a scant few hints and clues.'

Helewise thought how best to encourage her. To point out that she'd just announced she was dying, and might well be dead before Faruq returned, the secret dying with her, seemed unnecessary and very cruel. Besides, surely Hadil could see that for herself. Instead, she said, 'You told me your home was Jerusalem. Was it there that your grandmother came across this – this evil thing that came into your family?'

Hadil shot her an angry look, as if reprimanding a child for not paying attention. 'My grandmother didn't come across it!' she snapped. 'She was his child, and *he* found it. Then, when the men of my great-grandmother's family attacked and killed him, they searched his garments and found the treasure he had hidden inside his tunic. I *told* you that!'

'And it was he—' who *was* he? – 'who found it?'

'He must have done. He was a rotten-hearted man and he did a truly wicked thing, and my

235

kinsmen and I cannot escape it no matter how we would wish to. Then, as if that wasn't bad enough, we have had to bear the legacy of the evil that he unleashed on us. It is our responsibility, you see,' she said urgently, 'for her father should have known better, and left it on that devil's body so that it would have been buried with him.'

'And—' Helewise chose her words carefully – 'and over the years since, members of your family have been trying to put right what has been done by this – er, this evil thing?'

'*Yes!*' said Hadil, as if it was quite obvious. 'Because it was my ancestor's fault. Her father – his name was Harun, which is the same name as Aaron, as you would say it – realized that the treasure was too large to dispose of all at once, for our family was poor and to have been discovered with even that small amount of wealth would have raised suspicions. So, he sold a part of it here, a part of it there, until all was gone.'

'And so, in order to track it all down, you have had many different trails to follow,' Helewise said, trying to make sense of the tale.

'Oh, yes,' Hadil agreed fervently. 'So many, and all to a successful conclusion except this last one! And how far we have come, my son and I. We thought, when we had crossed the Inland Sea and arrived in the great port where we disembarked, that our journey was approaching its end, for, although we had many days still to travel, at last we were in the land that we sought – or so we believed.' Her expression darkened. 'When we reached our destination, and discovered it was no longer there but had been taken here, to England, I thought at first that I could not go on.' She sighed. 'But I did. Now, though, Faruq has to continue alone, for all that still he does not fully understand.'

Helewise was praying for guidance. *Should I say what is in my mind, dear Lord?* She waited. She thought an answer came.

She summoned her courage and said, very gently, 'Hadil, if you die before Faruq returns, who will tell him the remainder of the story?'

Slowly Hadil nodded. 'Yes,' she sighed. 'Yes.' She glanced up at Helewise, who saw with surprise that there was quiet humour in Hadil's eyes. 'If you are telling me that I should reveal the truth to you so that you may pass it on to my son, then you are quite right.' She sighed again. 'He is a fine man, and I feel in my bones that he will succeed. He deserves to know why he has had to do what he is doing, does he not?'

'I think so, yes,' Helewise said.

But Hadil turned away, settling herself more comfortably. 'Soon,' she said, suppressing an enormous yawn, 'I shall tell you.'

Fourteen

The King, his army and his peripatetic court had arrived at Swineshead Abbey. Josse, tired, aching, hungry, thirsty and cold, had been anticipating the comforts of the evening and the night with increasing eagerness as they slogged through the last three or four miles. Unfortunately for Josse, and for all the others in the King's train, Swineshead Abbey was a Cistercian foundation and the guiding principle of the Cistercians was austerity.

The King and his close group were greeted at the gate by the porter, repeatedly bowing double, as if to make up in obeisance for what the accommodation lacked in luxury, and escorted to the abbot. Josse watched, amused, as King John endured a long speech of welcome from the elderly monk, with many comments about the great honour being bestowed and his doubts as to whether the abbey could possibly be worthy. He was not, it was clear, the only person present to have these misgivings. The King was already wearing an expression of mixed dismay and disgust, for the monks' greyish-white wool habits were none too clean and the place stank of cabbage, muck and sweat.

When the abbot at last finished, the King's party were escorted by the guest master and installed in their quarters. There were tiny, windowless stone cells for the King and the most important of his lords, in which it appeared they were to sleep on narrow, shelf-like benches with one thin blanket apiece. Josse and the rest of the King's company were shown into the communal guest quarters, where they would sleep on the floor. Everyone else – the whole of that vast procession – would make shift as best they could in the yard and outside the walls.

There were long stone troughs in the yard and

cold water for washing, and hardly anyone bothered. The King, Josse reflected, would be furious. He was renowned for being fastidiously clean and probably hadn't bathed since Lynn.

Yves, staring round and scratching at a fleabite, said quietly, 'I don't hold out much hope of a decent supper, do you, Josse?'

Geoffroi, coming to join them after seeing to their horses, looked from one brother to the other in dismay. 'But I'm famished!'

Josse slapped his shoulder. 'So are we all, son. We'll just have to hope for the best.'

The monks were not called upon to feed more than the King's inner circle, but nevertheless it was obvious that this was a challenge which they were going to find extremely hard to fulfil. Almost immediately after John's arrival, an anxious, desperate flurry of activity had commenced, and eventually – far too late for hungry travellers – they were summoned to eat.

There was no table on a raised dais here, where all men were equal, so the King was placed at the top of one of the long, bare trestles where the monks ate. The meal was served. As Josse took his first doubtful taste, his spirits sank even further, for in the roughly hewn wooden bowl set before him was a sort of beige mush, comprising various vegetables, a great many beans, and one or two leaves of herb plants to provide a minuscule amount of flavour. There were chunks of coarse bread set out in baskets at intervals along the table, and Josse followed the example of everyone else and grabbed a couple before they all disappeared.

Geoffroi kept up a constant, soft-voiced muttering as he shovelled up the meagre, tasteless fare. 'They work, don't they?' he said to Josse. 'Isn't that the purpose of the White Monks, to work hard and to pray?'

'Keep your voice down,' Josse warned. 'Aye, you're right. It's a severe life, and they settle well out of the way of temptation, in lonely spots such as this.'

'Then if their purpose is to work,' Geoffroi replied with ruthless logic, 'surely they need to *eat* properly?'

Josse, wiping his bowl with the last of his bread, and with the troubling sense of only having taken the very edge off his hunger, couldn't really argue.

Yves, who had already finished and was watching the King, nudged Josse. 'Look,' he said quietly. 'The monks know they've failed to provide food fit for a king and the poor souls are trying to make amends.'

A dish of meat – mutton, Josse thought – was being offered to King John; there was a lot of it, and Josse realized with a stab of pity that the monks had probably sacrificed a month's meat ration. The King picked at it, selected three or four pieces, then waved the platter away. The remainder was fallen upon by the lords seated closest to him, and the platter was empty long before it passed down the table to Josse and his companions.

The guest master, the cellarer and the abbot were standing in the doorway, heads together in a muttered conversation, the abbot shooting worried glances at the King. Then, as if they had come to a decision, the cellarer hurried away, returning shortly afterwards with a jar of some sort of liquor and a sealed stoneware pot. He bowed to King John, and Josse heard him say, 'My lord King, may we offer you some peaches and the first of the new cider? The peaches were rather good this summer, and we have laid down some of the finest to see us through the bleak winter months, preserved in a honey solution.'

Without a word the King indicated his silver cup, and the cellarer filled it. The King took a sip, swilling the cider round his mouth. It seemed that the whole refectory held its breath. Then, with a curt nod, John drained his cup and held it out for a refill.

Then he stuck his knife into the jar of peaches, stabbed half of a fruit and ate it. It must have been acceptable, for quickly he ate four or five more. Then, a hand on his belly, he pushed the cellarer away.

He ate no more food. But he went on drinking.

'I believe,' Josse said privately to Yves as the evening wore on, 'that he drowns his rage and his sorrow at the loss of that baggage cart.'

'And, perhaps, the lives of the men who died,' Josse added.

Yves sighed. 'So it is to be hoped. But life is cheap, and precious objects hard to come by.'

During the night, the King was taken ill.

Josse, deeply asleep between Yves and Geoffroi, was woken by the sound of running feet. He knew, even as he struggled out of sleep, that something was very wrong. There was a mood of fear and he could hear monks talking in loud, worried voices. Not waiting for his companions to wake properly, he leapt up from his hard bed and ran out into the passage, falling into step behind a young monk carrying a large bowl and running towards the King's quarters.

King John lay half on and half off his shelf of a bed. He had been copiously sick on the stone floor and the tiny room reeked. There was a mess of faeces on the harsh sheet. John was only half-conscious, one hand clasped to his belly, moaning in pain.

The young monk leaped forward, just in time to catch another gush of vomit. An older, grey-haired monk beside Josse leaned close, introduced himself as the infirmarer and said, 'You have been travelling with him. Do you know what ails him?'

Josse led him a few paces back down the passage. The King might appear to be barely conscious, but it wouldn't do at all for Josse's words to be overheard. 'He suffered in this way back at Lynn,' he whispered. 'Then, as perhaps now, an incautious consumption of alcohol was at the root of it.'

The infirmarer nodded sagely, as if drunken kings vomiting up great puddles on the cell floor were a daily occurrence. 'And what is the remedy?'

'Plenty of good, clean water. He should be encouraged to keep drinking, even if it comes straight back up again.'

The infirmarer made a face. 'Oh. A busy night,

then, for our young monks emptying the bowls.' Even as he spoke, the young monk in the King's cell came hurrying out and another replaced him. 'I will go and see about the water.'

As the long night went on and the King showed no signs of improvement (in fact, Josse thought anxiously, he seemed even worse), the monks began to try other remedies. He had no idea what they were, and found himself wishing that Meggie was there. He watched the monks' efforts, none of which appeared to bring much relief. He found himself wondering how hard they were really trying, realizing belatedly that he might have made an error in attributing John's sickness to over-indulgence. For these Cistercians were vowed to a severe life of self-denial, poverty and simplicity, and thus would have little sympathy for a man who made himself so ill through his own lack of self-control, even if he *was* a king. And, Josse fumed to himself, greatly disturbed by the continuing sights, sounds and smells of the King's continuing distress, in all likelihood the monks looked upon painful and distressing sickness as a punishment from God that must without doubt have been earned, and they expected other men to do as they did, and accept it with joy, since it offered the chance of earning forgiveness.

None of which, Josse concluded, was availing the poor, suffering King in the very least.

13 October 1216

By morning, it was evident that King John was extremely unwell. 'Dysentery,' pronounced the infirmarer firmly. 'Either that or rather too lavish partaking of the preserves and the new cider.'

Josse overheard him say that to the guest master, two not terribly sympathetic men viewing a sinner's divine punishment with a certain amount of complacence. *I would wager*, Josse said to himself, *neither of you dared say that to the patient himself.*

The infirmarer and the abbot tried to persuade their royal guest to rest and attempt to recover his strength. But John refused to listen. He would not remain bed-bound and, contrary to advice, the moment he could keep anything down he demanded wine. The Cistercians had no wine and so could not indulge him. Unfortunately for the King's suffering, contorted guts, many of his lords had their own supplies and were only too pleased to gain a little favour by supplying it.

It seemed to Josse, hovering close to the King's cell and watching and listening closely, that John was suffering from some sort of paranoia. 'He doesn't trust anybody,' he reported anxiously back to Yves and Geoffroi. 'The monks in particular seem to make him absolutely furious, and just now he hurled a vomit bowl at that sly-looking monk who assists the abbot and told him not to show his face again.'

'Why doesn't he trust them?' Geoffroi asked. 'Does he think . . .' Disbelief flooded his innocent face. 'Surely he doesn't believe anyone's trying to *poison* him?'

'I don't know, son,' Josse admitted.

'You look sad, Father,' Geoffroi said. 'Why

don't you go and talk to him? It might stop you worrying, and it would undoubtedly comfort him.'

'I'm not sure that it would,' Josse said. He wasn't at all certain he wanted to run the risk of having a bowl of vomit hurled at him. Even when very unwell, the King was a good shot.

'Geoffroi is right,' Yves added, glancing affectionately at his nephew. 'You showed me that letter the King wrote. Yes, Josse, I know he sent it to many men, but how many do you think had that personally written appeal?'

Josse looked from his brother to his son. Not wanting to appear weak and unwilling to either of these men he loved, he agreed to try.

To his surprise, the King both knew who he was and seemed to welcome him. 'I am sick, old friend,' he muttered. 'I do not know what ails me. I have been sick from drink before, but not like this.'

Josse could well believe it. John hadn't looked healthy since the great feast at Lynn and its aftermath. Now he looked truly terrible, and Josse thought he had lost quite a lot of weight.

'How can I—' he began.

But the King interrupted. Leaning closer to Josse, he said quietly. 'I keep having visions. It's this fucking monastery, and these fucking bare-arsed monks – they make me think I'm back in my horrible prison of a cell at Fontevraud where they penned me up as a child. Remember?'

He seemed so desperate for Josse to say he did, that without thought Josse said, 'Aye.'

'There you are, then!' said the King. Confidingly

again, he said, 'They couldn't turn me into a monk then, no matter what privations they imposed and what threats my devil of a father made, and they won't now!'

Josse, about to protest that nobody would dare even to try to turn a king into something he didn't want to be, realized King John wouldn't have heard if he did. He was lost in hallucination; even as Josse watched, he put out a hand and tried to push an invisible attendant roughly away. 'Get out, you bastard! Don't you dare come near me!'

Then, just as abruptly returning to the real world, he said courteously, 'Pass me my silver cup, will you? I think I'll have some more of that wine.'

There was little Josse could do but obey.

He watched as the King drank his wine. To his amazement – for he would have thought more alcohol would be the worst thing – the King seemed to rally. A little colour infused his pale, sunken cheeks. He met Josse's eyes, and a faint smile stretched his wide mouth. 'Not dead yet,' he murmured. 'See?'

The he sat up, swung his legs round off the bed and placed his feet firmly on the floor. 'Give me your hand, Josse,' he commanded.

'My lord King, ought you to—'

'Shut up, Josse.'

Josse watched as the King's personal attendants were summoned to help him wash and dress. When he had been prepared to his own satisfaction, John told Josse to fetch his captains. Shaky on his feet, leaning on his body servants, the King went out to meet them.

'We move on,' he said in a loud voice. 'Make the necessary preparations. We ride early tomorrow.'

The bravest of his officers dared to begin a protest. 'My lord, surely you should—'

But King John turned on him like a wildcat. 'You think the attack in the north will wait while I lie recovering on my sick bed, do you?' He strode over to the officer, almost spitting with anger right in the man's face. 'I have loyal barons in the north, men I'm relying on to fight beside me when Alexander makes his move, but even now they'll be wondering if they have chosen the right allegiance. All the time I waste my time here in this ghastly place, they'll be steadily deciding I'm not worth fighting for and, for all you, I or any of these fucking monks know, every last one of them is on the point of joining the rebellious forces allied against me.'

Courageously the officer had one last try. 'But could representatives not be sent on your behalf, my lord King? A message could be sent, and—'

'*I have to do it myself!*' King John roared. The great cry seemed to weaken him, and he leaned briefly on the shoulder of the stouter of the two attendants. 'I must act,' he added, more quietly. Then, with words that Josse thought were almost unbearably poignant, he whispered, 'There is nobody else I trust.'

Meggie was sick with frustration and worn out with trying to keep her fast-growing fear at bay.

For three days now she and Faruq had been searching for the King and his train, but they

247

had found no one who was capable or willing to tell them where he was.

'Would you not think,' she cried to Faruq, 'that a king attended by servants, courtiers, loyal old knights and a huge amount of baggage, not to mention several hundred soldiers, might be quite easy to locate?'

'I would,' Faruq agreed solemnly. She had the distinct impression he was trying not to smile.

'I'm *sure* they know!' she burst out. 'So why don't they tell us? What is the reason for the secrecy?'

'They do not trust us, any of them,' Faruq said. 'You are a woman and I am a foreigner, and so neither of us is worthy to be told the truth.'

But Meggie hardly heard. '"Make your way to Sleaford," the man at Spalding told us,' she ranted, '"or maybe Newark would make better sense". And what he meant by *that*, I really couldn't say.' She scowled, furious with the man for being so vague. With herself for not obtaining better advice. 'So we race off to Sleaford, but there was no sign of the King's imminent arrival and, moreover, nobody there seemed to be aware he was even *expected!*'

The last word was a shout of fury. Faruq, nodding sympathetically, murmured, 'It was indeed frustrating.'

'So we thought that meant he wasn't going that way, and, increasingly desperate in case we missed him, we flew like the wind to Newark. And then . . .' She broke off. It still pained her to think about what they'd been told at Newark.

Faruq edged closer to her. They had made

248

camp for the night, and were sitting either side of their small fire. They'd eaten a good supper: despite the sparse population in the area, and what seemed to an outsider to be vast stretches of lonely, misty, watery ground, dotted with the occasional low hill, crisscrossed with waterways of every size from tiny ditches to small rivers, there were settlements here, with inhabitants who farmed their land efficiently and were able to sell – or occasionally give – food and drink to travellers. Tonight they had eaten fresh bread, eggs and thick slices of bacon fried in their own fat in the little metal tray that Meggie had stowed in her pack and that they had used as often as they had something to cook in it. There had been a generous flagon of excellent ale to drink, which they were sharing between them.

'It was a large disappointment to be greeted at Newark with such news—' Faruq began.

Meggie grinned. 'I think we'd say a *big* disappointment.'

'A *big* disappointment.' He echoed her emphasis carefully. 'Thank you. Yes. I watched your face while the man at the gates spoke to you, and I saw very clearly your distress.'

The King was indeed on his way to Newark, the gate guard had said. Well, that had been the latest report, although it was quite possible the plans would change. Then he'd added, almost as an afterthought, 'They're saying he's unwell.'

'What exactly does *unwell* mean?' Maggie asked. Faruq, knowing the question wasn't for him, didn't answer. It was in any case about the twentieth time she'd asked it. Then a sound

249

between a sob and a laugh broke from her: 'It can't be what I'm so afraid of, can it?'

Faruq took her hand. She was surprised at how comforting his touch was. 'You cannot know,' he said calmly. 'All you have been told is that King John is not well, but I think you must ask yourself how worried the man at Newark appeared to be. If he had learned that—'

'If he'd been told the King had camp fever or something, he'd have been extremely worried, wouldn't he?' she said eagerly, twisting round to look at him. 'But in fact he seemed only mildly concerned.'

'And he only added that the King was unwell after he had answered your enquiry, whereas had the King and all his train been in peril of infection, he would surely have told us that important piece of intelligence at the outset.'

Meggie, who had long accustomed herself to Faruq's somewhat formal and elaborate way of speaking, heard only about every other word, but that was enough. 'Yes. *Yes*,' she said emphatically. 'So really I don't need to worry that . . .' But she couldn't say it.

'That your father, your brother and your uncle are in danger,' he finished for her. 'No. I do not believe there is cause for concern. Not in this respect.'

They sat for some time in easy companionship. He still held her hand. With their free hands, they slowly and steadily drank the last of the flagon of ale.

'So,' Faruq said presently. 'What shall be our plan for tomorrow?'

She sighed. She had been thinking about the same matter, although, thanks to the ale, with marginally less anxiety than usual. 'I would very much like to go out and search for them,' she said eventually, 'for, although you have reassured me about the possibility of sickness in the camp, I can't shake a sense that I need to find them, urgently, because . . .' She trailed off. 'I don't know.' She had tried and failed to put from her mind the frightening images she'd seen in the Eye of Jerusalem. Now, as if those were not enough, she was beset by other apprehensions, which she feared even to think about. 'Something's happened, or something is going to happen, and I sense evil.'

'As do I,' he agreed surprisingly.

'You do?'

'Meggie, you know by now something of what brought my mother and me here. We believed what I search for so desperately was in the vicinity of Queen Isabella, and, on finding that was not correct, I concluded that it had to be with the King.' He looked at her intently, his light eyes reflecting the fire's small flames. 'Now that we are so close, I know I am right. I too sense evil, and I have a fair idea whence it emanates.'

'But surely that's not possible!' she protested. 'Wherever the King is with this tainted, dangerous thing, he's not just up the road, and I can't believe you can feel evil over a distance of many miles!'

He didn't answer, other than with a faintly dismissive shrug.

Which in a way, Meggie realized, was in fact a

251

great deal more alarming than if he'd vehemently defended himself and said, *Of course I can!*

She waited until the shiver of fear had subsided. Then she said, 'In answer to your question, I would very much like to set off and look for them. But, since we have no idea from which direction they'll be approaching, that seems pointless, so I suggest we stay here, in this quite comfortable camp, and wait for them to come to us.'

Fifteen

14–15 October 1216

The King, his household and his long train were on the move again.

The monks at Swineshead Abbey had been unable to deter him from setting out, and Josse, watching as the abbot, the guest master and the assembled monks stood in line to bid their King farewell, thought that to a man their disapproving expressions said, *You are being very foolish in thus risking your health, but you are a king and we are merely monks and therefore we wash our hands of you.*

He wasn't sure he blamed them.

On the first day out of Swineshead they travelled as far as Sleaford, a distance of a little over a dozen miles. For King John, capable of travelling almost three times that in a day when really pressed for time, it was unbelievably slow.

But King John was not himself. Josse was riding close behind him and could see John's distress all too plainly. The King was vomiting periodically, not stopping but leaning sideways in the saddle and retching weakly, producing a mere thin yellowish liquid that splattered feebly on the ground. His posture, bent almost double for much of the time, suggested that his stomach was cramping, his guts tying themselves in knots. He was bloated with wind, his belly swollen like that of a gravid woman, and he was straining to pass it, with little success. He had emptied his bowels catastrophically earlier, crouched by the side of a road behind the inadequate shelter of a hazel break, and he was very evidently sore and uncomfortable. He was flushed and sweaty-faced, clearly running a fever, which appeared to increase as the day went on.

The night was spent in Sleaford. The King, according to the rumours, retired very early and refused all food, although managed a cup or two of wine.

The next day followed the same pattern.

White-faced, in agony, King John ground his teeth as he rode to keep from crying out. Sitting in the saddle must surely be torment, Josse thought with deep pity, yet John utterly refused to stop and rest. But the King's great courage failed in the mid-afternoon and he called a halt, his attendants racing off to seek somewhere to make camp and spend the night, and finding lodgings in an isolated, all-but-derelict convent, where the semi-roofless cloister offered the only

253

shelter for everyone except the King, who was found a bed in a tiny cell. Josse and his companions were too far away to overhear any distress he might have suffered as they all tried to sleep, which, he reflected guiltily, was probably to their advantage.

It was late in the evening at the Sanctuary, and, as Josse tried to make himself comfortable in a ruined convent somewhere deep in the Lincolnshire fens, Helewise stood in the doorway, enjoying her usual few moments of peace, looking out into the darkening forest before closing the door and settling for the night.

It had been a very hard day, brightened only by a visit from Tilly and some of her children, bringing fresh supplies and staying only for an all too brief exchange of news. Since neither of them had any, there was little else to talk about.

Helewise missed Josse so intensely that it hurt.

Tiphaine had returned in the afternoon. Together they had stood over their patient. Throughout the day, Helewise reported to the old herbalist, Hadil had barely stirred, but spent the long hours in a state that might have been sleep but was most probably the coma that leads eventually to death.

'What ails her?' Helewise asked softly, as much to herself as to Tiphaine. 'Her arm mends, or so I assume, for there is no inflammation and she says it does not pain her much. The blow to her head, too, appears to be healing.'

Tiphaine didn't answer for a few moments. Then she said, 'She's old and tired, my lady, and a very long way from home. This mission you speak of obviously preoccupies her to the extent of obliterating all else, yet here she lies, helpless, unable to participate any further, so that full responsibility now rests on her son's shoulders.'

'And he does not return and sends no word,' Helewise finished. She sighed. 'Yes. It is enough to daunt the stoutest heart.'

A further period of silence ensued. 'She still refuses to explain this mission?' Tiphaine asked after a while.

'She did undertake to do so,' Helewise said, 'but I fear she has forgotten. Now, I'm not sure if she will.'

She might have been mistaken but, as she said the words, she thought she saw a very faint movement of Hadil's eyes under the closed lids.

As twilight fell, Tiphaine had muttered that she had to go, and Helewise got up to see her out.

Now, still leaning in the doorway, Helewise turned reluctantly to go back inside. She banked down the fire in the little hearth, unrolled her bedding, poured a mug of water and was about to settle down when Hadil said, 'I haven't forgotten.'

Helewise had to think quite hard to understand what she meant. When she did she said, trying to keep her voice calm and not betray her eagerness, 'If you feel strong enough, Hadil, I should very much like to hear your tale.'

Hadil propped herself up on her pillows, and

Helewise hastened to help her. 'I do feel sufficiently strong,' she said and, indeed, Helewise observed that there was a faint flush in her cheeks. 'I am ready to speak, and you shall hear my story. You'd better make yourself comfortable,' she added, 'for it is a long one.'

Helewise sat down on her own narrow bed, pulled up a blanket, rearranged her pillows and waited.

'There was once a knight,' Hadil began, 'and he belonged to the Order of the Knights Hospitaller. He cannot have been a good or honourable member of the Order, for he had been given a severe and degrading punishment. He had been beaten and, afterwards, as soon as he had ceased to bleed, he was sent to work digging the grave pits in the Akeldama.'

Helewise had no idea what the word meant, but she had no intention of interrupting Hadil when she had only just started.

'Oh, but there was such a need for graves back then,' Hadil went on. 'There was a fine new hospital, built by those knights, but it was already inadequate. The fighting was as fierce as ever and so there were always numerous dead who were taken straight out for burial, and so many died afterwards of their wounds. Also, sick men nursed in close proximity are vulnerable to disease, and many terrible maladies affected those long wards. At the height of summer and in the depths of the winter cold, as many as fifty bodies had to be disposed of daily, and the parsimonious Hospitallers, always unwilling to spend the smallest coin if they could avoid it, preferred to use their own men from the punishment detail rather than employ the local men, who they would have to pay.'

They had taken a vow of poverty, Helewise thought. *It was not from choice that they saved money wherever they could.*

'So, there he was, that rogue of a Hospitaller, enduring his punishment,' Hadil was saying. 'They said he came from the north, and that was surely correct, for he was considerably taller than my people and fair-haired, and his eyes were blue. The punishment was harsh, but it had not been imposed in retribution for the worst of his crimes, for only a very few people knew about that one.'

'What did he do?' Helewise asked.

'He raped a young woman,' Hadil replied expressionlessly. 'Well, she was a girl, in truth, and barely even on the cusp from childhood to womanhood. Her name was Fadila, and that means in our language "virtuous".' She smiled wryly. 'That is so sad, I always think. It was a little time after that terrible deed that he was caught and tried for one of his many other crimes; two or three weeks, perhaps a month. And, in case you were about to ask, I do not know what the other crimes were. He was a thief, I do know that, and probably not unwilling to use his fists and become embroiled in a brawl at the least provocation. Perhaps he had simply taken time off without permission. That, I am told, was quite common.

'He was digging deep in a hole, sweaty, exhausted and dizzy from the heat, without a drop of water to refresh him,' Hadil continued.

257

You can't know that! Helewise thought. But she didn't say so aloud. She was becoming entranced by the story, and if Hadil was embroidering the plain facts a little, it hardly mattered. 'Then, all of a sudden, his spade struck something that he knew straight away wasn't the heavy clay soil. What was it?' Her eyes rounded and her eyebrows went up, dramatically miming the question. 'Was it a skull? Had he inadvertently dug into an earlier grave? Mystified, intrigued, he checked that no overseer or senior knight was watching, then swiftly he bent down to investigate.

'He had uncovered a bag; quite a sizeable bag, made of some sort of thick cloth, heavy with clay deposits. At first he thought that was the only reason for its considerable weight as it lay in his hand. Then, as he gave it a little shake, he realized he was mistaken. Crouching down in the trench, careful not to be seen, he unfastened the drawstrings and peered inside.

'When he saw what the bag held, he knew he had found something of great value, for, even after he was aware what the contents were, still he was surprised at the weight. It was as if each of the items within was somehow more *dense* than it ought to have been. "What a concentration of precious metal I have found!" he said to himself, crowing silently as he rejoiced in his skill, his cunning and his luck. He knew better than to take his treasure away with him when at long last work was finished for the day, for the prisoners on the digging detail were routinely searched as they left the burial field.'

'He went back later?' Helewise asked.

'He did,' Hadil replied. 'By good fortune, that night marked the end of his week of punishment, and he was released. He returned under cover of darkness to the place where he had been digging earlier, and found his treasure without difficulty. He brushed off the sticky clay and tucked it safely away inside his tunic. Then, keeping to the shadows, he made his escape.

'He believed himself to be so clever, so cunning!' Hadil's eyes narrowed with hatred. 'He believed himself alone, unobserved. But they were waiting for him. Three men – Fadila's father, her brother and her cousin, the son of her father's brother – stood concealed in the darkness. All three were tough, well-built men, and their blood was hot with fury. The honour of striking the first blow went to Fadila's father, and, while one of the others pinned the rogue knight's arms behind his back, he bunched up his fists and administered the sort of beating that normally kills a man. But he was fit and strong, that Hospitaller, and, despite a lashing and a week of punishment, he was strong enough to break free from the imprisoning hands and fight back. The four of them were making a great deal of noise, of course, and soon a guard came hurrying out from his post on the city walls to see what was happening. But his presence, far from calming the men, served only to enrage them further. When the father and son stood still at last, panting, sweating and bleeding, it was to discover the guard, the nephew and the rogue Hospitaller lying dead on the dusty ground.'

'*Three* dead?' Helewise gasped.

'It surprises you, yes?' Hadil asked. 'It surprised the father and his son, too, and, once they came down from the terrible heights of their blood fury, they were aghast at what they had done. "Father, I cannot believe that this has happened!" the son said in a horrified whisper. "What have we done? Where did all that terrible violence come from? Oh, that guard, who only came to investigate the noise, and my poor, poor cousin!" He sobbed.

'"I do not understand either," his father muttered. "We came with the intention of only giving that rogue a beating, to make him pay for what he did to Fadila, and you must believe me when I tell you that murder was not in my mind." His son assured him that he did. "But, just now, when we were fighting, it was as if . . . as if someone, or something, had taken me over. As if some terrible demon of violence rode me, screaming in my ears to go on, hit harder, kill, kill, *kill!*"

'His son nodded. "I do believe you, my father," he said, "for it was the same for me."

'Nevertheless and despite their guilt,' Hadil continued, a shrewd look on her face, 'they still decided to search the dead Hospitaller, for they were poor men and could not afford to pass up the opportunity. And so—' abruptly her expression changed, and now she looked grief-stricken – 'and so that is what he did, Fadila's father, and by that simple action of theft, he set into motion the dreadful trail we have had to follow ever since. For he unleashed evil that night. What he took from the rogue

Hospitaller should have been re-buried, as swiftly as possible, and the man and his son should have put it from their minds and forgotten all about it.'

'But they were poor!' Helewise protested. 'The temptation was too great.'

'It was, oh, it was,' Hadil agreed mournfully. 'And yet I believe they knew full well that something was wrong. It is always said that the very moment when Fadila's father first held up the bag of treasure, he realized it was too heavy. And, in addition, he ought to have understood that the treasure was dishonest.'

'Dishonest?' It seemed an odd word.

'Yes! Do you not see? The rogue Hospitaller had only retrieved his treasure a very short time ago, and already it had betrayed him and brought about his death.' She leaned close to Helewise. 'It was accursed,' she whispered. 'It was so very heavy because it was weighed down with guilt.'

Accursed, Helewise repeated silently. *It betrayed him. It was weighed down with guilt.* In the comfort and security of the little room, she felt a shiver of dread.

And this evil thing, whatever it was that had been in that bag, was still in the world. It was the reason for Hadil and Faruq's long, long journey, and for their presence here in England.

'Quite soon they became uneasy, Fadila's father and his family,' Hadil resumed. 'They felt an inexplicable urge to rid themselves of what they had found, and so they divided the contents of the bag into five separate lots and sold them.

261

For a great deal of money, I might add. From thenceforth, the family's fortunes improved, and they were never again among the poorest of the city. But what a price was extracted for their new affluence!' She sighed heavily.

'Bad things happened around that treasure,' she went on, not giving Helewise the chance to comment. 'The rogue Hospitaller was dead within hours of unearthing it. The guard and Fadila's cousin died with him. And the tale of woe went on, for the taint did not relent, and still the task does not end . . .'

Her voice trailed off. Helewise realized the old woman was very tired. She put out her hand, gently taking Hadil's. 'What a burden you have borne, you and your family,' she said softly. Hadil's drooping eyes opened widely again, and she shot a look at Helewise. 'Of course I know that it's your own family you speak of,' she added. 'It's obvious from your story, and besides, although you don't remember, you've already told me that it was the men of your great-grandmother's family who beat the rogue Hospitaller. Fadila was your great-grandmother, wasn't she?'

Slowly Hadil nodded. 'Yes.'

'What became of her?' Helewise asked.

'She was fortunate, considering what had been done to her,' Hadil said, 'because when she grew up a good man named Zahir was prepared to take her to wife, despite the fact that she had been violently raped and was not a virgin. They had a large family, and she lived to a good age.'

262

'And from one of those children, you and Faruq are descended,' Helewise murmured. 'And you—'

'I knew her,' Hadil interrupted. 'For the first twelve years of my life, I saw my great-grandmother Fadila at least twice a week, and sometimes more.'

Slowly Helewise nodded. What a powerful woman she must have been, she reflected; not only to have overcome the horror of rape, make a good marriage and produce a family, but also to persuade her descendants that it was up to them to put right the evil their kinsmen had unwittingly released on the world.

'This is the very last of it,' Hadil murmured, as if she had followed Helewise's thoughts. 'Once Faruq comes back and tells me it is done and he has succeeded, we can go home.'

Then, as if suddenly she had been drained of all energy, she sank back into her pillows. Her eyelids drooped. Helewise, leaving her to sleep, lay down in her own bed and tried to settle, although the vivid images in her mind suggested that might not be easy. She was just going through the tale, trying to commit it to memory so that she would be able to repeat it to Faruq, when very softly Hadil said, 'Soon, quite soon, I shall tell you the rest.'

Not many moments afterwards, her deep, regular breathing suggested she had fallen into a profound sleep.

Sixteen

16 October 1216

The morning on which King John left the derelict convent in the Lincolnshire fenland and set out on his last journey ushered in a truly terrible day.

Josse, riding a little ahead of Yves and Geoffroi and only a rank behind the King, could not begin to understand how John had even managed to clamber up into the saddle, and surely he only remained sitting there by sheer willpower. After only three miles, that willpower failed. Turning to those riding nearest, he muttered something. Josse saw his face and suppressed a gasp, for the King was deathly white – his skin looked almost transparent – and he had bitten his lower lip in an attempt not to cry out.

But he was still the same old John. As the attendants leapt down from their horses and began asking their anxious questions – 'What is the matter, my lord King? What should we do? How may we help you?' he silenced them all with a great bellow.

'I'm sick and in agony, you useless, unobservant bunch of whore's bastards! I can't ride another step!' Then he let himself slide down out of the saddle, slumping on to the ground. The beautiful chestnut gelding, mildly curious, bent his graceful neck and gave his master a nudge, and the luxuriant ginger mane softly brushed the deathly pale face. It was the gentlest of nudges, almost as if the horse was offering sympathy, but nevertheless the King groaned in agony. Josse, hurrying over to see if he could help, saw that John, his eyes screwed closed, was sweating and panting, bent double, a hand to his stomach, and in so much pain that he could barely draw breath.

The King opened his eyes and saw the men clustered anxiously around him. 'Don't just stand there staring at me!' he yelled. 'Can't you see what's needed? Fashion me a litter – I'll have to be carried. Just for a while,' he added.

But the men who heard the command scratched their heads, at a loss to know what to do. 'We haven't got any wood,' said one. Yves and Geoffroi, riding up to the little group in the middle of the road, enquired what had happened. Someone muttered a terse few words of explanation.

'We'll make a cradle,' Yves said. 'I've seen it done – one of my men at Acquin was charged by a she-boar and her tusk opened his thigh from testicles to knee. We wrapped up the wound to slow the bleeding, then a bright lad cut down two slim willow saplings and tied them together with a blanket. Or we could use a cloak, I suppose, provided it fastened all the way down the front and was made of good, thick fabric.'

Geoffroi, understanding before Josse did what Yves had in mind, drew a strong blade from his pack and ran back down the road to where a

265

small group of willows stood bravely upright against the prevailing wind off the Wash. As he was trimming off the side branches, Josse, comprehension having dawned, said, 'How do we carry it?'

Yves straightened up from helping Geoffroi. 'A man at each end of the two willow poles?'

'Aye, perhaps, but if we made the frame out of four poles rather than two, it'd form a firm square that could be tied between two of the horses.'

'We'd move faster that way,' one of the King's body servants said in a low voice. 'And we need to reach help as soon as we can.'

The hastily conceived plan was effected and put into practice. The King's improvised bed, padded out with his men's spare cloaks and blankets, was hoisted off the ground and secured between two destriers. The horses, however, were uneasy at this strange, unaccustomed load, and the men leading them found them all but impossible to control. The swift but smooth-paced walk that had been envisioned soon proved impossible.

And the King, the cuts on his lip bleeding again from trying not to howl in pain, finally screamed at them to stop. The litter was unfastened and the horses led away. Four of the brawniest men took their places.

When Newark was in sight and there were only a couple of miles to go, John roused himself from a brief sleep. 'I will ride now,' he said, in the sort of voice that was never questioned.

He couldn't manage the beautiful chestnut

266

gelding, for the horse was highly strung and required his rider's full attention. So one of the lesser men of the train was summoned from the ranks further back and ordered to give up his horse, an amiable, plodding grey mare with a sway back and a patient air. Then – although every man there would far rather he hadn't witnessed it – they all watched as the King was helped into the saddle.

Grey faced with pain, eyes screwed up against the daylight as if it pierced him, upright on the old grey mare, the very tension in his body proclaiming the effort it took, King John rode the last mile and a half into Newark.

The dignitaries of Newark came out to meet him. He was escorted to the bishop of Lincoln's castle and, as he and his inner circle rode through the narrow streets, Josse watched in admiration as he stretched his sore lips in a smile like a rictus and returned the eager greetings of the crowds who welcomed him.

Once inside the castle, however, he collapsed.

They took him straight to the quarters that had been prepared for him. Up a narrow spiral stair – circumnavigated with enormous difficulty, since the King was now unconscious – and into a wide room that took up most of the floor area of that level, off which there was a private chamber where, at last, the King was laid on a soft bed.

Josse stood aimlessly in the outer room, wanting so badly to help but having no idea how to. Presently, with a bustle of attendants and some muttered conversation, a man in monk's garb arrived.

'That's the abbot of Croxton,' a man close to Josse muttered. 'They say he has medical knowledge and a reputation as a healer.'

The abbot remained in the inner chamber for some time. When at length he emerged, someone – one of the attendant monks – whispered a question, and the abbot shook his head.

Josse was so absorbed in the drama that, when Geoffroi sought him out, he had to take hold of his arm to get his attention. 'What is it, son?' Josse demanded, frowning.

Geoffroi said, 'There's someone who's asking for you.'

'But I can't come *now!* The King . . .' He stopped. Had he been about to say, *The King needs me?* But then it wasn't really very reasonable to think that, for what in heaven's name could he do to help?

'Very well, but I mustn't be long.'

With enormous reluctance, Josse followed Geoffroi back down the narrow stair and out into the courtyard.

Meggie was waiting for him.

For a few moments he simply stared at her, quite unable to deal with the fact that she whom he most wanted to see was standing there before him. He found he was praying: a simple prayer of gratitude, repeated over and over again: *Thank you, dear Lord. Thank you.*

He took her in his arms, pulled her close and hugged her. He felt the strength of her arms as she hugged him back, and heard her say softly,

'I have found you, and Geoffroi tells me all three of you are well.'

He kissed the top of her head. 'We are.' Then, loosening his hold so that he could look down into her face he said, 'Dearest, you are needed – come with me.'

He led her up the spiral stairs. As they emerged into the outer chamber, the abbot of Croxton came striding out of the little room where they'd put the King, his attendants hurrying in his wake. Noticing Josse, the abbot paused briefly just in front of him.

'I have provided what comfort I can, both of a physical and, more crucially, of a spiritual nature, but I fear he has made himself extremely unwell,' he said in a low voice. 'He stinks of stale alcohol, which of course is the very worst thing for a man in his condition to have imbibed.'

'He had to do whatever was necessary to keep him travelling onwards,' Josse replied, stung by the abbot's critical tone to defend his King. 'He—'

The abbot waved a dismissive hand. 'Yes, yes, yes,' he said impatiently. 'I go now to prepare one or two remedies of my own, and in the meantime, don't let anything pass his lips.' He scowled ferociously, as if suspecting rebellion, then dived for the steps and hurried away.

The outer chamber seemed very crowded – Josse recognized the faces of many of John's group of close intimates – but the smaller room contained only the King and four body servants. Bending his head to enter in beneath the low

269

arch of the doorway, Josse held up a hand to Meggie, telling her to wait.

Josse approached the still figure lying on the bed. 'My lord King,' he said gently, 'I have someone here who wishes to help you.'

He watched as the eyelids fluttered briefly but remained closed. 'If it's the abbot, tell him I'm not ready for the sacrament yet,' John muttered. 'Bloody man would have me in my grave while I still draw breath. Stinks of fish, too.'

Josse smiled. 'It's not the abbot, I promise,' he said. 'May I allow her to approach you?'

The King opened his eyes as Josse said *her*, and stared up at Josse. 'A *woman*?'

'Aye, my lord.'

John gave a soft sigh. 'How long is it since I saw a woman?' he mused. 'I don't count those weird nuns at the convent last night. I'm not sure if they were even human, never mind female. Yes, yes,' he added impatiently, 'fetch her!'

Josse turned to the doorway and nodded to Meggie.

Meggie had already guessed who it was that her father had summoned her to see. As she stood there in the crowded room, she mentally prepared herself. She felt very apprehensive – not an emotion that normally troubled her as she approached a patient – and she didn't fully understand why.

She kept her eyes on Josse as he went over to the bed and spoke a few words to the man lying on it. When her father turned to beckon her, she was ready. She straightened her gown and walked into the little chamber.

Josse stepped back and she went to stand over the King. She stared down at him, her heart wrung with pity. She had been able to smell him from outside, and now, standing so close, the stench was overpowering. His tunic was crusted with vomit, his chemise was filthy, his hose were unspeakable.

She knew without even examining him that something was profoundly wrong. And then she understood, at last, why she and Faruq had been driven so relentlessly to find him. There *was* evil here, as both of them had well known.

She stepped away from the bed and went right up to the nearest attendant. She had no idea who he was, nor of his seniority. It didn't matter, and she was too angry to curb her tongue with courtly politeness. She said with quiet vehemence, 'Why has he been allowed to get into this state? You should be ashamed! Fetch hot water, soapwort, soft towels and clean garments, wash him from his hair to his feet, dress him in something soft and comfortable.' The attendant hurried away, and she returned to kneel down at the King's side.

It was cruel in the extreme, she thought, to allow a man as fastidious as the King to have become so filthy; mired in his own waste, soaked in sweat and stinking like a cesspit.

He looked at her and in the familiar blue eyes, dulled now with sickness and pain, she saw his humiliation.

She took his hot hand. 'My lord King, I have

271

sent for the means to bathe you and dress you comfortably. While we wait, please tell me what ails you, and what pain and discomforts you suffer. I have some knowledge of healing and I am here to help you.'

He looked at her for some time. Then he said softly, 'Limestra.'

She was very surprised. She had thought him too ill to recognize her, but not only had he done so straight away but also, it seemed, he had remembered how they came to know each other. 'Yes,' she said, smiling. 'Still I await those lessons in swordsmanship that you promised to give me.'

He shifted on the bed, wincing. 'You will have to wait a little longer, my Meggie.'

My Meggie.

Controlling the painful emotions, she said briskly, 'Now, tell me what is wrong.'

If he was embarrassed at the change from man and woman to patient and healer, he gave no sign. With admirable frankness and brevity, he listed his symptoms. Then, while the attendants hurried back with everything she had ordered and set about cleaning him up, she asked to be shown to somewhere with a good fire where she could boil water and begin preparing the remedies.

Firmly she put her horror at the King's condition to the back of her mind. *He doesn't need me or anybody else feebly weeping over him*, she told herself, *he needs a capable healer*.

She went through her pack to check what supplies she had – it made good sense, when travelling, to be well prepared – and she asked the plump, kindly woman who had shown her to the little room with the hearth and the jars of fresh water if she could supply what Meggie lacked. Soon she was concentrating so hard on the various tasks that everything else faded.

The King had described a complex set of symptoms. Meggie, at a loss to think of any sickness that encompassed them all, decided to treat them piecemeal. He complained most of the pain: agonizing pain, in his head and in his belly. 'It feels as if my guts are in knots,' he told her, 'and I am bloated like a sheep's carcass on a flooded river. There can be nothing left in me, and I pass wind constantly, yet the bloating will not subside.'

She had asked his permission to put a hand on his belly. It was grotesquely distended and as hard as a rock.

Against diarrhoea she prepared a thick oat-based drink containing water pepper and lady's mantle. To counter the spasms she prepared a strong-smelling mixture of peppermint, fennel and dill. He needed above all to sleep, so finally she set to work with chamomile and lime, adding a very carefully measured amount of the highly efficient but potentially deadly poppy milk that she always kept tucked in a secret pocket in her pack.

She decided to prepare one more remedy, although she hoped very much that it wouldn't be needed. She had surreptitiously put her fingers on his wrist to feel his heartbeat, and what she'd

273

detected had concerned her. She had dried foxglove leaves with her and, as she set about her remedy, she remembered Tiphaine – she'd been Sister Tiphaine then – showing her what to do.

In a time of such fear and distress, the sweet, peaceful memory was doubly welcome.

Lastly, because she knew he was a man who prized cleanliness and must be profoundly upset by his own stench, she prepared aromatics, crushing together lavender and rosemary so that their strong, fresh, invigorating smell filled the air.

She became aware that the plump woman stood in the doorway. As Meggie looked up, she said, 'They're ready for you.'

And Meggie went to treat her patient.

Faruq had found a place in which to conceal himself while allowing him to keep close watch on the quarters in the castle given over to the King's use. He had been waiting for the right moment for what seemed hours, although he suspected it was only the tension that gave that impression.

He'd been alarmed when the big, thick-set young man came running up to Meggie, but then they'd started hugging each other, and Meggie was laughing and exclaiming with relief. Even before she'd turned to Faruq and said, 'This is Geoffroi. He's my brother,' Faruq had marked the resemblance and already guessed. Geoffroi had dashed back inside and, very shortly afterwards, her father had appeared and hurried her away.

He wasn't worried by Meggie's absence. Anticipating that they might need to separate, they had sought out a meeting place. Whichever one of them emerged first from the castle would fetch the horses from where they were stabled in the town and go to await the other.

He realized it wasn't a foolproof plan, but it seemed the best they were going to come up with.

Faruq had observed how busy the castle was. The building itself, the courtyard and the surrounding streets were hectic with rushing, anxious people, and nobody seemed to spare him a glance. In a moment of detachment he thought with absolute conviction: *Now. The right time is now.*

He made his way inside the castle to what must be the guest quarters and, tagging on behind a trio of men cursing and sweating as they carried a huge chest up the narrow steps, emerged into a large room where more men in the King's livery were unpacking food, linen, blankets, furs, ornaments, a beautiful altar cloth and a heavy silver crucifix. In the middle of the floor, getting in everyone's way, was a large wooden chest bound with bands of metal and bearing several locks which looked like a vast jewel box.

Faruq had come to precisely the place he sought. He felt again the strong conviction: *This is the moment.*

He slipped into the deep shadow formed where two walls intersected at an acute angle. Nobody noticed. Several people came past, all of them in a hurry, many of them yelling and all of them clearly anxious. Not one turned to demand who he was or what he thought he was doing.

He relaxed and let his eyes roam round the large room. Soon he spotted the area on which to concentrate. Fortuitously quite close to his place of concealment, two of the King's servants knelt before a huge box which carried the King's table-ware: knives, platters, bowls, some precious glassware carefully padded with handfuls of straw and, finally, emerging from a cocoon of soft sheep's wool, a glitter of gold and silver as the most costly items were unpacked.

'We should leave these in the chest and lock it,' one of the men muttered to the other. 'Surely he'll not be needing his best stuff, sick like he is?'

Then other man paused. 'Hmm. I don't know. When he wants something he wants it that same instant, and if one of us has to go round hunting for the keys before we can satisfy him, there'll be trouble.' He paused again. 'Leave most of the best stuff,' he said finally. 'We'll put out the pewter goblets, the silver cups and the two gold platters and we'll pray that'll do.'

Even as he spoke, he placed the objects on the shelf where he had been stowing the other objects.

Faruq knew it as soon as he saw it.

He drew an involuntary breath, slowly letting it out again.

At last.

Time had passed. He didn't know if it had been a long or a short time. He was concentrating so hard that he had no idea.

He had almost given up. It was *there*, only a few feet away. But there was always somebody in the room and, so very close to his objective, he dared not risk a hasty move.

Darkness fell and there was a flurry of activity as people dashed in, grabbed objects and dashed out again. The item for which he had travelled so far, however, remained on the shelf where the servant had put it. Faruq's hopes slowly rose.

Then, quite unexpectedly, the moment came. Briefly there was nobody in the room and, except for a trio of guards on the outer door, which opened on to the steps leading down to the court-yard, Faruq was alone. The guards were talking in a desultory manner, leaning against the walls, tired and bored.

And they were looking outwards rather than inwards.

Without pausing to think about it, Faruq stepped forward.

But even as he did so, there came the sound of running feet and a young man came flying into the room. His eyes were wide, his face was red and sweaty, and he began instantly to run his fingers along the shelves where the platters, goblets and cups had been arranged. Then, with a furious curse, he yelled to the men in the doorway, 'Where's the King's personal stuff?'

Faruq, back in the shadows, heart thumping with shock, prayed silently. *Don't let him take it. Don't let him take it.*

But then, with a sigh of relief, the young man selected an object and ran off.

Faruq wanted to slump to the cold stone floor

and curl up into the smallest possible form. *So close!* he wailed silently. *I was so close, and I lost it!*

He thought of his mother. How could he even begin to tell her? How would he . . .?

But then some sense of self-preservation roused him and he knew he had to leave. The doorway leading out into the courtyard was far too well guarded, but if he was discovered where he was, all alone in the dark corner and with no reason to be there, he'd be in trouble. There seemed no option but to slip out after the running youth.

In a well-disguised camp in a carefully chosen location, Jehan waited to see what would happen next.

Yann Duguesclin's spies had done their work well, and he had a far more accurate picture of the King's precise whereabouts and state of health than most of the people within the castle. His plans had been finalized, and the assassination detail knew what they had to do.

Jehan was by now in a state beyond anxiety and regret, and very nearly beyond fear. He recognized his extreme folly in so willingly and eagerly rushing to join in and support a cause he no longer believed in, but it was far too late now to do anything but endure.

For he had seen what Yann Duguesclin's fanaticism drove him to do when he sensed his great plan was being threatened. One of the men who had befriended Jehan was a fresh-faced, naïve youngster who, like Jehan, was a native of Brittany who had settled in southern England. He had a comely wife, or so he told them, and a little child, another on the way. Also like Jehan, he had been raised on tales of King John's devilish treachery; of the cruel slaying of his nephew, Arthur of Brittany, the beloved of his people, in order to clear John's way to the throne. He, too, had revenge in his blood, so that, when the opportunity arose to act, he hadn't hesitated.

But this pleasant young man had changed his mind.

Believing Yann Duguesclin to be an honourable and reasonable man, he had gone to him and asked to be excused. 'I thought I could be part of this, you see,' he had said apologetically, 'and I was desperate to help strike the blow.' He had hung his head. 'Seems I was wrong. I'm no killer, sir. I miss my wife and I want to go home.'

In a strike as fast as a snake's, Yann Duguesclin had drawn his knife and cut the young man's throat. As he lay at his feet, horribly liquid gurgling sounds coming out of him, Duguesclin wiped his knife and said calmly, 'Nobody leaves.'

When he closed his eyes at night and tried to sleep, Jehan still heard those terrible noises.

I am here till the end, he told himself.

He didn't know exactly what that end would be, and he found he had neither the ability nor the will to think beyond it.

Throughout the long night, Meggie tended the King. To begin with her remedies seemed to ease his symptoms, and he revived sufficiently to summon wine, served in a silver cup. He drank a little, pronouncing it good, but didn't finish the draught.

She didn't know exactly when the realization came that he was dying. He had moments of lucidity when he talked, even joked, with the men who incessantly and insistently clustered around him. Meggie wished they would all go away, but she knew that was not the way of it when a king lay fighting for his life.

She slept briefly. Josse came to find her and, taking her hand, led her away to a small room where he, Yves, Geoffroi and about a dozen other men had bedded down. Her father tucked her up in his own bedroll, and the warmth, the familiar smell, were like a restorative.

And so the sixteenth day of October rolled unnoticed into the seventeenth.

Seventeen

17–18 October 1216

Meggie stayed with the sinking King for as often as she was allowed. His state of mind was now vacillating quite dramatically. Sometimes he was lucid; making logical, practical plans for the next few days and weeks, turning over the likely progress of the struggle in the north with common sense and a realistic assessment of his strengths and weaknesses. Sometimes he was the vibrant, charismatic blue-eyed man she had encountered in her own forest home. Once he said, holding her hand, 'We should both have had the courage, you and I, Meggie, to follow that particular path and see where it led us.'

She knew what he meant, for she had felt the same herself, more than once.

She responded with a suitably light, flirtatious remark.

But her heart ached at his use of *should have*. He knew, just as she did, that they had run out of time.

For sometimes – most of the time, now – he simply lay there, eyes closed, occasionally moaning in pain but more often unconscious.

In the kitchens and out in the courtyard, men muttered the rhyme composed by a French seer back in the reign of King John's father: *Henry the Fairest shall die at Martel, Richard the Poitevin shall die in the Limousin, John shall die a landless king lying in a litter.*

It hurt Meggie to hear it. She didn't think he could hear – he was probably beyond that now – but, aching for him, suffering with him, she discovered she had a very strong urge to hit anybody who hurt or upset him.

The abbot of Croxton came back. John seemed to quite like him, and greeted him with an attempt at a smile. It was rare for him to treat a man of God with kindly tolerance, and Meggie wondered if that was an indication that he knew death was

281

close. The abbot was a comfort, that was clear; he heard the King's confession and administered the sacrament.

Late in the day, the King drew upon his last strength and, summoning the grandest of the lords attending him, listened intently while one by one they swore their oath of allegiance to his elder son, Prince Henry, appointing William Marshal to act as regent until the young prince was of age and also to act as his guardian. Josse had come to join Meggie, comforting her simply by his strong, loving, safe presence, and they stood together in the outer chamber, straining to hear, wondering how Queen Isabella would feel about William Marshal's appointment.

When the gaggle of lords and clerics had gone and John was lying back exhausted upon his pillows, Meggie went to return to his bedside. Josse stopped her: 'Go and breathe some fresh air,' he said softly. 'I'll sit with him for a while. He seems to like a friendly face from the old days,' he added, as if his offer had somehow been boastful.

She gave him a hug.

When she came back, Josse was standing in the doorway, looking back at the sleeping King with a strange expression on his face.

'What's wrong?' she asked urgently.

He came out of his reverie and gave her an apologetic grin. 'Nothing – no change. He's just been dictating his will.'

She went back into the little chamber.

She took up her position by the bed. Four of

the King's body servants stood in the corners. The outer chamber was full of important men.

We're all waiting, she thought.

As the light began to fail, lamps were lit. There was only one lamp in the little room, and the light was soft and forgiving. It probably wasn't sufficient for anyone to observe that she had taken the King's hand. She didn't really care if they did. Nobody, she believed, should die without someone holding their hand if there was anyone there to do it.

Night fell. As midnight approached, a strong wind suddenly blew up, blowing and buffeting round the castle, howling.

John died an hour after midnight, and the wind rose briefly to a gale.

Everything changed in that moment.

Meggie was ushered out of the little chamber. Not that she wanted to stay, for she had said goodbye and she had sensed the moment when the King's spirit had fled. *There is nothing to stay for,* she thought as she stumbled out into the outer chamber. *I do not care what becomes of the body.*

The abbot of Croxton returned, with his cortege of monks. There was a lot of praying, and the smell of incense. Then they began on the corpse. The heart and intestines he would take away, he announced in a sepulchral tone. He would oversee the embalming process, which his monks would carry out. Towards daybreak, when the eastern sky was just starting

283

to show a pale line on the horizon, more monks arrived to stand vigil. Mass was said for the King's soul.

Meggie found a quiet corner, lay down on the floor, and fell asleep.

Early in the morning, Josse found her. He sat down beside her and gently placed her head on his lap, stroking her soft hair. Presently she awoke. She stared up at him. 'He's dead.'

'Aye, I know.'

'He was peaceful, at the end. He'd told them all he wanted them to do, and I suppose that helped.'

'That's good.' Then, for that seemed inadequate, he added, 'It was well that you were there, sweeting. Both your remedies and your presence were a comfort.'

But she didn't answer.

She struggled to sit up, looking around her, a bemused expression on her face. 'I was dreaming . . .'

He waited, but she didn't elaborate.

'Yves and Geoffroi are downstairs,' he said presently. 'They're ready to go.'

She looked puzzled. 'Go? Oh, yes. Of course.' Then – and he sensed she was making an effort to speak of practical matters when her mind was clearly far away – she said, 'What will happen now? With the rebel barons, I mean, and the threat from the north?'

He thought for a few moments. 'It's most unlikely that the rebel barons will oppose Prince Henry's accession,' he said very quietly. 'The ones who have allied with Alexander of Scotland will probably abandon him, for there was only any point in fighting with him while John was King, and they'll have no quarrel with the new order.'

'What about Prince Louis, and the invasion in the south?' she whispered.

'The same, I believe, will apply,' Josse replied. 'I hope so, anyway. With any luck, Prince Louis will realize that support is gradually fading away and go back where he came from.'

'What about you, Father?' she asked. 'You'll go home – you, Yves and Geoffroi?'

'Aye, we will. Geoffroi can barely wait to set out.' He hesitated. 'But surely you will be with us?'

She was getting to her feet, and didn't answer. Turning to him, she said, 'I'll come down and see them.'

Puzzled, more than a little worried, Josse followed her down the steps, across the huge ground-floor chamber and out into the courtyard.

She hugged Yves and Geoffroi, exchanging a few words with them. Then Geoffroi turned to Josse and said, '*Now* can we go home?'

'We can, son.' Josse smiled at him. 'In fact, I have a task for you, for while the King was dictating his will, somebody asked what was to become of that fine chestnut gelding he set such a store by. His glance just happened to be on me at the time, and he's bequeathed the horse to me.' He dropped his eyes modestly as Yves exclaimed with pleasure. 'He said he wanted his favourite horse to go to a loyal old friend, and he chose me.'

Geoffroi's face lit up with delight.

'Before you utter a word,' Yves said to him very firmly, 'you're not riding him all the way back. We're going to rest my old Hector, since he's still favouring that sore foot, so the three of us'll ride your horse, your father's horse and the chestnut.' He grinned. 'Josse and I have already agreed that he and I will draw straws for who goes first with the chestnut.'

Josse turned to Meggie, who had been standing silently beside him. 'Now, tell me what's happening,' he said firmly. 'I had assumed you'd be riding with us, and that we'd find the time for you to tell me what you're doing here?' Despite himself, he found he'd turned the remark into a question.

Meggie shook her head. 'I can't leave with you, Father, although it's possible I'll catch you up on the ride south. I'm not alone, and I'm sort of responsible for the person with me.'

Josse frowned. 'Who is it?'

'Remember how I was summoned to Hawkenlye Abbey to tend an old woman?' He nodded. 'It's her son.'

'But why can't he—'

'Oh, Father, it's far too long an explanation and it'll have to wait,' she said with rare impatience. 'I'm really sorry' – his dismay must have shown in his face – 'but I must go.'

She stood on tiptoe to kiss him, hugged her uncle and her brother, then, without another word, hurried away.

She had been thinking so hard. The King was dead – she couldn't dwell on that yet – and she didn't really understand why he had died. She knew that her remedies ought to have helped. He might have remained sick and weak for days, perhaps longer, but *he shouldn't have died.*

She made her way through the mass of people. Although it was still early, it seemed that the entire population was abroad. She knew where she must go and what she must do there. She hoped fervently that she wasn't too late. As she emerged into the large room with the little chamber leading off it, she began to pray.

Against all expectation, immediately she saw what she had come for. She strode across the room and picked it up, instantly turning and hurrying away. Her heart banging and jumping with terror, she told herself, *Stay calm. You're only doing what everyone else is doing – clearing up, tidying the room – and if you act just as they do, you'll be safe.*

She crossed the outer room. Descended the spiral stairs, even managing to exchange a remark with the woman just ahead of her about how tricky the narrow steps were to negotiate when your hands were full. She strode across the vast space whose wide doors opened on to the courtyard, and she merged with a large band of women heading out towards the town.

Presently she broke away and walked calmly off down a side street. She doubled back, once, twice, three times. When she was quite sure nobody was either following or watching her, she slipped away and set off for the place where she and Faruq had agreed to meet.

* * *

He was waiting for her. He was sitting on a low rise beside the stream that flowed between the willows, and the horses were tethered among the trees, peacefully grazing.

He stood up as she approached and, to her great surprise, put his arms round her. She thought she felt him sob.

'What is it?' she asked. 'Are you hurt?'

'No, no, but I wish I was!' he cried. 'Meggie, it was there, I saw it, I almost had it, but I was a coward and I hesitated, and someone came and took it!'

She took his hand and led him into the shelter of the trees. The undergrowth was thick and well grown, and she didn't think either they or the horses would be visible from the road. She said calmly, 'We're going to have something to eat, and we'll tell each other what we've been doing. I have . . . there's something I have to do – a test, I suppose – and I'll tell you about that too.' She glanced at him, and all at once she was quite certain that she knew the truth about the things that had mystified her. 'Then we shall sleep, and, later in the day, we'll set off south.'

Eighteen

Josse and his party set out almost as soon as Meggie had run off. Josse waited hopefully for a few moments in case she changed her mind, but then Yves took his arm and gently ushered him away.

It was a relief to leave, and he had to admit it. As they rode off he turned round for a last look at the place where King John had died. There had been orders not to spread news of the death. *But how could you keep such a thing quiet?* Josse thought. The castle was thronged with people, busy saddling up and leaving. The large contingent of Flemish knights that the late King had recruited to fight for him had clearly heard the news, and they were packing as swiftly and efficiently as if there was a prize for the quickest. Quite a lot of those scurrying off down the road, Josse observed, were bent double under large packs and had presumably been helping themselves to anything portable that they could hide away. Then, suddenly, it occurred to him that this was what a place always looked like when the King's train rolled away. If somehow you hadn't learned of John's death, he realized, there would be nothing to say this morning was different from any other morning.

Progress was slow to begin with, for most people seemed to be going in the same direction and it was difficult for the three mounted men – one of them leading a fourth horse – to make a way through the crowds. But gradually they overtook the foot traffic and the carts, and the road opened up before them.

Josse was still distressed and not a little angry that Meggie wasn't riding with them. Yves, guessing what troubled him, said, 'Josse, she's a grown woman and used to making her own decisions and looking after herself. She'll be all right.'

His brother's words had, as they always did, comforted him.

The weather was depressing. The wind that had risen in the small hours had dropped as suddenly as it had begun and the mist had come creeping back, now covering the ground to a depth of about eight or ten feet and making visibility poor. The mist bore droplets of moisture that soon permeated cloaks and hoods. It was very cold.

Presently they came up behind a big group of riders who had left the castle earlier. There wasn't room on the narrow track to pass, and, Josse reflected sourly, they weren't in a hurry any more. He, Yves and Geoffroi resigned themselves to waiting until the road widened.

Jehan was waiting with Yann Duguesclin's three killers. They were on the edge of a small pine wood just outside a town. He understood that the King had been staying in a castle in the town and was to leave this morning: the spies watching from a distance had reported very early on the activity around the castle that meant King John was on the move again.

Jehan didn't know why he was with the three silent men. His job had been to stay close to them to tend their horses. He'd done that, but he couldn't understand why they insisted he rode out with them this morning. What were they doing? Was this yet another mission to gather intelligence about the King's movements? But surely the spies had already told them where he was going next – north, to Lincoln, as soon as he was feeling better. The fact that he was moving out this morning implied he was, so why—

Just then one of the silent men broke into his thoughts. Pointing, he said very softly, 'There.' The other two followed the line of his outstretched arm.

'You're sure?' one said.

The first man nodded.

'Then the plans have changed,' the second one muttered, 'for that road doesn't lead to Lincoln.'

The first man didn't reply, other than with a faint shrug. Then all three put heels to their horses and set out on the road south. Nobody said a word to Jehan. After a moment, he kicked the bay gelding into a lively trot and went after them.

The weather was awful. The rain had set in, and what had begun as a light drizzle hardly distinguishable from the swirling mist was steadily intensifying. The ground was quickly becoming sodden, and many little streams and brooks were beginning to flood. The mist had worsened. Riding at the back of the column meant that they had to force a way through ground already churned up by hooves, wheels and feet. When Josse suggested to Geoffroi and Yves that they try to loop across open ground to the right, returning to the road ahead of the large, slow group, they readily agreed.

The manoeuvre was proving to be a good idea. They had elected to overtake at a spot where there was a low, flat-topped bank beside the road, and cantering along it was a relatively easy matter. Quite a lot of those riding in the long train stared up at them, and a man muttered audibly, 'Flashy buggers.' Turning to look back, Josse noticed that several other riders were copying them.

Yves, who had been looking at the people they were passing, gave a mild exclamation of surprise. 'Oh, look, Josse,' he called, 'there's that young lad I spotted back at Lynn – the deaf one I thought was a spy. I wonder what he's doing here? I haven't seen him for days.'

Josse turned to where Yves was pointing. He saw a young, pale face, staring up at the three riders on the top of the bank. *He's only a boy*, Josse thought.

The lad's eyes met Josse's. He stared for a moment, his mouth open. Then an expression of growing horror flooded the thin face and, frantically turning in the saddle and looking all around, he gave a strange, wordless cry.

The archer had his target in his sights. He stood utterly immobile, arrow nocked to the bow, hands steady. The mist swirled then cleared again.

The arrow flew, straight and true.

Jehan Leferronier, because of a freak little breeze that parted the mist just as the arrow struck, saw who had been hit, and understood what would inevitably happen.

And he knew he could never return to his forge in the woods above Hawkenlye Abbey.

Riding along the bank behind his father and his uncle, Geoffroi was trying to control the spare horse as well as his own. Even for him, very used to the ways of horses and extremely strong, it was a struggle. To add to his frustration, some of the others in the slow procession – who had copied Josse's idea and clambered up on to the bank – had managed to get between Geoffroi and his two companions. Now he was separated from Josse and Yves by a group of five mounted men, a couple of lads on ponies and a determined old boy staggering along under a huge sack. When the mist swirled thickly, as it was doing now, Geoffroi totally lost sight of his father and his uncle.

The pair of big, broad-shouldered, barrel-chested men, and the younger, very similar one who always rode with them, had become a familiar sight over the days and weeks. The knights from Acquin, people called them. One of the older pair – nobody was sure which one – was a boyhood friend of the King, and one of the faithful old knights who had been summoned to John's aid. They were amiable and courteous. People treated them with respect, but at the same time found themselves liking them. Watching them now, riding up there on top of the bank and cleverly managing to get past the slow, tedious train, many people smiled.

When one of the figures gave a cry and fell, nobody – including the young man racing towards them, the son of one and the nephew of the other – could tell which of the pair it was.

* * *

Just before the terrible cry rang out, Geoffroi had frozen. He *knew.*

The instant before the arrow found its target and the knight from Acquin was killed, Geoffroi was already trying to press forward, yelling, screaming at those impeding his path to get out of the way. He had a terrible moment of precognition: he could see figures in the mist . . . a crush of men on horses, but among them two men whose outlines were very familiar, as the very shape of people who are deeply loved is instantly recognizable.

Then there came the whistle of an arrow through the air . . .

There were the two broad figures. One had fallen to the ground to lie face down in a deep puddle. In horror, Geoffroi thought: *It's not a vision, it's real.*

His own cry frozen in his throat, tears flowing down his face, he strained to see past the crowds now surging up on to the bank, through the mist and the rain. The two bulky, broad-shouldered outlines that were all he could make out were so alike and he didn't know which one had fallen.

Oh, Lord, whose turn was it to ride the King's horse? Which out of his father or his uncle was dead?

For he *was* dead, whichever one it was. They were crying out the news, passing it from one to the other. 'Yes! *Yes!* Oh, dear God, yes! One of the big knights from Acquin, the pair of brothers who always ride side by side! No, I don't know which is which any more than you do!'

One was lying on the sodden ground. The other, bending over his fallen brother, was shocked into silence and could only put his strong arms around the still body.

And then someone said, 'This is terrible! We must let them know back at Newark!'

'What's it to them?' someone replied harshly. 'They'll have enough to worry about.'

'But don't you see, you fool?' cried the first man. 'Somebody – one of the senior lords, maybe that William Marshal – needs to *know!*'

'But—'

'This was an attempt on the King's life, you bloody fool!' the first interrupted. 'It's his horse, isn't it? That lovely chestnut gelding is so distinctive, with that long mane and tail and the star on his brow, and nobody else rides a horse like that.' The mutterings in the crowd rose to a crescendo, and through it someone cried, 'Someone's just tried to kill the King!'

Geoffroi, so stuck by horror and grief that his mind seemed to have come to a total halt, slowly slid off his mare's back. He stood on the path that ran along the bank, clutching tight to the two sets of reins. Yves's Hector stirred uneasily. Automatically Geoffroi soothed him.

He didn't understand.

They were saying someone had tried to kill King John, but how could that be right? The King was already dead. Geoffroi's father had told him so.

But someone was dead. Someone lay, broad-shouldered, big, huddled in a still heap in the mud.

That someone, Geoffroi thought, *is either my kindly, affectionate, funny uncle, or my beloved father . . .*

And I can't see which one.

Although he pushed, shoved, shouted and finally screamed, using his elbows, his fists and even his feet, the great throng of people, high on the thrill of sudden, violent, dramatic death right in their midst, wouldn't move out of the way and let him through.

There was sudden hectic activity down on the road.

Geoffroi spun round to look.

Two riders were about to leave. One was heading back the way they'd just come, to Newark. The other was facing south.

Someone called out to him. 'He lives in Kent, quite near Tonbridge. Go to the sheriff there and make sure he understands he must take the news to the family!'

'Tonbridge,' the rider repeated.

Then he raced away.

For some moments Geoffroi stared dully after him.

Then he bowed his head as the pain engulfed him.

In the Sanctuary on the edge of the great forest, Helewise was awake soon after dawn. There were too many anxieties crowding her mind to allow much sleep. She lay still in the soft, dim light, thinking.

Late the previous evening she had had some visitors: her son Dominic and her grandson, Ralf.

It was a huge relief to see the young man. She'd been told of the fall of Dover Castle, and, in common with the rest of the family, had been very worried about Ralf's fate.

Having given her a very tight hug, Ralf told her what had happened.

'Hubert de Burgh wrote to the King for permission to surrender once he knew it was hopeless,' he said, 'but he anticipated the King's approval and moved as much stuff out as he could before Prince Louis could get his hands on it. Then he told all of us who could walk, and who weren't involved with someone really important, whose absence the French prince would notice, or else engaged in some vital task, to get out.'

'But how could goods and men leave the castle if it was besieged?' she had asked.

'That's one of the great advantages of being inside!' Ralf said. 'You get to know the place, especially when you're shut up and can't go out. Beneath the castle there's a maze of tunnels in the chalk cliffs, and thankfully Prince Louis didn't know about them. I was with a group that emerged right down on the shore, and then we managed to get a fisherman to take us along to Rye, and I walked home.'

Ralf, then, was safe, she thought now, and the relief flooded her again. And, from what Dominic had told her of the rest of the family, everyone else was all right, too. There had been many more unexpected guests at the House in the Woods, according to Dominic, and it seemed to have become a focus for the archers and the other fighters in the forest.

I am all the more glad, Helewise thought rather disloyally, *that I am here.*

It was still early, but, having gone through her other concerns, all that remained was Josse. Lying in bed worrying about him was not helpful, so she quietly got up, went outside, had a quick wash and put on her outer garments. She built up the fire and put water on to boil. As Hadil began to stir, Helewise had a hot drink and some thin porridge ready for her.

Hadil took the drink and gratefully finished it, but she ate only a couple of spoonfuls of the porridge. Then, eyeing Helewise closely, she said, 'Do not reprimand me this morning for not eating, my lady, for you, I perceive, have eaten even less than I.'

Helewise bowed her head. 'Yes.'

'What ails you?' Hadil asked kindly. 'You are tired?'

'No, not really,' Helewise replied. Then, in a burst of confidence, she said, 'I am very anxious because someone I love very much is far away and I have had no news.' As soon as the words were out of her mouth, she wished she could have pulled them back, for wasn't Hadil anxious for precisely the same reason? 'I'm sorry,' she added quickly, 'I shouldn't have spoken, for you have your own worries.'

Hadil nodded slowly. 'Indeed, which is why I understand yours so well.' She reached behind her, trying to pile up her pillows, and Helewise hurried to help. 'That's better, thank you. Now, the best thing for both of us, I think, is for me to continue my tale, so, if you are ready, I shall begin.'

Helewise, who had been thinking of ways to encourage Hadil to do just that, could only nod and say, 'Please do.'

'Well, now, I told you, did I not, that the treasure stolen by Fadila's father was soon deemed to be dangerously evil, and so he and his family divided it into five lots and disposed of it?'

'You did,' Helewise agreed.

'Good. They disposed of it very profitably, as I believe I also said. But then, as the years went by, gradually it became clear exactly what they had unleashed upon the world.' She paused, frowning, as if searching for the right words. 'It was as if possession of any part of the treasure, even if it were to be melted down and made into a new object, carried the taint. Over time, dreadful tales reached the ears of the family, and the common feature was always the same: betrayal, leading to despair, destruction and death. And so, as first Fadila's children and then her grandchildren grew to maturity, they conferred together and came reluctantly to the realization that it was up to them to put right what Fadila's father and brother had put wrong.'

Helewise frowned. 'What a burden that was. It was brave of them all to accept the responsibility, for it must have been a heavy one.'

Hadil gave her a long look. 'It was. As I was about to say,' she went on before Helewise could ask more questions, 'Fadila's daughter Basma and her son – he too was called Faruq, and he was my father – began the long toil. They did well, at great cost to themselves, and by the time it was my turn to take up the responsibility, only

299

two items remained. One I found and destroyed.' The memory of pain crossed her face. 'Then, when my son was old enough, I told him the family's tale – or rather, I should say, as much of it as I thought he ought to know – just as my father told it to me; like me, my father, my grandmother and my great-grandmother, he accepted the burden. We had managed to trace what had become of the final fifth of the rogue Hospitaller's treasure, and together we set out on the long, long trail to find it.'

She paused, then said meekly, 'May I have a cup of water? It is thirsty work, telling tales.'

'Of course.' Helewise leapt up.

'Although my ancestors were called upon to make many journeys in the fulfilment of their mission,' Hadil went on, sipping her water, 'just as my son and I have done, it became clear, as he and I began our own search, that a part of the treasure did not immediately leave the area in which the knight had originally dug it up. In order to explain, I shall digress and tell you a little of the history of the country that is my home.' She sipped again. 'Around the end of the eleventh century, a great new force of western lords descended on the region. One great lord was known as Hugh the Devil, and he was the sixth duke of that name who originated from a place in France known as Lusignan. He was the leader of a family of power, wealth and influence who were determined to push themselves to the forefront in Outremer.' She smiled wryly. 'Outremer is what these outsiders called my land, for, to them, it was over the sea. Ourselves, we call it by a different name.'

She did not say what the name was.

'Hugh the Devil sought power,' she continued. 'He craved it, coveted it, and at the thought of it his blood flowed hot, as does that of other men at the sight of gold, or a beautiful woman, or fine wine, or a table groaning with food. He did not much care how his power was achieved, and when a sorcerer offered to make him a magic silver goblet that would lay low his enemies, he didn't even stop to think but commissioned it there and then.'

'A *sorcerer?*' Helewise was greatly surprised. Hadil had been speaking calmly and reasonably, and the sudden mention of magic and sorcery, casually thrown into her narrative, was unsettling. Especially as, judging by her expression, she appeared to accept such things as totally believable.

Hadil ignored the interruption. 'Hugh the Devil's goblet was a beautiful thing. It was made of ancient silver; silver which had already been in the world and through men's hands for a very long time and in several different guises, now melted down and formed into this new shape. It consisted of a wide, shallow bowl set upon a graceful stem that opened out into a firm, weighty base. The rim of the cup was set with opals: milk-white opals in which flashes of brilliant blue, pink and green lay hidden; and fiery orange opals which, when they caught the light, almost hurt the eye with their brightness. Because Hugh

301

had caused it to be made, it became known as the Devil's Cup.'

The Devil's Cup. Helewise repeated the words silently. They sent a shiver through her.

'Not that Hugh ever used it himself, of course. He was far too canny for that since, if truth were told, he was a little in awe of the sorcerer and his magic, and did not entirely trust him not to have imbued the cup with the power to harm its owner as well as its owner's enemies.'

She stretched, wincing. Then, before Helewise could offer help, went on. 'Hugh the Devil hadn't got where he was by taking risks. Once the cup was safely in his possession, he ordered one of his most trusted knights to dispose of the sorcerer.'

And 'dispose of', Helewise thought but didn't say, was undoubtedly a euphemism for 'kill'.

'In time, the power of Hugh the Devil's family in the east waned, along with that of all the other western lords, and eventually they all returned to where they had come from. Hugh the Devil's descendants went back to France: to their ancient lands in Poitou, to the north-east of Bordeaux and the wide estuary where two great rivers combine and spill into the sea. There they picked up the reins of power as if they had never been away. The Devil's Cup, naturally, went with them.' She glanced at Helewise, her eyes narrowed. 'And, in time, they found the perfect use for it.'

And, as she revealed what that use was, at last Helewise began to understand.

*   *   *

It was evening.

Helewise stood in the little clearing outside the Sanctuary. Hadil was dying, and both of them knew it. For now, she was as comfortable as Helewise could make her, and had fallen into a deep sleep. Although Helewise tried to spend as much time as she could sitting beside her, holding her hand and speaking calmly and quietly, occasionally she needed to take a short break. She wondered if Tiphaine would be back before nightfall. The old herbalist had been at the Sanctuary earlier, willingly taking on the care of the small stream of visitors while Helewise stayed with her patient.

Hadil will be dead within the week, Helewise thought.

It was as if, she reflected, having told her tale and made absolutely sure that it would be passed on to Faruq when he returned, there was nothing left for the tired old woman to live for.

I will stay with her until the end, Helewise resolved.

She was taking a last deep breath of the clean forest air, about to return inside, when she heard someone approaching along the path beneath the trees, from the direction of the House in the Woods.

Josse, she thought. Her heart gave a leap of joy.

But it was not Josse who appeared in the clearing. It was Gervase de Gifford. His face was grave.

Helewise made herself stay calm. There might be many innocent reasons for the sheriff of

Tonbridge to ride over to see the family at the House in the Woods – although just then she couldn't think of a single one – and he had undoubtedly come on to see her for mere courtesy's sake.

But she knew, even before he had spoken a word, that he brought terrible news.

He hurried forward, taking her hands in his. Hers suddenly felt very cold.

'My lady, word has come from the north, swiftly relayed via a series of fast horsemen,' he began, his clear green eyes fixed on hers. 'A rider arrived early this morning, and I undertook to pass his news on to you.' He drew a breath. 'It is very bad, my lady.'

'Tell me.' She was quite surprised that her voice was steady.

'Men have reported that one of the two big brothers from Acquin has been killed.'

One of the two big brothers from Acquin . . . At first she heard the words with absolutely no comprehension.

Then she understood. *'Which one?'* The words flew out before he had finished speaking.

He held her hands more tightly, and his taut, strained face was close to hers. 'Nobody knows. The report is confused – the messenger set out too quickly, it appears, hurrying off before the picture was clear.'

'But . . . but how could they *not know*?' she whispered.

'I have been asking myself that all the way over here,' he replied. 'The conditions were appalling – mist, very sodden ground, extremely difficult going. It's hard to determine exactly what happened, because the message has been passed on from messenger to messenger several times and it's obviously become distorted. As far as I can tell, the two of them – Josse and Yves – were bringing the King's horse back to London, and—'

'To London?'

His eyes fell. 'My lady, I should explain. King John is—'

'Not *now*,' she interrupted sharply.

He understood.

'One of them, Josse or Yves, was riding King John's horse, but we don't know which one,' he said. 'Seen from a distance, or even from close to, they are very alike, those two. But it seems he was mistaken for the King – because he was riding the King's horse – and someone shot him.'

Hope flared. 'He may not be dead!'

'He is, Helewise,' Gervase insisted gently. 'The arrow was very well aimed and pierced the heart. It would have been very quick,' he added, as if this would console her.

'But . . .' She was struggling to understand. 'But why were they bringing the King's horse south? Did the King not require it himself?'

Gervais hesitated. Then he said, 'The King is dead.'

Abruptly Helewise couldn't feel her legs. She slumped, and Gervais caught her and supported her, reaching out for Tiphaine's little stool, in its place beside the door of the Sanctuary, and helping her to sit down. Presently Gervais placed a mug of cold water in her hand, and obediently she drank some.

After some time she whispered, 'When will I know?'

And, his voice breaking, he said, 'As soon as word reaches us down in Tonbridge, I will come back. You have my word.'

She looked up at him. *I should thank him for taking the time and trouble to seek me out*, she thought. 'Thank you,' she said politely.

Gervais had tears in his eyes. 'Oh, my dear lady, no need for thanks! If Josse is dead, I . . .' But, perhaps realizing such speculation wasn't tactful, he stopped. After a little time, he said, more calmly, 'Will you go back to the House in the Woods? The family should perhaps be together, so that you all may comfort each other.'

But she shook her head. 'I should go back, yes, Gervais.' She gave him a tiny smile. 'But I cannot.' The prospect of having them all weeping, worrying, grieving, speculating, draining her, needing her strength when she had no strength to give, was quite appalling. She looked straight into his eyes. 'If Josse is dead, the greater part of me will go with him. Until I know—' she choked back a sob – 'I do not want company.'

'But you—'

She held up a firm hand, stopping him. 'I have a patient to care for.' She indicated inside the Sanctuary to the sleeping Hadil. 'Tiphaine stays here with me from time to time. She and my patient,' she concluded in the sort of tone she had once used with recalcitrant novices, 'are all the people I want.'

After a moment he gave her a look of total understanding. Then, getting up, he gently kissed her cheek and hurried away.

Nineteen

Time passed. Helewise, not knowing if it was hours or days, lived in a sort of trance. Tiphaine had returned, and now she stayed at the Sanctuary, not speaking often, sharing the care of Hadil, a quiet, solid presence which Helewise discovered she needed as she needed to breathe.

Hadil was still alive, although now she rarely woke from her deep sleep. It was, Helewise thought, watching her, more like unconsciousness. The coma that led gently to death.

When her son comes home, Helewise thought, *I will tell him what she told me.*

There was no more news.

She didn't know how to endure the agonizing wait. Other than the silent and rock-like Tiphaine, there was nobody she could lean on. They were, she realized as if it were a revelation, all used to leaning on *her*.

And then, in the long hours between midnight and dawn one night, she suddenly thought, *I can lean on God*, and then was amazed at herself that she hadn't thought it before.

But I am not myself, she concluded. *I haven't*

slept, I have barely eaten, and then only when Tiphaine refused to take no for an answer.

God, she felt, would understand.

As soon as it was light enough to make out the path through the forest, she tapped Tiphaine on the shoulder and said very softly, 'I am sorry to wake you but I need to tell you I shall be absent for a while. Will you stay with Hadil?'

'Of course,' Tiphaine murmured. Then, turning on her side, she slept again.

Bless you, dear sister, Helewise thought, *for not asking me where I'm going.*

But perhaps Tiphaine knew.

She walked the path without having to think about it, one foot falling softly after the other, just as she had done countless times over the years. Presently the trees began to grow less densely, and then the vale opened up before her and there was Hawkenlye Abbey, the lamps of one or two early risers penetrating the dim light of dawn.

She did not go on down to the abbey. Crossing the patch of grassy, open space, she opened the heavy door and slipped into St Edmund's Chapel. In front of the large block of sandstone that formed the altar, her eyes on the simple wooden cross that was the only ornament, she sank on to her knees.

'I do not have the words to pray, dear Lord,' she said aloud. 'I can only beg you to be here with me, hold me up, until . . .'

But she couldn't manage the rest of the sentence. Not that it mattered, since she was quite sure God knew anyway.

* * *

After a time, she realized she was no longer alone. Someone was moving very quietly up the aisle towards her, and presently this person knelt down at her side.

'Do you remember,' Caliste's soft voice asked, 'how you and I first met?'

And Helewise, without opening her eyes, for she knew full well who it was, said, 'Of course I do. You were little Peg, left as a baby in a bundle on the doorstep of the kind Hursts one night, named and cared for as one of their own by that kind-hearted family, and you stayed there with them, obedient and hard-working, until you were fourteen, whereupon you presented your-self at Hawkenlye Abbey and asked to be taken in as a postulant.'[4]

'Remember how you felt?' Caliste asked softly. 'You thought I was far too young and that I didn't have a vocation.'

Helewise smiled despite herself. 'I also thought you were far too beautiful and utterly different from practically everyone else I knew.' *As indeed you were*, she thought, her eyes open now and staring into Caliste's midsummer-blue-twilight gaze. *You were a child of the forest, and the gods that your ancestors worshipped predated the loving God you have given your life to by many thousands of years.*

But what an exceptional nun Caliste had become.

Now Caliste put her arms round Helewise, rocking her gently.

'I pray and I pray,' Helewise whispered, 'but

[4] See *Ashes of the Elements*.

309

I don't really know what I pray for, because if it is Yves who is dead, then I know that Josse will have lost something of himself and he'll never really recover, and if it's Josse, then I-I . . .'

She couldn't go on.

At long last, her tears began to flow and, once she had started, she didn't seem to be able to stop.

And other nuns had now joined them, coming quietly, soft-footedly into the little chapel.

Sister Liese the infirmarer. Sister Madelin, middle-aged now, composed, tall and thin, with wiry strength. Sister Philippa the artist, who long ago made the *Hawkenlye Herbal*, beautiful and graceful in youth, serene and lovely in age. Sister Bernadine, in charge of the abbey's small collection of precious manuscripts, austere, pale, detached.

In a show of such gentle, perfectly judged kindness that it made her weep the more, they came and quietly gathered round her, so that she was enfolded by their love. And Caliste said, 'Dearest Helewise, it is done. Whatever has happened, it is over and cannot be changed. Let God hold you up, for he knows of your pain and has you in the palm of his hand. And, just in case you can't quite feel him, we are here, his representatives, and we will support you.'

Meggie and Faruq were waiting for a boat to take them across the Thames estuary. It was evening, and Meggie had discovered she couldn't bear the thought of settling for the night on the

310

northern shore. Ever since Newark, she'd been haunted by a growing dread. Something was wrong, and the desperate anxiety was robbing her of sleep and had totally taken away her appetite. Had it not been for Faruq's coaxing, she wouldn't have eaten at all.

He stood silently beside her now, holding the horses. They were on a low promontory leading out into the estuary, on one side of which was a wooden pontoon where the ferries berthed. One was approaching, and she was preparing the words with which to persuade the ferryman that he must do one last crossing before he went home for his supper.

She knew she was being unreasonable. They'd passed several possible places to spend the night – a tavern a few miles short of the coast had looked and smelled particularly inviting – but she had insisted they go on. Turning now to look at him, she said, 'I'm sorry. I can't explain, but I just know I have to get home.'

He nodded.

The ferry had tied up. It was a broad, squat boat, riding low in the water. The passengers alighted and, just as Meggie stepped forward to speak to the ferryman, a party of half a dozen riders came clattering on to the pontoon, the leader demanding loudly that they be ferried to the Kent shore straight away. The ferryman sighed and stood back for them to come aboard, and Meggie, Faruq and the horses followed.

Some time later, in the soft light of their little fire, Faruq said, 'We are alike, Meggie, for both

311

of us accept the truth of things we sense as well as that which we see, hear, smell and can touch.'

She realized straight away what he meant. 'Yes,' she agreed. 'And thank you, in case I haven't said it before, for not even asking me to explain why I am so driven to get home.'

'You know somehow that something has happened,' he said calmly, 'just as, when we had at last arrived in the area where the King was, I knew that evil was close.'

'And you were right,' she said quietly.

He was staring at his pack, lying beside him in the shadows. 'I want to look at it again,' he whispered.

She knew she should have stopped him, but her desire to stare again at that malign object was far too strong. 'Go on, then.'

He opened his pack and took out a small bundle. He unwrapped the length of cloth, fold after fold dropping on the grass. Then, with a gesture worthy of a priest at the altar, he placed what was concealed in the cloth on a flat stone beside the fire.

It was the perfect place for it, for the flames seemed to set the jewels on fire.

She said, 'It's hard to believe how malicious it is.'

He nodded. 'Yes. But you proved it. Back at Newark, when first you showed it to me, we put water in it and you dipped in that beautiful sapphire.'

'The Eye of Jerusalem. Yes, that's right, I did.' She didn't want to think about what had happened. Out here in the darkness, all alone but for Faruq, it was too frightening. 'Put it away,' she said abruptly.

She guessed he, too, was scared. He wrapped the beautiful object in its cloth and shoved it back inside his pack.

In the morning, they rose early and, after a swift and fairly meagre breakfast, set off south.

Others making the same journey ahead of them were already home.

She was not at the House in the Woods. When at last he and Geoffroi rode into the courtyard, the family and the household who flew out to welcome them, to fall on them with love and grief, told them she was at the Sanctuary.

Pausing only as long as good manners and kindness demanded, he left his horse with Geoffroi and walked on.

My brother is dead, he thought. He had been thinking the same thing constantly, all the long way back. *I have loved him all my life, although our lives took us in different directions and we did not see as much of each other as we'd have liked. Until I knelt there in the mud beside his fallen body and saw that there was no hope, I had never realized how much I am going to miss him.*

He increased his pace.

It was evening, and the autumn night was fast closing in. A light burned in the Sanctuary and the door stood slightly ajar.

She must have heard his approach.

Suddenly the door was flung right open, and light spilled out into the clearing. She called out in a tight, strained voice, 'Who is it?'

313

He advanced.

But of course she couldn't see him properly, for he was in darkness and she had only just emerged from the light of the interior.

She took a step, two steps. He could see her face now. The agony of this interminable time of his return was written plainly. She looked as she would no doubt look when she was a very old woman.

He said softly, 'It's me.'

And then she was in his arms, weeping, laughing, hugging him so tightly that he could barely breathe.

She said, 'Oh, my dearest love, your brother. Dear Yves, and you loved each other so long and so well. Oh, I'm so, so sorry.'

He gave a muffled moan of pain. The loss was so raw, and kindness made the grief overflow. He didn't speak, and she reached up and put her hand on his cheek, feeling his tears.

Then, as if she could bear no more, she buried her face in his chest and wept.

She wept for a long time.

It was, he thought with a puzzled wonder, a sort of breakdown.

And it formed itself into the final factor in the decision he had been beginning to make ever since he had left home all those days and weeks ago; the decision that had slowly and steadily been hardening since his beloved brother fell dead in the mud beside him with a perfectly placed arrow in his generous and loving heart.

Now, at last, he recognized that it was irrevocable.

'I'm home to stay,' he said in her ear. 'We're old, my dearest love, you and I, and, even given good health and enough to eat, we won't have that many more years together.'

She raised her wet face and looked straight into his eyes. 'Do you mean it?' she demanded. 'Oh, Josse, don't make the promise if you won't be able to keep it.'

'I do mean it,' he said, so roughly that it sounded like a curse. 'I'll not leave home again.'

Twenty

'I think,' Josse said as, having called for quiet, he stood in the circle of his household, 'that we have a story to piece together, and that, if we are patient and allow each one their turn, we shall succeed and, at last, understand.' There were a few murmurs of assent. 'But first, please join me as I raise my cup to the dead.'

There was a noise of benches and stools dragging on the stone flags of his hall as everyone stood up.

'To King John, God rest him,' Josse said.

'King John,' echoed up into the high roof.

'And to his successor,' Gervase de Gifford added. 'To King Henry.' Once more the voices repeated the toast.

It was Faruq who spoke next. 'To my mother, Hadil,' he said, his voice strong. Hadil had almost managed to last until her son's return, dying in the late afternoon of the day before. Faruq had been in time to arrange her burial, at sunset of the next day, attended only by Helewise and Tiphaine, the women who had cared for her so well. Afterwards, he and Helewise had talked alone long into the night.

Finally, Josse stepped forward again. 'To my brother,' he said, his voice breaking.

This time the cups and mugs were raised in silence. Yves's death was too recent and sharp a grief, and nobody trusted their voice.

Yves's body had been brought home to the House in the Woods. Josse had worried anxiously about where his brother should rest, and said several times to his kin that he ought to take him back to Acquin.

It was Geoffroi who persuaded him otherwise. 'He came to find you, Father,' he said. 'His wife was dead, his sons managed Acquin well enough without him, and he chose to live out his life with you.' Before Josse could reply he went on, 'When you die, you'll be buried at Hawkenlye, won't you?'

'So I hope and pray,' Josse replied.

'Then Uncle Yves should be there waiting for you.'

Yves had been buried that morning, and the Hawkenlye priest had conducted his funeral in the abbey church. The numbers who had turned out to say farewell to Josse's brother had been astonishing and, even amid his sorrow, Josse had found comfort.

Slowly he sank down into his big wooden

chair, and, taking this as a signal, everyone else began to move.

Several people, having come up to speak to him, slipped away, for they had nothing to contribute to the story Josse needed so much to understand. Gervase was one of the last.

'I am sorry for your loss,' he said. His voice was stiff.

'Thank you,' Josse replied. Then, catching the sheriff's expression, he said, 'Gervase, I know that, since that business with Lord Benedict, relations between our two families – between us – have been awkward.'[5]

Gervase gave a rueful laugh. 'Yes, so they have.'

'Let us put all that in the past, where it belongs,' Josse went on. 'You came here to my family, to Helewise, when you all thought – er, when you heard the news – and I know how much your presence meant to them. Life's too short to let a good friend turn into an enemy.' He stood up, holding out his hand, and Gervase took it.

'It is indeed,' Gervase agreed. He smiled. Then, with a bow, he turned and strode out of the hall.

Geoffroi and Faruq drew up a couple of benches on either side of Josse's chair and then the two of them, together with Helewise and Meggie, sat down. Josse turned to Faruq. 'I think that, if you feel able, it is for you to begin,' he said. 'I understand from what I have already been told that you were vowed to silence by your late

[5] See *The Winter King*.

mother, and felt you could reveal very little of your purpose in coming to England. If you feel that her death releases you from your vow, we who have been bound up so closely in your quest would very much like to hear your story.'

Faruq sat with his head bowed. Slowly he nodded. 'You have every right, sir,' he replied. Then, looking up, he stared straight into Josse's eyes. 'My mother did indeed make me swear to keep the secret. But . . .' He seemed on the point of saying something more – something that, from his expression, affected him deeply – but with a small shake of his head he said, 'This is my tale, and I'll tell it as briefly as I can. Some of you—' he glanced at Helewise – 'know some of it; indeed, may know more than I do.' He smiled grimly. 'I come from Outremer, and my family's home is Jerusalem. There, nearly a hundred years ago, a girl was raped by a member of the Order of the Knights Hospitaller. Not long afterwards, when he was being punished for another crime, he was put to digging graves outside the city walls, and he dug up some treasure. He hid it, then went back by night to fetch it. As he crept away, the father, brother and cousin of the raped girl set upon him, and he and the cousin were killed. The father searched the body and stole the treasure, but very soon he and his family realized it carried a stain of evil. They divided it into five lots and got rid of it. The girl grew up to marry and have children, and, as the years passed and evil tales reached their ears, her descendants came to accept that, by disposing of the treasure – to their own great financial

318

advantage, it must be said – they had unwittingly released a terrible evil, and it was their responsibility to rid the world of it. I do not know the details of what happened to four of the five lots, for my mother never told me. But it was her task, and therefore mine as her son, to ensure the discovery and the destruction of the fifth and last portion.'

He paused, clearing his throat. Meggie got up and, pouring wine into a cup, handed it to him. He murmured his thanks and drank a few sips.

'We – or, I should say, my mother – knew that the last portion of the treasure had gone into the manufacture of an object made to the order of one of the Frankish knights of Jerusalem, a man who came from the Lusignan family. Like most noble families who traced their rise to power and wealth to the early tenth century, the Lusignans of Poitou included both the good and the bad. Hugh II Carus, called the Kind, built the castle at Lusignan, but one of his successors, Hugh IV Brunus, was a hectic, turbulent lord who made up his mind that his family were too good to be small-time lords and needed a bigger stage. It was he who began his family's rise to prominence, first in Europe and then in Outremer. He was followed by Hugh V the Fair and Pious, and he by Hugh VI the Devil, whose nickname speaks for itself. He threw himself into the First Crusade, and his reputation was dark. He wanted to look like the important lord he knew himself to be, and the wealth and luxury of his household in the East grew rapidly. He purchased locally made luxury items, their cost and quality increasing as his wealth grew.'

He paused to sip more wine. Josse, glancing at Helewise, was about to speak – to make some comment about the Crusades being violent times – but she shook her head.

'Hugh the Devil commissioned the manufacture of a very beautiful silver chalice decorated with opals,' Faruq went on. 'Both the milk-white sort whose depths include flashes of vivid colour, and the brilliant orange fire opals. But the beautiful cup was not for Hugh the Devil's personal use. In fact, the very opposite was true, for the cup was dangerous.'

'But I have—' Josse began.

'Let him finish, Josse,' Helewise said quietly. He met her eyes, and she sent him a loving smile.

'In time,' Faruq said, 'Hugh the Devil's descendants abandoned their rich and profitable lands in Outremer and returned to Lusignan, and he took the silver cup with him. We can't say for certain, but it seems likely that, being both beautiful to look at and a highly efficient and subtle weapon, Hugh kept it close and, when he sensed death was near, made sure to pass it on to his heir. With a full and very careful account of what it could do,' he added grimly.

Josse couldn't contain himself any longer. 'And this cup was what you and your mother came here to find?'

'It was,' Faruq said calmly.

'And you . . . but you . . .' He took a breath and began again. 'You'd better tell us, I think.'

Faruq smiled faintly. 'My mother and I landed

320

in Marseilles, and we proceeded north into the Lusignan lands. We found it relatively easy to make our enquiries, for one or two of the Lusignan family had intermarried with people of our race and we were welcomed as compatriots in a foreign land. Nobody suspected our true purpose, and in the end it was simply a matter of asking about the Devil's Cup. But it was no longer there.'

'Where had it gone?' Geoffroi asked. Josse looked at him. Of all of them, Geoffroi knew the least, and Josse well understood his puzzled expression.

Faruq turned to him. 'I know where it went although not why,' he said.

'I believe I can help,' Helewise said. She shot a sympathetic glance at Faruq. 'Your mother spoke at length to me before she died. She was all too well aware that she had kept much of the tale from you, and she told it to me in the expectation that I would pass it on to you.' She hesitated, and Josse had the impression she was collecting her thoughts.

'More than a century after Hugh VI acquired his cup, his successor Hugh IX le Brun became betrothed to Isabella of Angoulême, the young daughter of Count Aymar Taillefer. But she was stolen away from her bridegroom by John of England, newly crowned and in search of a new and more exciting wife. It was an outrageous act and ultimately an unwise one, for by his action John had aroused the fury of two powerful families, the Lusignans and the counts of Angoulême, and they united in enmity towards him.'

'As if he didn't have enough enemies already,' Josse observed softly.

'But what happened to the Devil's Cup?' Geoffroi persisted.

'I will explain as well as I can,' Helewise said, 'although much of what I say is but Hadil's conjecture.' She paused. 'We do know that somehow the Devil's Cup travelled from Poitou to England, and it was Hadil's suggestion that somebody in one of those two wealthy, influential and tetchy families – it was probably one of the Lusignans, who were said to have felt King John's insult the more keenly – decided to take revenge. He – or perhaps she – managed to add one more precious and glittering item to the vast array of gifts included in Isabella's baggage train when she set off for married life with her new bridegroom.'

'The Devil's Cup,' breathed Geoffroi.

Josse was looking at Faruq in admiration. 'Your mother discovered all this?'

'Obviously, yes,' Faruq said. He smiled. 'She was a clever woman, and also an extremely determined one. She took her responsibility very seriously.'

'So Queen Isabella had the cup, you're saying.' Meggie was frowning. 'Did she know what it was? What it could do?'

Helewise spread her hands. 'Who can say? Hadil did not wish to give a definite opinion, although she pointed out that the cup had been in the family of her former fiancé for a long time, so perhaps she had heard tell of it.'

Meggie was silent for a few moments, still

322

frowning, obviously thinking. Then she said slowly, 'The Queen comes across this beautiful, dangerous object that one of the family she was meant to have married into has so thoughtfully put in with her vast array of wedding presents. Why did they do that? Did they want to harm her as a punishment for marrying John instead of Hugh?'

'I should not think that is likely,' Faruq replied, 'for everyone would have known that girls have no say in the choice of their bridegroom.' His eyes were fixed on Meggie's, and Josse, watching intently, sensed a power of some sort between them. *Interesting*, he thought.

Meggie grinned. 'Go on, then. Tell us what you *do* think is likely.'

Faruq returned her smile. 'I would rather defer to the lady here' – he indicated Helewise – 'so that she may voice my mother's thoughts.'

'I will,' Helewise said. 'Hadil told me that she had originally believed that Isabella had no idea what she had been given, and what it could do. From all we are told, anyway, she did not object to being married to John of England and, as a newly wedded wife and – after a few years – a mother too, she would have had no need of the Devil's Cup anyway. No doubt it was relegated to the back of the cupboard and, for a long time, overlooked.'

She turned to Faruq. 'So you and Hadil came on to England from Poitou,' she said, 'very anxious because you believed Queen Isabella was in danger, and hoping that by finding the Queen you would also find and be able to destroy the Devil's Cup.'

'Yes, my lady,' Faruq said politely. 'That was about all I knew. But it wasn't with her, at Corfe Castle. I asked, and I was told it had probably been sent off with all the other luxury household objects in the King's baggage.'

'But if she did know, did she . . .?' Geoffroi began. But, as if the thought was too dreadful to voice, he stopped.

'Did she, knowing what the Devil's Cup could do, deliberately make sure it was packed among his luggage?' Josse said it for him. With a snort of anger he added, 'Little good it did her, for it was silver and he was used to gold. He told me himself how much he treasured his gold cup, which had been a present from his mother when . . .'

Suddenly he stopped.

Nobody said a word.

'But he lost his precious gold cup when the wagon was overturned in the water,' he said.

The silence extended. Josse, looking round at the semi-circle of faces, wondered if they were all asking themselves the same questions he was.

Did Isabella know what the Devil's Cup could do?

Did she really want to kill him?

But to make such accusations would be treason, he thought. Isabella was no longer Queen, but she was mother to the new King.

Just in case any of these people he cared for so deeply might be having any ideas about justice, he said very quietly, 'All that we have just said remains here, within these four walls.

324

Each of you must give me your most solemn word never to speak of it to anyone else.'

One by one they all did as he commanded.

Not one of them needed to ask why.

And Josse thought, *This is not the moment to raise that dreadful suspicion, even if doing so wasn't so dangerous to my family. Now that John is gone* – he felt the familiar stab of pain – *it is everyone's task to ensure that the transference of power is effected as calmly and swiftly as possible.*

It was likely, he reflected, that the French invasion would quickly fizzle out. The barons had no argument with John's heir, and surely they too would want peace restored and Louis gone. Without their support, Louis would very soon see there was no future in staying.

There will be peace under the new king, Josse thought. Perhaps there would even be certainty and prosperity, which was more than his father managed. Was it really the time to upset the fragile promise of the new regime with a terrible accusation based on nothing more than an ancient legend and a lot of speculation?

No. It wasn't.

After some time Josse emerged from his reverie. Glancing at Meggie, he said, 'I think that the moment has come for us all to see it, don't you?'

She spun round to stare at him. 'How do you know we've got it?'

'I didn't until a short while ago. But when Faruq described the cup, I was about to say that I'd seen it, only Helewise interrupted.' He turned to Helewise and gave her a smile. 'I noticed that Faruq instinctively put a hand down to that pack, lying on the floor beside him, and I guessed.'

'It is there, yes,' Faruq said. He unfastened the pack and extracted something wrapped in white cloth. He unwrapped it and, following Josse's pointing hand, put it down on the edge of the hearth where they could all see it.

'You went back for it, Meggie?' Josse asked. 'You risked so much?'

She must have detected the reproach in his voice. Spinning round to meet his eyes, she said, 'Yes. Perhaps it was stupid, and it's true that the penalty for being caught stealing it, or even with it in my possession, would have been severe.'

'They'd have hanged you, and him too, probably.' Josse glared at Faruq.

'Don't blame him, Father, it was entirely my idea,' Meggie said sharply. 'And, as to why I was prepared to take the risk, it was because I didn't know why the King was dead.'

'Because he had dysentery!' Josse shouted. 'He'd been ill for days, and exhausted, and so many men had turned against him, and . . .' He found he couldn't go on. He dropped his face in his hands.

He sensed someone beside him. He felt his daughter's soft hair brush his hands and she said, so softly that he thought he was probably the only one to hear, 'I know you grieve for him, Father. You're not the only one, I promise you.'

Still perched on the arm of his chair, she straightened up and said, 'I'm not claiming to have an infallible cure for dysentery, but the various remedies I gave to the King ought to have afforded at least some relief. Instead, his condition became worse and worse, and I had to accept that he was dying before my eyes, despite everything I had done.'

'You're sure that's not just your pride as a healer speaking?' Geoffroi asked. Josse, wondering if she would take offence, realized immediately that she must have heard the earnest honesty behind the question.

'I did wonder, but I'm pretty sure it's not,' she said. 'But, anyway, I just had to know. I'd seen him drinking from that silver cup. He didn't eat, he didn't drink much, and that was the only vessel that he used. So, after he died and when everyone was racing round like ants in a ruined anthill, I went back and took it.'

She got up and walked over to the hearth. Looking up, she nodded at Faruq, and he passed her a jug of water. Slowly, carefully, she poured some into the cup. 'This is good, fresh water,' she said, 'and all of us have been drinking from the jug.' She paused, then added softly, 'What happens next must therefore be caused by the silver cup.'

Then she reached inside the bodice of her gown and took out the Eye of Jerusalem.

Josse gave a soft gasp. It had been a long time since he'd seen it, and he had forgotten how lovely it was; how it caught the firelight, reflecting pools of bright blue into the air.

He watched – they all watched – as Meggie lowered the stone into the cup.

For a moment, nothing happened. 'Wait,' Meggie said softly.

Then a thin wisp of yellowish smoke rose up from the surface of the water.

Meggie lowered the Eye further under the surface.

Now the water was bubbling gently, like a pan of liquid coming to the boil. And the wisp of smoke had become an acrid, dense little cloud, and it stank of rot; of brimstone; of cunning and betrayal; of the worst of violence; of evil, deadly things.

A quiet voice – Geoffroi's – said in a tone of utter horror, 'Oh, dear God, save us!'

Josse stepped closer to him and briefly touched his shoulder. 'Steady, son.'

Geoffroi pulled away. 'But it's foul, awful!' He stared around at them with frantic eyes. 'Can't you sense it too? Something's come into the room, something dark and horrible – oh, stop it, *stop it*!'

Josse said, 'Enough,' and Meggie took the stone out of the water.

The poisonous little cloud was already beginning to disperse, and the mood of despair was lifting.

Geoffroi, embarrassed by his terror, hung his head.

But Helewise said, 'Dear Geoffroi, you only expressed what all of us were sensing, and there is no need to feel ashamed.' Raising her eyes to look at each of them in turn, she went on, 'There is a reason for our reaction and, if I may, I shall explain.' She paused, and her glance lingered on Josse. He nodded for her to go on.

'Hadil told me why it was that she and you,

Faruq, and your predecessors were willing to give their lives to retrieve every last object containing elements of the treasure that the rogue Knight Hospitaller had unearthed in the potter's field in Jerusalem, and that the father of the girl he had raped had stolen from his corpse.' She was watching Faruq closely. 'You know this?' she asked quietly. Very briefly he nodded. Then it was his turn to hang his head.

'Some might say that it can be no more than a legend,' Helewise continued, looking at Faruq with compassion, 'but then legends can sometimes be based upon fact. This legend was persistent, and the events that attached themselves to it over the years served to suggest it just might have contained an element of truth.' She paused, and Josse had the impression she was nerving herself to go on.

'Just before she died, Hadil told me about the origins of the treasure that made up a substantial part of the Devil's Cup, and where they believed it had come from.' Once again she stopped, this time reaching out a hand to Josse. He took it and instantly she clasped it so hard that he winced.

Then, her voice quite steady, she said, 'What the rogue Hospitaller dug up was the bag of coins given in payment to Judas for the betrayal of Christ.'

And on the hearth, the quiet flames reflecting in its smooth silver sides and making sparks of fire in its rich jewels, the Devil's Cup stood, its terrible power hidden, nothing more than a beautiful, precious object.

* * *

329

One by one, all of them drifted out of the hall and into the fresh air. The foul yellow cloud had long dissipated, but it was as if some lingering, faint smell was still there. As Josse left, he made sure to prop the door wide open to air the hall.

Helewise sought out Faruq. She said, 'There is one further thing I must tell you, for I promised your mother that I would.' She glanced at Meggie, standing at his side. 'It's . . . er, it's quite a personal matter.'

Faruq smiled. 'I would prefer Meggie to hear too,' he said. 'We have been through much together, and I have learned that I can trust her.'

'Very well.' Helewise drew a breath, for what she had to tell him was not easy. 'You believe, or so I understand it, that your great-great grandparents were Fadila and Zahir, who married her when she grew to maturity despite her earlier, dreadful experience.'

'Yes, that is quite right.'

She knew just by looking at his face that he had no idea what she was about to say. She gathered her courage and went on.

'Your mother told me that she had one last secret, and, although she had thought to take it to the grave with her, in the end she found she could not bear the thought of you, her beloved son, not knowing the truth.'

'Go on.' His tone was terse.

'Faruq, you have been led to believe that your great-great grandmother was little more than a child when the Hospitaller raped her, but I'm afraid that is not quite true. She was on the point of becoming a woman, and the rape took place

330

just as she was becoming fertile. She conceived a child by that evil man, and that child was your great-grandmother Basma. She was, your mother told me, eight years older than her half-brothers and sisters.'

Faruq's face was stony. He said through white lips, 'I had no idea of this.'

'Yes, so your mother said, and she told me to tell you how very sorry she was to have to break it to you.'

A strange expression was spreading over Faruq's handsome face. 'I have his blood in my veins,' he said in a voice of deep repugnance. 'That vile, evil man, who raped a child, is my ancestor.'

'Nobody has any control over their forebears,' Helewise said firmly. 'Your mother knew you would react in this way and she told me to say that she too had her time of revulsion and rejection of her own history. She overcame it, however, and so must you.' She moved closer to him, and his distress was palpable. 'This does not change you, Faruq, for you have always been the person you are now, with the forebears you now know you have.'

'But he was a terrible person.'

'Yes, he was,' Helewise replied. 'But he is dead and gone, and you must balance his evil with the good that is in all your other ancestors, those brave men and women who took on a great and dreadful task. A job,' she added, 'that, thanks to your mother and you, is now complete.'

Slowly he nodded. 'Yes,' he said. Then, with a very faint smile, 'I'm taller, broader, fairer-skinned

331

and lighter-eyed than almost everyone I know at home, as are many of the men in my close family. Now, at least, I know why.'

Then, turning to Meggie, he made her a graceful, formal bow.

'As this kind lady just pointed out,' he said gravely, 'my family's great task is now done, and I cannot tell you how relieved I am. But my own part in it could not have happened without you, Meggie. From the depths of my heart, I thank you.'

And, to judge by Meggie's expression, astonishing her as much as it did Helewise, Faruq took Meggie in his arms and kissed her.

Postscript

Jehan's forge had stood cold and dead for many weeks now. He had gone, and would never come back. Later rumours, steadily turning to legends and becoming fixed in local folklore, told of the man with the dark skin who wore his long, black hair wound up in a cloth, who had a gold hoop in one ear and whose dark eyes flashed out the fire with which he lit his furnace. He was guilty of a terrible deed, the tales said, for through his actions the beloved brother of a kind, benign giant was transfixed with an ill-placed arrow that Jehan had believed to possess magic powers, until those powers betrayed him. He could not live with his guilt. His tears of remorse fell into his furnace and made a great swirl of silvery steam, and he rose up into it and disappeared.

Perhaps Jehan Leferronier would have been gratified that history did not remember him as an evil man, only a misguided one.

The forge furnace in the old charcoal burners' camp was relit on the last day of the October that King John died. Geoffroi d'Acquin stoked it, fired it and tended it, for he had learned well from Jehan Leferronier, and was preparing to step into the footsteps of the Breton blacksmith. He would continue to provide the growing population of Hawkenlye with a smithy throughout his long life. It was his hope, as he put the flame to the wood that momentous day, that in time he would have sons and daughters who would continue the tradition.

It didn't occur to him not to think of women in that capacity, for his dear sister often worked alongside him, and she was almost as strong and as skilled as he.

The furnace had been going for some hours when those invited to attend slowly arrived in the clearing. The household from the House in the Woods were all present, from the eldest, Josse, to the youngest, the infant daughter who was Tilly and Gus's first grandchild. Ninian and Eloise came, with their children; Dominic and Paradisa; even Leofgar and Rohaise, with most of theirs. With the death of King John, rifts in many families were healing, Helewise's among them.

At the last minute, silently, unobtrusively, the abbess of Hawkenlye slipped in from the shade of the trees, the old herbalist Tiphaine just behind her.

Meggie stood beside Faruq, and he held an object in his hands. He held it up. It was utterly beautiful, but they knew now that it was also utterly evil.

The furnace was roaring now, its heart white-hot. Meggie, Geoffroi and Faruq stepped forward. Geoffroi nodded to indicate that the time was right. Faruq held the silver cup high for a long moment, and the flames sparked glittering flashes from the fire opals and, from the pale ones, lit brilliant rainbow colours of blue, green and yellow.

Then, crying out words in his own tongue, he threw the Devil's Cup into the fire.

They let the fire go out that night.

It would be the final time that this happened for many a year, but there was a reason. The evil in the silver coins that had gone into the Devil's Cup would persist for as long as those coins remained in the world, and so they raked through the ashes until every last contorted lump of metal had been found, enclosing them in a heavy old piece of sacking.

Meggie and Faruq rode to the high cliffs above the sea and Faruq hurled the sacking package into the water. It seemed to Meggie that a big wave rose up to greet it. But she might have been mistaken.

Josse d'Acquin kept his promise. He was, after all, a man who usually did.

Late in the evening of the day that Meggie and Faruq had thrown the last of the metal from the Hospitaller's tainted bag of coins into the sea, he and Helewise sat side by side by the hearth in his hall. The advancing night was chilly and the first hard frost of the autumn was predicted. Everyone else had gone. Gus, Tilly and their family were in bed, as was Geoffroi, and Meggie and Faruq had set off for the little dwelling beside the forge.

'He seems rather taken with her,' Helewise said, breaking quite a long silence.

335

Josse gave a snort that might have been interpreted to convey virtually anything.

'I think,' she said, 'you're going to have to elucidate.'

He chuckled. 'I would if I knew what it meant.'

She smiled. 'Go on with you. Tell me your opinion.'

He paused to think. 'I agree with you that Faruq is attracted to Meggie, but that's no surprise. For one thing, she's a beautiful, comely woman – aye, I know full well she's my daughter, but it doesn't alter the fact; and for another, she's just helped and supported him through this mission of his *and* the death of his mother. She's everything to him at the moment.'

'But you're not sure it will last,' she finished for him when he didn't continue.

'Who can say?' he said shortly. He didn't like to think of Meggie believing in this young man's love for her, then discovering, once she'd given him her heart, that it was only a temporary infatuation.

As if Helewise had read his mind, which wouldn't have surprised him, as she so often did, she said, 'My dearest, don't worry about Meggie. She has, I think, recently learned a very valuable lesson about herself. She was in love with Jehan Leferronier, and set up home with him believing it was what she wanted. Believing, I'm quite sure, that love would lead to commitment, marriage, children. But, once these gifts were hers for the taking, she realized that wasn't the role for her after all.'

He turned to her, astounded. 'How on earth

do you know all this? Has she been confiding in you?'

She laughed. 'I keep my eyes and ears open, Josse. And she most certainly hasn't confided in me.' She glanced at him, and something must have told her that imagining his beloved daughter spilling her heart to Helewise rather than him had cut deeply. 'If she were to confide in anyone – which, in truth, I can't really see her doing – it would be you.'

He knew he shouldn't have been as pleased as he was with her reply. 'Go on,' he said.

'I think, for what it's worth, that just now Meggie is enjoying being with Faruq. They've shared a great deal. She is far more affected by the death of the King than she is admitting, and the fact that Faruq was there with her means that he is important to her at present.'

'D'you think he'll stay?'

She shrugged. 'Who knows? Meggie will survive, whether he does or not.' She hesitated, as if not certain whether to continue.

But it was his turn to read her thoughts. He decided to say it for her. 'She's like her mother,' he said very quietly.

And Helewise murmured, 'She is.'

He stared out at the flagged floor on the far side of the hearth. There, just there, warm and snug in a pile of furs, he and Joanna had first made love. Images flashed through his mind, and for a while he was back there in the past. It might have been that very night that Meggie had been conceived.

Joanna was gone, but her spirit lingered. Quite

often he sensed her presence, and always, always, she was smiling, enfolding him with love, giving her blessing on his life.

Love doesn't die, she had said to him the last time they had met as living, breathing human beings. *That is the one rule of the universe that cannot change.*

He smiled at the memory. *How right you were, sweeting*, he thought.

She lingered there with him for some time more. Then quietly, gently, she slipped from his mind and was gone.

Beside him was the woman he had loved for as long as he could remember. He'd loved her before Joanna, all through the turbulent years when Joanna had been a part of his very soul, and she had been there when Joanna had departed.

He turned to look at her, but she was gazing down into the gently dying fire.

He reached out and took her hand.

'I meant what I said, you know,' he said. His voice sounded gruff.

She smiled. 'Which particular bit?'

'You know full well,' he said reprovingly.

'Yes, but tell me anyway.'

'I'm not going adventuring again. I went this time because King John sent me a summons and he included a note just for me. I couldn't refuse him!'

'No, I know,' she said quietly.

'I've served three kings, Henry, Richard and John, and that's enough,' he went on. 'I've never met this lad who's to be the new King, and I don't want to. He's not ten years old yet, so he'll

338

be surrounded with men trying to make him do this, that and the other, and hopefully some of them will bear in mind the lad's interests and those of the realm at least as much as their own. Whether they do or they don't, I want no part of it. Not,' he added modestly, 'that anyone's likely to ask me.'

'It was hard for you too when King John died,' she said.

'Aye, it was.' He felt the tears well up in his eyes. He blinked them away. 'Known him from a boy – unreasonable, pig-headed, arrogant, loveable, capricious sod that he was.' He gave a laugh that was almost a sob. 'But, God knows, I'll miss him.'

'And there's Yves,' she said very softly.

Yves.

In all the fierce, urgent activity of the last days, Josse hadn't had nearly enough time to think about Yves.

He had lost people very dear to him before; nobody got to his age without that. But as the immediate shock had faded, he came to realize that nobody's death had affected him like that of his brother.

He had noticed, with a part of his mind that seemed to stand back and observe him, that an element of grief consisted of a succession of what felt like punches to the heart. Some aspect of his loss would occur to him: *Yves will never walk by the water in the evening again,* or *he still smiled that quiet smile of his that he had when we were children,* or, *he won't see his grandchildren grow to maturity.* Sometimes this punch was relatively minor, necessitating no more than a brief pause in whatever he was doing while he quietly absorbed it into himself and let it pass. Sometimes – far more often, in those early days – the punch would have the power to bring him to a total stop while the pain endured and he would stand there, tears falling down his face, and suffer the agony of loss all over again.

Sometimes the images of Yves's death crashed into his mind, driving out whatever he was thinking about or doing, and he saw again that terrible moment when the arrow struck. Yves had died almost instantly. That was the one, the only blessing: the archer had been an expert. Josse had fallen from Alfred's back, stumbling, rushing to his fallen brother, cradling his beloved head in his lap, crooning words of comfort, reassurance.

Yves's brown eyes had met his own, just for an instant. He whispered, 'Oh, dear!' and Josse had seen a faint smile.

Then blood had welled up out of Yves's mouth and he died.

There was a long time of mourning ahead. Josse sensed it waiting for him, patient and calm. It was as if grief said to him in a kindly voice, *When you're ready, here I am.*

Again he felt the tears form in his eyes. Even as they did so, Helewise gave his hand a squeeze.

I'll get through it, he thought. *I am lucky, for I have someone beside me whose support and love will not waver.*

He knew, then, how it would be. Perhaps it was Joanna who allowed him the vision; perhaps it was Yves, his benign shade still lingering. But he could see the years ahead, here with Helewise. Living quietly, lives gradually more restricted as they aged together, but always there would be contentment. Always love.

It was, he thought, more than enough.

They sat in silence for quite a long time.

Then he said, 'Ah, well, the fire's dying. Shall we go to bed?'

Author's Note

The cause of King John of England's death is not known for certain. He seems to have had a bout of food poisoning, perhaps dysentery, at King's Lynn, although the symptoms may just have been the aftermath of a colossal blow-out and rather too much to drink. He was sufficiently recovered, anyway, to set out from Lynn a day or so later. This was the journey across the Wash that led to the loss of part of the baggage train.

Contemporary accounts say that it was the terrible news that Dover Castle was about to fall to Prince Louis that led to a recurrence of King John's sickness. It is indeed possible that a low, depressed state of mind can lessen the body's defences so that a lurking illness can once again break out, but it doesn't seem likely that this could apply to either food poisoning or dysentery, which surely require the ingestion of a causative agent of some kind.

Regarding the suggestion of hostile action by the Queen, with or without the assistance of the Lusignans, there is of course nothing in the record either to support or refute this.

Three years after John's death, his widow Isabella married Hugh X de Lusignan, the son of the fiancé of her youth.